THE PEPPERMINT TEA
CHRONICLES

Other titles in the *44 Scotland Street* series

ALEXANDER McCALL SMITH

THE PEPPERMINT TEA CHRONICLES

A 44 Scotland Street Novel

First published in Great Britain in 2019 by
Polygon, an imprint of Birlinn Ltd
West Newington House
10 Newington Road
Edinburgh
EH9 1QS

www.polygonbooks.co.uk

9 8 7 6 5 4 3 2 1

ISBN 978 184697 483 0
British Library Cataloguing-in-Publication Data

A catalogue record for this book is available on
request from the British Library

Typeset by Studio Monachino
Printed and bound by Clays Ltd, Eliograf S.p.A.

This is for Lorraine Veitch Rutherford

1

The Plight of Cats in South Australia

Domenica Macdonald, anthropologist, resident of Scotland Street, and wife of Angus Lordie, portrait painter and long-standing member of the Scottish Arts Club, sat in the kitchen of her flat in Scotland Street. She was immersed in a magazine she had bought on impulse at the local newsagent's, and so did not hear Angus when he asked her about her plans for the day.

"I said," repeated Angus, "are you going to be doing anything very much today?"

"I'm sorry," said Domenica, looking up from her magazine. "I didn't hear you. I'm reading something here that I can hardly believe."

"Ah!" said Angus. "Oscar Wilde."

"What about him?"

Angus tried to remember exactly what Oscar Wilde had said – he had pronounced on so many things – but found that he could not recall the precise words. "He said something about his diary being sensational reading. Or somebody else's diary. I don't really remember . . ."

"It doesn't matter too much if you can't remember exactly what he said," Domenica reassured him. "Wilde will undoubtedly have more to say. Uniquely, perhaps, among those who are no longer with us, he continues to make witty remarks from beyond the grave – people impute them to him, you see. The volume of his quotations grows daily. This article, though, is about cats in South Australia."

Angus was puzzled. "What about them?"

Domenica shook her head. "They're to be confined."

"In what sense?"

She looked down at the article. "Apparently cats in South Australia have been eating too many birds and small mammals. They're very destructive, cats."

Angus glanced down at his dog Cyril, who was lying under the kitchen table, one eye firmly closed, but with the other slightly open, allowing him to watch his master. Angus was sure that Cyril knew when the conversation concerned him, or in more general terms had something to do with canine issues; the flicker of an eyelid, almost imperceptible, was enough to reveal that Cyril was listening, waiting to see whether the situation developed in such a way as to be of interest to him. Cyril's vocabulary, like that of all dogs, was limited to a few familiar nouns – *walk*, *bone*, *sit*, and so on – and one or two adjectives, *good* and *bad* being the most important ones. Beyond that, Cyril's intellectual life was no more than Pavlovian. So when anybody mentioned the Turner Prize, an institution that for Angus stood for everything that was wrong in the contemporary art world, Cyril would dutifully raise a leg. This was not a gesture of contempt, of course, but was a trained response, instilled in Cyril through the use of rewards. Angus found it amusing enough – as did most of his friends – but Domenica had expressed the view that it was childish. Many of the things that men do are childish in the eyes of women, but this was egregiously so.

"Really, Angus," she had said when she first saw Cyril performing his new trick. "That's a bit adolescent, surely."

Angus was unrepentant. "I have little time for the Turner Prize," he said. "I have no taste for its pretentiousness. I dislike the way it is awarded to people who cannot paint, draw, nor sculpt." His eyes widened; he became slightly red, his breathing shallow – all fairly typical reactions provoked by the Turner Prize in those of sound artistic judgement. "You are *not* an artist if you merely make a video about paint drying or pile a few *objets trouvés* in a heap. You just aren't."

Domenica shrugged. "Calm down," she said. "Installations make us look at the world in a different way. They must have some artistic merit. They challenge us. Isn't that what the Turner Prize is all ab—?"

She had stopped herself, but it was almost too late. "Don't say *Turner Prize*," blurted out Angus. "Not when Cyril . . ."

But he, too, had spoken without thought of the consequences. "Cyril," he shouted, just as the dog, impervious to the fact that they were indoors at the time, prepared to pass judgement on installation art. "No, Cyril! Sit!"

It had been the right – and timeous – counter-command. Cyril, confused, forgot about the Turner Prize and lowered his hindquarters, waiting for further instructions.

Now, with Cyril somnolent below the table, the discussion of feline destructiveness continued. "Yes," Angus mused. "Murderous creatures. Birds, in particular. The Royal Society for the Protection of Birds gets hot under the collar about cats."

Domenica pointed to the article. "This," she said, "tells us what Australian cats get up to – and it makes sobering reading. Nearly four hundred million birds are killed by cats in Australia every year. A lot of those cats are feral, of course, but pet cats, it says, get through over forty million a year. Some of those are threatened species too." She looked up at Angus. "Four hundred million, Angus. Four hundred million."

Angus sighed. "It's what cats do, I suppose. Nature's red in tooth and claw, isn't it?"

Domenica referred to the article again. 'They take their wildlife seriously in Australia, of course. And so . . ." She looked down at the page. "People have to keep their cats under control in cities. You can't let them wander around."

Angus frowned. "But you can't keep a cat under control. They're not like dogs. They don't accept our authority."

"According to this," Domenica went on, "in South Australia you have to keep the cat in the house or in a cage in the garden. You don't have any option."

Angus looked out of the window. Freedom: everywhere, it seemed to him, the boundaries of freedom were being encroached upon. Passports, regulations, prohibitions, requirements pinched at the lives of us all, and now this. No cats stalking about in the garden; no cats lying on walls in the sun, watching us; no cats leading their parallel lives in the gardens of other cats, or other people; cat doors, the symbol of cats' liberty, a thing of the past, a reminder of what used to be.

"That poem," he muttered.

"What poem?"

"That Christopher Smart poem. He wrote it when he was in the asylum. I learned chunks of it as a boy. There was a teacher who believed in poetry. We loved him. He was gentle; he didn't disapprove. And then he died."

Domenica listened. Yes, she thought. Great teachers are like that: they believe in something – poetry, physics, it can be anything, really – and they are loved, but often do not know it. Then they die, and are loved all the more.

"He – Christopher Smart, that is – listed all the merits of cats. He said: *For his motions on the face of the earth are more than any other quadruped. For he can swim for life. For he can creep.*"

"No longer," said Domenica.

Below the table, Cyril cocked an ear. He was unaware of the subject of discussion, of course, but he hated cats. He resented their freedom and their arrogance. Their humiliation would be heaven for him – justly deserved, and none too soon in its coming.

2

Angus Thinks about Freedom

"I can see the point, of course," said Angus. "We have to protect species, and cats are certainly a threat to birds. But . . ."

Domenica nodded. "You can't have unfettered freedom. We certainly can't, and nor should cats have it. There has to be a compromise."

Angus looked thoughtful. "You say we can't have that freedom. It's interesting to think about what the reach of *we* is: we as individuals, or we as bigger groups – nations and so on? They're separate issues, aren't they?"

"Yes, I suppose . . ."

Angus cut Domenica short. "You see," he continued, "people talk a lot about freedom at the individual level – liberal individualism has secured that particular conversation. But what about freedom at a higher level: the freedom of nations? Have we given up on that, do you think?"

"You mean sovereignty?"

Angus nodded. "Yes, I suppose I do. Isn't it the same thing? The right of self-determination?"

"It still exists," said Domenica. "There was some discussion of it in the paper the other day. It was about Woodrow Wilson and the rights of nations to determine their future. The Americans have always disliked other people's empires. Their own, of course, was a different matter . . ."

"Unacknowledged."

"Yes, but to be fair to then, it was different from the old European empires. And they do take freedom seriously, the

Americans. They really do. They fight over it in the courts all the time. They still seem to believe in freedom. I'm not sure if we do."

"No," said Angus. "There are plenty of people only too ready to stop other people from saying things with which they disagree. It's grossly illiberal, of course – intolerance, in fact – not that they'd see it as such. The intolerant never do. How few of them look in the mirror and confess their intolerance? Or their pride?"

Domenica smiled. "Looking in the mirror is a useful exercise. Looking straight into it and describing yourself. Who likes to do that?"

"Narcissists?" suggested Angus.

"Perhaps. But their descriptions are rarely honest. In fact, they're compliments rather than descriptions. There's a difference."

Angus remembered something. "Bruce Anderson – you've met him in the Cumberland Bar."

"The building surveyor? The one with the hair?"

Angus nodded. "Yes, him. His hair's cut *en brosse* and he puts gel on it. It smells of cloves. Which makes me think of dentists. Cloves trigger Proustian memories for me – when I was a boy my dentist must have used oil of cloves."

"What about Bruce?" asked Domenica.

"I saw him in the Gents at the bar," Angus said. "He was standing in front of the mirror, staring at his reflection, grinning with satisfaction."

"Well, he is good-looking, after all. If you look like him, what you see in the mirror won't be exactly displeasing."

Angus wrinkled his nose with distaste. "Good looks are something that should be accepted with proper diffidence. It's rather like having money, or an enviable talent. Like being able to play the piano rather well, or having a low golf handicap. You don't parade it. You close the piano lid modestly when somebody comes into the room, and you say *Just practising*, or *I never seem to get that particular piece right*. That's what you say. You don't boast *I'm a bit of a Paderewski*. Or, *mutatis mutandis*, Tiger Woods."

Domenica laughed. "I hate to say it, Angus, but you sound distinctly old-fashioned. Expectations have changed. If you have it these days, you flaunt it. You blow your own trumpet. You bask in your good fortune, and you don't care if it makes others feel inadequate."

Angus sighed. "So it seems. But I still believe we should be modest."

Domenica agreed. "Oh yes. You and I should be modest – and I hope we are. But I suspect we're in a minority. Have you seen anybody's CV these days – their résumé? People trumpet their achievements to the rafters – and beyond. They tell you themselves how marvellous they are; how good they are at doing this, that and the next thing. How popular they are. How effective."

"Do people believe them?" asked Angus.

Domenica doubted it. "I suspect they disregard it. That's the trouble with formulae of any sort. People get to know that it's no more than going through hoops – uttering the necessary shibboleths."

"Noise," said Angus.

"Yes, noise. It's rather like these mission statements that clutter up the announcements and advertisements of public bodies. They signal their virtue. They tell us how they're there to serve us and how they are even-handed in everything they do. Of course they should be even-handed; of course they should behave correctly, but the problem of this constant signalling of virtue is that it weakens the message when the message really needs to be put across. People just don't hear it any more because it's always there. The message loses its power. People don't see it because it has become so omnipresent, so ritualistic."

"Yes," said Angus. "It's interesting how . . ."

But he did not finish; Domenica had more to say. "I have a Russian friend," she said. "I met her at a conference. She teaches anthropology at St Petersburg University. She told me that in Soviet days people got so accustomed to strident propaganda – you know, those great red posters and so on – that they simply did not see it. They filtered it out – they didn't see it. And when she told me this, we were sitting with somebody from Los Angeles, and she said, 'It's odd that you should say that because we're the same with adverts. We don't see the billboards all over the place. We don't hear the inane jingles on the radio. It's there, of course, but we become blind to it.'"

Angus tapped a finger on the table. "How did we get on to this?" he asked.

"Sovereignty," said Domenica. "We were talking about freedom and sovereignty."

"Ah, yes."

"And you said . . ."

Angus remembered. "I said that we no longer seemed to be all that concerned about nations – or states, perhaps – having the right to control their future. I wondered if we were losing that altogether."

"Or just being realistic?" asked Domenica. "We're all interdependent now, aren't we? John Donne *redivivus*?"

"Yes, but . . ." He was not sure how to go on. He felt uncomfortable about giving up freedom, and yet so many people seemed to be enthusiastic about doing just that. Perhaps the idea that a country could control its own destiny was just no longer possible, not in the world in which we now lived. Brussels. London. Berlin. Washington. Places where there's real power. Not us, not us. Not small people like us. He thought of Hamish Henderson and his lovely lament, *Freedom Come All Ye.* One might try to sing that, he thought, but what if the choir has gone away – or no longer cares?

3

Aberdeen

"But speaking of freedom," said Domenica. "What about downstairs?"

Downstairs was the flat below, the home of the Pollock family – of Bertie Pollock, now, at last, seven; of his young brother, Ulysses, one-ish; and their father, Stuart Pollock, formerly a statistician in the Scottish Government. It was also the home of Irene Pollock, of course, enthusiast for the works of Melanie Klein, former counsellor at the Carl Gustav Jung Drop-in Centre in the Edinburgh New Town, and now a registered PhD student in the University of Aberdeen. This fact would make Scotland Street her home only for brief periods – weekends, for the most part – while for the remaining five days of the week she would live in a small shared flat in the university area of Aberdeen.

Irene had taken the unusual step of leaving her family behind in Edinburgh while she went back to university. For many, this was as outrageous as it was inexplicable.

"That woman," Domenica had observed, "has responsibilities. She has a small child – not much more than a baby – and poor little Bertie. She has a husband too – poor man. And yet she gaily waltzes off to Aberdeen to undertake some half-baked PhD. Can you credit it?"

There were two reasons why it had been easy for Irene to take herself off to Aberdeen. The most important of these was that Stuart's mother, Nicola, having been deserted by her Portuguese husband, was now back in Scotland and had been prepared to move out of her rented flat in Northumberland

Street in order to look after the boys. Nicola had little time for Irene – in fact, she had no time for her at all – and felt nothing but relief that Irene had largely left Scotland Street. She loved her grandchildren, and was only too pleased to step into the maternal shoes vacated by Irene. She had time on her hands, and filling it with the demands of two small boys was, in her view, an inestimable privilege.

The other factor that made Irene's departure relatively easy was the encouragement that she had received to pursue her studies in Aberdeen. In Stuart's view, the marriage, which he had never had the courage to end, was effectively over. It suited him that Irene should have a new goal to pursue, and that she should choose to do that in a city other than Edinburgh. There was something between her and Dr Fairbairn – Stuart was sure of that – and he did not resent it in the least. In fact, he was relieved that Irene should become the emotional responsibility of somebody else. So he came up with no objections when the move was first mooted. His difficulty then was to try not to appear too enthusiastic. Irene had a habit of doing the opposite of what she thought Stuart wanted, and he was concerned that if she sensed keenness on his part, then she might change her mind and stay after all.

Bertie was too young to show such tact. "That's a wonderful idea, Mummy!" he enthused. "I've always thought you should do a PhD."

"Have you now, Bertie?" Irene responded. "Well, I must say that's very supportive of you."

Bertie nodded solemnly. "And I'm sure it's a good idea to do it in Aberdeen," he went on. "Aberdeen's a jolly good place to do a PhD, Mummy."

"Do you think so, Bertie?" said Irene.

"Yes, I do." He paused. "And you can go and live up there, can't you? It would be best to go up there and spend all your time on it. You could come back every other year, maybe . . .

for a visit. Or you could phone us if you didn't want to do the train journey. A phone call would be fine."

"Bless you, Bertie," said Irene. "I'll come back every weekend. Mummy wouldn't want to leave her boys too long."

"But we'll be fine, Mummy," protested Bertie. "We have to learn to stand on our own two feet."

Irene laughed. "But Bertie, Ulysses can't even stand properly yet. He'll need Mummy to look after him."

Bertie bit his lip. He knew how Ulysses felt about his mother. It had been obvious right from the very beginning of his small brother's life, when Ulysses had spontaneously and copiously thrown up whenever his mother approached him. Bertie had diagnosed this as fundamental antipathy, and although loyal to his mother in the face of all her scheming had attributed this to her ill-fated attempt to start Ulysses on music lessons at the age of eight weeks.

"I gather that a six-year-old recently auditioned for the Conservatoire in Glasgow," Irene had remarked to Stuart.

"Ridiculous," had been his response, which had brought forth a severe rebuke from Irene.

"That, Stuart," she lectured him, "is exactly the sort of attitude that destroys potential. What if Leopold and Anna Maria Mozart had not given their son music lessons when he was very young? What if Leopold Mozart had said 'Ridiculous'?"

"You don't want to hot-house children excessively," Stuart had protested. But his heart was not in the argument, as he knew that he would lose – just as he had lost every argument with Irene, on every subject, throughout their marriage.

Bertie realised that in so far as Irene would return at weekends, he would probably still have to endure his yoga and saxophone lessons, both of which took place on Saturday. His psychotherapy appointments, however, were another matter, as these were usually scheduled for Thursday afternoons when, according to Irene's new timetable, she would be safely up in Aberdeen and therefore unable to take him to his psychotherapist in Queen Street.

He had hardly dared hope – and his pessimism was justified: before she started her new life, Irene had extracted an undertaking from Stuart that Bertie would continue in therapy.

"I can't emphasise it enough," she said to Stuart. "Continuity in these matters is of the essence – the very essence. If Bertie is to grow up neurosis-free, then he must continue in therapy. He needs it, Stuart, he needs it . . ."

"Like a hole in the head," muttered Stuart, *sotto voce*, but not quite *sotto* enough.

Irene's glance told him she had heard. "I'll be watching you, Stuart," she said. "Aberdeen is not all that far away, you know."

Would that it were further, thought Stuart.

4

Ranald Braveheart Macpherson's Book Club

Irene's departure for Aberdeen had been easy for her, but difficult for Stuart. On the day on which she was due to drive up to Aberdeen in the family's old Volvo estate car, its back seats flattened to allow room for her luggage, he suggested that Bertie and Ulysses be sent to Nicola's flat.

"I don't want them to see you going," he said to Irene. "It's not going to be easy for them."

He almost choked on the words as the reality of what was happening struck home. This woman was about to leave her two small children. She might be intending to return at weekends, but the brute fact of the matter was that she was leaving home. Any parting would be a wrench, even one in which a fundamental pathology lay at the heart of a relationship; a parting was still the end of something, and he did not want his sons to see their mother drive away. That could not happen – it simply could not be allowed to happen.

Irene looked at him. "We've discussed this," she said. "You assured me that the boys would have emotional continuity."

"I know, I know, I know. You don't have to tell me that."

She sighed. "So why now? Why talk about their experiencing trauma just when I'm about to go?"

He returned her stare. Irene had always had a good complexion, with skin that seemed much younger than her years. How old was she? He suddenly realised he was not sure. She was two years younger than he was, and so she was thirty-eight. And he saw that around the edges of her eyes there were tiny crow's feet developing. It was such a human thing to happen to a face; she was all mind, all theory, all domination of the world, and yet here was ordinary humanity touching her, ordinary being-in-the-world staking its claim.

"I don't want them to see you go," he insisted.

"It's only for five days," she said. "I'll be back at the weekend."

He shook his head. "No, you won't."

She raised her voice. "I beg your pardon?"

"I said: you won't be back. I don't want you."

She moved towards him. He felt his heart beating faster.

"What did you say, Stuart?" she hissed. "Have you taken leave of your senses?"

He gasped. He had never been able to stand up to her. He could not. It was impossible.

He looked down at his feet, at his suede shoes that were showing their age now, and had become shabby. His shoes. His shoes. He suddenly felt ashamed of them. "All right," he said. "Come back."

She seemed relieved. "Yes, I will. Just as we agreed. Remember our agreement, Stuart?"

He nodded. "Yes, I remember." He paused. "But at least let me take them round to my mother's. At least let me do that."

She hesitated. "If it means that much to you. I don't think it's necessary, but if you really want it."

"I do."

"All right. I'll say goodbye here and then you can take them round to her."

He hated the way she referred to his mother as *her* or *she*. "She has a name," he muttered.

"Nicola, then."

"Yes, that's her name." He paused. "And she's the one who's going to be stepping into the breach."

Irene sighed. "You're being very petty, Stuart."

He felt raw. There was a persistent, numb wound somewhere

within him. He had always felt that way when he witnessed human conflict or bad behaviour. He felt dirtied by it, and the feeling of dirtiness soon became a feeling of regret at the way the world was, at the thought that people could treat one another so badly.

Bertie and Ulysses were in the sitting room. Bertie was reading and Ulysses was in his bouncer – a strange construction in which he could sit, supported by straps that were in due course attached to heavy-duty rubber bands.

Bertie looked up as Stuart entered the room. "Has Mummy gone yet?" he asked.

Stuart tried to sound cheerful. "Not quite yet, Bertie."

"Has she forgotten to go?" asked Bertie. There was a note of disappointment in his voice.

"No," answered Stuart. "She hasn't forgotten. But you could say goodbye now and I'll take you round to Granny's."

Bertie closed his book. He was reading Walter Scott. "Rob Roy was very fierce," he said.

Stuart grasped at the straw. "I'm glad you're enjoying it, Bertie."

"I am," said Bertie. "Ranald Braveheart Macpherson and I have started a book club, you know."

"Oh yes?" said Stuart brightly, bending down to release Ulysses from his bouncer.

"We're going to read *Rob Roy* and then *Kidnapped*, which I've already read but Ranald says I should read again. That's by Mr Stevenson, Daddy. Did you know he built lighthouses?"

"His people did," said Stuart. "I'm not sure whether he built any himself."

"They made one out on the Bell Rock, Daddy," Bertie continued. "It was right out at sea and they had to wait for the tide to drop before they could build it. Every day the bits they had just built were covered by the sea until the next low tide. It was jolly hard, Daddy."

"I bet it was, Bertie. And what a good idea to have a book club. Just like Mu—" He stopped himself. He did not want to mention her. It was ridiculous, he knew, but he did not want to mention her – not just yet.

Bertie did not notice the caesura. "The only problem is that Ranald can't really read yet. He can, if he goes very slowly, but it takes a long time for him to get through a whole page."

"That could be a problem in a book club," said Stuart. "What do you do about it, Bertie?"

"I'm the one who reads the books," replied Bertie. "Then we talk about them. Ranald tells me what he thinks after I've told him what the book is about."

Stuart looked away. I want to cry, he thought. I want to cry, but must not, must not; not in front of Bertie.

"We'll go and see Mummy quickly and then I'll take you to Granny's." He got the words out somehow.

And now, in the kitchen, Irene took Bertie in her arms, planting a kiss on his forehead. "You're going to be a good boy, Bertie, aren't you?"

Bertie nodded.

"And then Mummy will come back to see you very soon. On Saturday. How many sleeps away is that? How many sleeps until Saturday?"

Stuart turned away. He felt his stomach heave; sobbing did that to him; it *racked* him.

5

Scotch Pies

Stuart's mother, Nicola, had been married to a Portuguese wine-grower, Abril Tavares de Lumiares. It had not been an unhappy marriage, but it had not been strong enough to survive the efforts of their housekeeper, Maria, to displace Nicola in favour of herself. To achieve the objective of prising Abril away from his wife, the housekeeper had invoked the assistance of the local priest. This priest had never been happy with the presence of a Protestant Scotswoman in a house long noted for its piety and general support for the Church. In his view, Nicola was a historical aberration – a weed planted in a Catholic vineyard that could justifiably be resisted. The marriage itself could in time be annulled; the priest had spoken to the bishop, who took the view that marriage to a Protestant was indicative of such mental reservation – and possibly even mental instability – as to negate the consent necessary for the marital bond. There would be little difficulty, he thought, in having the whole thing set aside, leaving Abril free to marry the housekeeper, who happened to be the priest's cousin. That, of course, was an irrelevant detail, but it did have a bearing on a promise that the housekeeper had made to send her cousin on a pilgrimage to the Basilica della Santa Casa in Loreto once she found herself in charge of Abril's finances.

The campaign proved to be remarkably easy. Although they lived in reasonable harmony, Abril and Nicola had drifted apart in their interests and Maria's repeated whisperings had convinced him that God wanted him to marry her. In addition, she was considerably younger than Nicola and Abril, who had begun to experience that mid-life anxiety that derails so many otherwise uxorious men, found himself increasingly drawn to the housekeeper. With God added to the equation, it was an unequal battle, and while Nicola was visiting Scotland, she received a letter from Abril in which he revealed that he had decided to leave her for the housekeeper.

It was a dent to her *amour propre*, as any desertion must be, but it proved unexpectedly transient. Nicola found that she was happy to be back in Scotland, where the climate suited her better. And it was her place, after all: she had been brought up in the Borders and once again seeing that gentle, rolling countryside, with its well-kept farms, she was reminded that the landscape in which we spend our childhood remains the backdrop against which our inmost lives are led.

Abril Tavares de Lumiares had been generous in his provision for her, and although she was prepared to roll up her sleeves and get a job, Nicola would have enough to live on without finding employment. In addition to the divorce settlement, she had modest resources of her own, inherited from a childless aunt in St Andrews. The major part of this legacy had been invested in shares in the Clydesdale Bank, a bank that had not been enticed by any of the heady temptations that spelled ruin for other financial institutions. That investment had held its value, as had the other major asset in the aunt's estate that now passed to Nicola – a small pie factory in Glasgow. This factory, formerly trading under the name *Pies for Protestants Ltd* but now called *Inclusive Pies*, employed no more than three people. It did not make a large profit, but it had never encumbered itself with debt.

Inclusive Pies made mutton pies of a sort that is consumed only in Scotland and known as the Scotch Pie. These pies are made in a hot-water pastry mould, with space between the rim of the pie and the pastry lid, below which the meat is to be found. This space can be filled with a variety of unhealthy fillings, baked beans or mashed potato often being thought suitable. In the case of the pies sold by Nicola's pie company, this space was taken up with extra grease, skimmed off the large vats in which the mutton filling was cooked. When the pie was heated, this grease would liquefy, giving off a smell of the nutmeg that had been added to it.

Extra grease has always been popular in Scotland, and the pies found a ready market. But an additional stroke of marketing genius had made them perennially popular: this was their name, which was the *Pure Dead Brilliant Scotch Pie (Nae Messing)*. People liked that. They did not like their food to be messed about with, and any product that assured them that this had not happened was bound to succeed.

When Stuart revealed to Bertie that his grandmother owned a pie factory in Glasgow his eyes opened wide with awe. "Real pies, Daddy?" he asked.

"Yes," answered Stuart. "Mutton pies. They're called Scotch Pies, Bertie. You should ask Granny to get hold of one for you. I'm sure they'd send one over from Glasgow."

In Bertie's mind, the fact that the pies came from Glasgow was an additional attraction. He had long wanted to live in Glasgow, where he imagined he would be free. There was no psychotherapy in Glasgow; there was no yoga to speak of; and now there were mutton pies. This promised land, only forty miles away by train, was a world to which Bertie had always felt drawn. Now here he was with a real Glasgow connection – and to a pie factory at that.

On the day Irene left for Aberdeen, Nicola returned to Scotland Street with Bertie and Ulysses and a bag she had extracted from the fridge of her rented flat in Northumberland Street. She kept the contents of this bag secret, in spite of several polite but pointed questions from Bertie, until now, around the kitchen table in Scotland Street, she revealed four *Pure Dead Brilliant Scotch Pies (Nae Messing)*.

"I thought we might all have one for our tea," she said, unwrapping one of the pies from its greaseproof paper.

"Even Ulysses?" asked Bertie. "Mummy usually just feeds him on carrots."

Nicola and Stuart exchanged glances.

"Even Ulysses," said Nicola. "Babies love Scotch Pies over in Glasgow. That's what they feed them over there."

"Do they give them Irn Bru in their baby bottles?" asked Bertie.

Nicola smiled. "Possibly, Bertie. They do a lot of things differently in Glasgow. It's a city of great character."

The pies were put into the oven and heated. The smell of mutton and nutmeg filled the room. Stuart sat down. He closed his eyes. He felt happy.

6

Boyle's Law and Business Growth

Big Lou had been unsettled by an article in the business section of *The Scotsman* newspaper. "Any business that is not going forwards," the writer of this article warned, "is going backwards. That's a law of business physics. If you don't go forwards, you go backwards."

These three sentences had made her stop and frown. It was a proposition that she had heard time and time again: a business had to expand if it was to succeed; you could never stand still; you had to grow. It was essentially the same advice, however it was dressed up: here it was being presented as an immutable law, of the order of the laws of gravity, or of Boyle's law . . .

Boyle's law . . . in the same way in which Proust's madeleine cake took him back to those mornings on which he went to say good-day to his Aunt Léonie in her Combray bedroom, the thought of Boyle's law triggered memories in Big Lou's mind of her classroom at Arbroath Academy. That was where she had learned physics, taught to her by Mr Donaldson, who seemed so attached to Boyle's law, while outside the sun was on the grass and the sky was filled with light, and that Gordon Thompson, who had smiled at her at assembly – he had definitely smiled, and she was absolutely certain that the smile had been directed at her – that Gordon Thompson was now walking between classroom blocks and he was carrying a pile of books for somebody, presumably one of the teachers . . . That Gordon Thompson, whose uncle had a fishing boat in Stonehaven and who had once said to her that he liked tall girls and Big Lou must be the tallest girl he knew. And there, on the board, chalked up by Mr Donaldson, who always seemed so sad about something or other – perhaps it was physics itself, the sheer inevitability of it, that made him feel that way – there on the board was Boyle's law reduced to a few letters: $P_1V_1=P_2V_2$. Propositions like that were so firm and, in a curious way, ultimately so reassuring: the world might be in a state of crisis, established orders might be crumbling, the country might be divided against itself, but P_1V_1 still equalled P_2V_2. That would never change.

The image of Mr Donaldson faded, as did that of Gordon Thompson, whom she had not seen since, eight years earlier, she had driven past him in Arbroath High Street and he had looked at her and then quickly looked away, as if embarrassed by something. She had wondered about that and decided that it must have been shame; she had noticed the same thing with a number of her old schoolfriends who had stayed in the area. If you had gone elsewhere, and then come back, they seemed apologetic about their continued presence, as if by staying in the place they had grown up they had somehow failed. People who went off to Edinburgh or London were adventurous – they showed ambition, they were prepared to swim in a larger pond. People who stayed in Arbroath were stick-in-the-muds, people who could not face the competition they would encounter in one of the cities. That was the feeling, anyway – that was the way some people thought about it. Of course, it was not true: it was harder, Big Lou thought, to find a job in a small place; there were plenty of jobs in Edinburgh or Glasgow, and you could always find something if you made a minimal effort. It was not so easy in the country; you had to be prepared to do anything and you had to be ready to hold several part-time jobs at the same time. In the city you could reinvent yourself; in the country you had to get along with who you already were, because everybody knew just who that was.

Big Lou had got away from Arbroath. She had given up the life she led on the family farm, Snell Mains, and gone up to Aberdeen to work in the Granite Nursing Home. A legacy from one of her charges there had allowed her to move to Edinburgh and buy the former bookshop that became her coffee bar. She had bought the shop's entire stock of second-hand books too, and had been reading her way through those since their acquisition. She wondered what Gordon Thompson would have made of that. He was a keen reader, she recalled, and was always getting into trouble with the school library for borrowing more books than he could read, and then taking too long to return them. She wondered whether he was still a keen reader and, if they were to meet again, whether they would find that they shared tastes in literature. They had read Lewis Grassic Gibbon at school because it was a novel of their place, their surroundings, and now she remembered what Gordon Thompson had said about it when they discussed it in the classroom. He had said, "I feel sorry for those people." She had been unsure what he meant. Was it because of the war, or the hardship of their lives, or because they were trapped in their small corner of rural Scotland where nothing would ever change? Would anybody ever feel sorry for her – stuck in her coffee bar day after day, seeing the same people, talking to them about the same things and getting the same views expressed back to her?

Was that what life entailed: not doing very much, and doing it every day, in the same place, following the same procedures and rules until you were told you were no longer needed? Big Lou sighed, and turned her attention back to the issue of business expansion. According to conventional wisdom, the fact that her coffee shop was not going forwards meant that it was condemned to go backwards. And if things went backwards, they would undoubtedly contract, and possibly collapse altogether.

Big Lou sighed again. She did not think that bald proposition about the need for expansion applied to her own business. She would ask Matthew about that, though, because he had a good understanding of business and knew how to read a balance sheet. Matthew was due to come in later that day and she could ask him then. He would be bound to know, as he read the business pages more assiduously than she did. He would tell her, and would settle this dispute about expansion. She hoped that he would say, "Lou, there's no need for a small business like yours to expand." But she feared he might shake his head and repeat the verdict of so many accountants and finance managers. He might well say, "Lou, you simply have to accept that the world has changed and that there's less room for small coffee bars like yours."

If he said that – and it was a possibility – Big Lou would stand up for herself. She had learned to look after herself, a long time ago, in the playground. She could do it again.

7

Schadenfreude

As Matthew crossed Dundas Street to Big Lou's café, his thoughts were taken up with Pat, whom he had left in charge of the gallery while he took his customary mid-morning coffee break. Pat was still working for him part-time – an arrangement that suited both of them well. From Matthew's point of view, it was useful to have somebody who knew what she was doing but who, at the same time, was flexible in her working hours. From Pat's perspective, the job was ideal because she was now enrolled for a master's degree at the university, and while that required she attend a certain number of seminars each week, it still left her time to earn some money. Working in a gallery, with a sympathetic employer like Matthew, was infinitely preferable to taking the sort of job that so many other students were obliged to make do with – working as a barista in a coffee bar, or, less glamorously, stacking shelves in a supermarket, both of which forms of employment tended to be paid at the minimum wage, or barely above it. Matthew paid more generously – in fact, he paid far too much, even in Pat's opinion, although that was not a matter she planned to take up with him.

On that particular morning, Matthew had been troubled by Pat's rather lacklustre greeting when she had arrived for work. Normally she smiled; normally she enquired after the latest doings of the boys, the triplets, Rognvald, Tobermory and Fergus, whose exploits she had always followed with lively interest. But nothing was said about them that morning, and Pat simply nodded mutely when Matthew announced that he was going over the road to Big Lou's.

He looked at her askance. "Is everything all right?"

She stared back at him, answering flatly, "Yes. Fine. Everything's fine."

It isn't, thought Matthew, as he crossed Dundas Street. He had seen this before, and it had always been to do with boyfriends. She needs somebody, he said to himself. She's fed up with being by herself. She needs a proper, decent boyfriend this time. Somebody who would be permanent, or at least semi-permanent. He paused. *The opposite of Bruce*. That was the answer. And she also needed to have a sense of where she was going, which at the moment seemed to be nowhere. *You're going nowhere*, he thought. That's what he should say to her: *You're going nowhere*. But that, of course, was not the sort of thing people liked to say to other people. As a general rule, those who were going nowhere did not appreciate being informed of the fact; and those who saw others going nowhere usually felt uncomfortable about pointing out another's lack of direction.

Big Lou greeted him warmly as he entered the café. She was fond of Matthew, for all his faults, which were, in her view – the view from Arbroath, essentially – typical of the faults of Edinburgh people in general: a certain satisfaction with the way things were in Edinburgh; a tendency to believe that things in Glasgow were, at best, all right (if that was the sort of thing one liked); an attachment to a number of holy places (Murrayfield and Myreside rugby stadiums, Charlotte Square, *et cetera*); and a quaint theology that dictated that those who lived in places like London only did so because their karma, negatively influenced by failures in past lives, so dictated. Big Lou did not believe that it was a misfortune to be English, but she knew that many in Edinburgh flirted with that view, even if they were hesitant to express it in public. Matthew, she knew, was not like that, even if others were.

"So, Matthew," she said as she ground the beans for his

coffee. "What's going on?"

"Not much, Lou," he replied. And then he immediately qualified his response. "Actually, I'm a bit worried about Pat."

Big Lou tamped down the grounds with the small, plug-shaped instrument that Matthew called her "coffee-packing-thingy". "Oh, yes?" she said. "What's wrong with her?"

"I think she doesn't know where she's going."

Big Lou raised an eyebrow. "Who does?"

"She barely said a word to me today," Matthew continued. "She normally asks after the boys. Nothing."

Big Lou shrugged. "People have their off-days, Matthew."

"I know that," he said. "But I think her situation is a bit grim. I was round at her flat last week – dropping in copy for a catalogue she's been working on. And I met her flatmates. They're seriously depressing, Lou."

"Oh, well."

"And I also think she doesn't like being by herself. I think she'd like to have a boyfriend."

Big Lou sighed. "Who wouldn't?"

"And I feel that she still has a bit of a thing for Bruce."

Big Lou shook her head. "Bad mistake," she said.

Matthew agreed. "Sometimes people just don't learn. We repeat our mistakes, don't we?"

Matthew's coffee was now ready and Big Lou passed him the steaming *latte*. "One consolation of being over forty," she said, "is that you have the pleasure of seeing people under forty fail to grasp things that you know they'll grasp when they're over forty." And then she added, "If you see what I mean."

Matthew took a sip of his coffee. "*Schadenfreude*," he said. "Which means—"

Big Lou cut him short. "Oh, I ken all aboot your actual *Schadenfreude*, Matthew. Don't think I don't know about that."

Matthew was apologetic. "Sorry, Lou. I didn't mean to be . . ."

"Condescending," supplied Big Lou. "No, but as it happens I've read all about *Schadenfreude*." She paused. "Pleasure in the discomfort of others. It's strange, isn't it?"

"Something to do with envy?" asked Matthew.

"Aye, envy's a gey powerful emotion, Matthew. Lots of folk want what others have."

Matthew sighed. "I know all about that, Lou. I suppose I'm pretty lucky . . ."

Big Lou nodded. "Aye, you are. And do you find that other people envy you? Do you notice it?"

Matthew did. He had much to be grateful for, and he was very much aware that those who have much to be grateful for must be tactful in their enjoyment of their good fortune. He had Elspeth and the triplets; he had his gallery, with his desk and the chair that gave such good lumbar support; he had . . . oh, one could spend a long time enumerating the things he had, and yet there was poor Pat, who had such an appealing manner and was so well informed on twentieth-century Scottish art, and she had nobody to go home to in the evening other than those dreadful flatmates.

"Big Lou," he said, "we must do something for Pat. We have to find somebody for her. A boyfriend."

Big Lou looked dubious. "Tricky," she said. "Matchmaking, Matthew, almost always ends in disaster."

"Nonsense," said Matthew. "Not true."

8

He Loved Him More than Ice Cream

Back at Nine Mile Burn that evening, as the late July sun painted the distant Moorfoot Hills with a mellow gold, Matthew drove slowly down the drive, thinking of his earlier conversation with Big Lou. He had not given much thought to her warning once he returned to the gallery; he had been too busy hanging a new exhibition to think about much else. But now, as the house came into view beyond the cluster of ill-behaved rhododendrons, he remembered her words. *You think you're helping people*, she had said, *and in reality you're making everything worse. I've seen it time and time again, Matthew. Dinna interfere; just dinna interfere.*

As he parked the car in front of the house, he saw the three boys, toddlers now, but steady enough on their feet and eager to get into every nook and cranny, every out-of-bounds kitchen cupboard; keen, with all the delighted enthusiasm of that age, to press buttons on devices, flick the switches of lights, and generally poke, prod and dismantle the world about them. There they were, their noses pressed to the window of the porch, with James, the au pair, standing grinning behind them. They loved James – they loved him as much as they loved their building bricks and their old-fashioned Noah's Ark; they loved him as much as they loved the Toffee Fudgie-Wudgie ice cream that Matthew occasionally picked up for them from Luca's ice-cream parlour at Holy Corner in Morningside. That fact Matthew had learned directly from Rognvald, who had remarked one day, à propos of nothing, "Please don't make James die, Daddy. I love him more than ice cream."

Matthew had been rendered momentarily speechless. The discovery of language by children brought forth the most extraordinary remarks, and one should not be surprised by anything. But this . . .

"I'm not going to make anybody die, Rognvald," he said. "James isn't going to die, my darling."

"Good," said Rognvald.

Matthew wondered what had occasioned this strange concern on Rognvald's part. Had Elspeth talked to the boys about death? Now he remembered: they had recently lost a budgie, and the boys had found the bird, small, blue, and lifeless, on the floor of its cage. Elspeth had come across them shaking the bird, trying to prise open its beak with a fork, and she had been obliged to explain to them that the budgie could not be brought back to life.

"He's gone to heaven," she said, aware, even as she spoke, that this explanation created as many questions as it purported to answer.

And that proved to be the case. Where was heaven? Did people go there too? Were there lavatories up there? These theological complexities, she realised, could not be answered, and she had brought the discussion to an end by giving a piece of toffee to each boy. This stuck their jaws together, and silenced them – a simple expedient, even if not one advocated in most contemporary child-rearing manuals. Later, when she told Matthew about it, he had said that he did not want to bring the boys up to believe in things that were not there. "Ghosts, heaven, all those things," he said. "Why fill kids' minds with non-existent clutter? They only find out the truth later on."

"And Santa?" asked Elspeth. "And the tooth fairy?"

Matthew hesitated. How dedicated a rationalist did one have to be to deny the existence of Santa Claus? One of his own clearest early memories was of the moment when he had been told of the non-existence of Santa. The truth had been conveyed to him by his father, as they stood outside in the garden of the family house at Fairmilehead. Matthew had been looking up at the night sky, which was clear, and studded by fields of distant stars.

"Which way is the North Pole?" he had asked his father. "I want to see if we can see Santa."

His father, bending down, had whispered in his ear, "You don't believe in all that, do you, Matthew? Now that you're a big boy, you don't have to pretend."

But he had not been pretending. He had believed in Santa in the same way in which he believed in Waverley Station or the Flying Scotsman, or any of the other things he could touch and see.

His father had continued, "You still get presents, you know, even if you don't believe any more."

That had calmed his fears, but it had still been an overwhelming, sad moment for him. Now, remembering that disappointment, he realised that Santa was the one myth that we might try to preserve when all others had been debunked or expired. It was a small sprig of hope in a relentless world, a tiny island in the shrinking domain of childhood innocence. Talking animals, A. A. Milne, counting rhymes, nursery stories were all being taken over by the mass-produced, de-cultured electronica of modern childhood.

Now he saw the boys wave, their faces full of excitement and smiles. To be welcomed back by dogs and children, thought Matthew – what a privilege that was; and suddenly, unexpectedly, he felt a cold hand of dread about his heart. These things, this love and warmth, were so vulnerable, given to us on the most temporary of terms. And yet we took them for granted, against all the evidence of every actuary there ever was; we assumed that they would last for ever. What was that poem? It was something of Auden's, he remembered, a poem he had heard recited in a film about weddings and a funeral, when the poet had said: *I thought that love would last for ever: I was wrong.*

James brought the boys out to greet him. They clutched at their father, hugging his legs; they bombarded him with questions and urgent news, delivered breathlessly. He thought: *I was wrong. I was wrong.*

Elspeth appeared. She kissed him. She said: "Come into the kitchen and talk to me while I make the boys' tea."

Matthew came from a home where they said *dinner* rather than *tea*. But now, in the warmth of this family welcome, he realised that it really should have been tea all along.

9

Bacon Without Nitrites

With the triplets safely in bed, Matthew, Elspeth and James sat down at the kitchen table. They ate there most evenings, other than when there were guests, when Matthew would lay the table in the dining room, setting out the place mats with their views of the Grassmarket, the Castle, and Heriot's; the silver candlesticks – Edinburgh hallmarked – that had been a wedding present from his late uncle, and the heavy Stuart Crystal glasses of which Elspeth's parents had divested themselves on downsizing. Around the kitchen table, the setting was much more contemporary: Danish cutlery, so advanced conceptually as to make it difficult to distinguish knife from fork; plates from a design approved by the Museum of Modern Art in New York; and cranberry-coloured glasses that Elspeth had first seen in *House and Garden* which sat very well with the shade of red she had chosen for their recently installed Aga. This, after all, was haut-bourgeois Edinburgh, although admittedly a few miles out of kilter.

James had been with them for two months now. He had joined the household at a time of real crisis. Clare, the Australian au pair who had preceded him, had been a success with the triplets, but had ultimately proved to be unreliable. She had taken up with Bruce, who had, much to Matthew's surprise, met his match in her. Clare was an extreme sports enthusiast, and had insisted Bruce accompany her on an ill-fated para-mountain-biking trip to Skye. Para-mountain-biking is one of the more dangerous of the extreme sports, involving, as it does, cycling over the edge of a cliff or down a steep hillside on a bicycle attached to a large kite-like wing. The theory is that the cyclist, along with the mountain bike, sails upwards, in the way of a glider caught in ascending thermals. The sensation is said to be like no other: the earth shrinks beneath one, the wind, unconstrained by any surrounding structure, envelops the rider with its touch, and by continuing to turn the pedals one feels as if one is actually riding across the sky.

It is not, of course, a sport for everyone, and Bruce, for all his courage, did not take to it. On that initial launch into the wind blowing in off the Minch, Bruce reached a height of several hundred feet before his supporting wing suddenly dipped and pushed him swiftly downwards. He managed to land, but did so with such force that he fell from the mountain bike, caught his left hand in the spokes of the front wheel, and suffered minor lacerations to his brow. Clare was concerned, but only momentarily so; she had come under the spell of the instructor, and joined him in laughing good-naturedly at Bruce's ignominious landing. After that, she and Bruce parted company and she went off to Callander with the instructor, last heard of at a folk music festival on South Uist. This left Matthew and Elspeth in urgent need of replacement domestic support. And into that vacuum stepped an unlikely candidate – James, the nineteen-year-old godson of Matthew's friend, the Duke of Johannesburg, who had sold them the house at Nine Mile Burn. James had left James Gillespie's School in Edinburgh, where he had been the winner of the German Language Cup, the Senior Art Prize, and the Lord Provost's Award for General Attitude. Matthew had been hesitant about taking on a male au pair; Elspeth less so. "Don't be so old-fashioned," she said to him. "These days it makes no difference. Boys, girls – it's all the same."

Matthew had struggled with this claim. Were boys and girls all the same? He knew that the days in which there were male roles and female roles were well and truly over, at least with regard to employment and public office, but he had a lingering feeling that the personal psychologies of men and women had not yet coalesced into a truly androgynous composite. It struck him that there were still differences of outlook, and that even if men had become gentler and more sympathetic, and women, by the same token, had become harder and less feeling, there were still members of both sexes who held on to the old categories of male and female interests. There were still plenty of men, Matthew felt, who did not much care about their appearance and therefore did not use facial moisturiser; these men were never more content than watching football or drinking beer, or indeed doing both of these at the same time, and in an unmoisturised state. These men still existed, and until they were finally rooted out and reconstructed they could not be entirely ignored.

Matthew was not sure that a young man would have the patience to cope with the triplets. And would he feel comfortable in doing the things that an au pair in charge of small children had to do? The boys were still imperfectly toilet-trained and that was not necessarily something that everybody could cope with. And would he be able to cuddle them and comfort them when they scraped their knees – as they were always doing – or acquired the bruises that were the inevitable concomitant of running around the furniture at low level?

Elspeth thought he could be capable of doing all of this, and she proved to be right. James soon revealed himself to be more than capable of looking after the boys, as well as being an enthusiastic house-cleaner. He cycled to the supermarket in Penicuik, where he did the shopping unbidden, but with economy and insight into the household's needs. He fixed the dishwasher when its complicated filter system clogged and regurgitated; and he was, they discovered to their delight, a talented and inventive cook.

So when they sat down to dinner that evening, the Danish cutlery and the MOMA-approved plates at the ready, it was to a meal concocted by James.

"I got hold of some scallops," he said. "And I've made some bacon to go with them."

"*Made* bacon?" asked Matthew.

It was Elspeth who answered. "James cures his own bacon," she said, "don't you, James?"

James smiled sweetly. "I do. I cure in a mixture of salt and spices. Which means there are no nitrites in it."

"You don't want nitrites," said Elspeth.

"No, you don't," said James, rising from the table to check up on a pan on the Aga. "And it's really quite easy. You get hold of a pork loin and you rub the salt into it. Really rub it in. And you mix the spices with the salt – nutmeg, cinnamon even – that sort of thing. Then you put it in a plastic bag and put it in the fridge for three days."

"It dries out in the fridge," said Elspeth. "Then it's ready."

Matthew gazed at James, who had returned to the table. James smiled back at him, the dimples in his cheeks appearing as his smile broadened. He is *very* attractive, thought Matthew – adding, very quickly, to women, that is. And then he thought: Pat? No. Ridiculous thought. Inappropriate. But then . . .

10

An Inadvisable Home Construction Project

The scallops and the nitrite-free bacon had been perfectly prepared.

"How do you do it, James?" said Matthew as he finished off the last morsel on his plate.

James looked down modestly. "It's not all that complicated," he replied. "The trick with scallops is not to wash them, of course. That stops them absorbing water. And then never overcook. That's rule number one when dealing with any seafood."

Elspeth agreed with this. "Some people wreck lobster," she said. "They boil it until it becomes all rubbery. It's awful."

Matthew nodded. He did not like rubbery lobster; in fact, he had become wary of eating lobster ever since, on a trip to France, he had seen live lobsters being tossed into a pot of boiling water with Gallic insouciance. He was sure he had heard their screams – high-pitched, whistling sounds – as they met their agonising deaths. People said that this was impossible; that lobsters had no voice at all, were mute, as oysters or mussels undoubtedly were; but even if that were true, he wondered how anybody could toss a living creature into boiling water. And yet, and yet . . . here was this bacon on his plate, and that had once been a pig, an intelligent, emotionally receptive animal that had perhaps experienced all the joy of nosing about in a muddy field and feeling the sun on its back.

He wondered about scallops. He felt no particular compunction in eating them as he very much doubted whether they had any of the attributes that made for moral status. A pig might have thoughts, might experience emotion; a scallop would hardly think, or even be conscious in the sense in which we thought of consciousness. Their watery existence, resting on the sand of some distant seabed, did not involve any real sense of a past, a present, and a future. Nor, he imagined, were scallops aware of the fact that they were scallops; unlike pigs, which were conscious of being pigs . . . Or were they? Did pigs know they were pigs, or did they think that everything around them was just part of an undifferentiated reality that revolved around, and created, an all-enveloping state of piggishness?

He became aware that Elspeth had said something about sauce, but he did not hear it. Nor did he pay much attention to the reply James gave. He said something about using a small amount of chilli, but then Elspeth asked, "Where did you learn to cook, James? Was it at home?"

They had met James's parents. His father was an accountant and his mother a primary school teacher. They had struck Matthew as being a fairly typical middle-aged couple; the father, Hugh, looked as if he was the type of man who might be able to cook. It was the Duke of Johannesburg, though, who had inspired James's culinary expertise.

"My uncle," the young man said. "Well, he's my godfather really, but I've always called him Uncle Joburg and I really think he's forgotten I'm not his nephew." He paused. "You know he's not a real duke? Well, not entirely, because his father never really got the dukedom that the government of the time had promised him. He felt cheated."

"As well he might," said Matthew. "Governments can't just promise to do things and then decide not do them."

"But that's exactly what many of them do," Elspeth pointed out. "They say something when they're out of power and then, once they're in, they do the exact opposite."

Matthew laughed. "I'm remembering the Lib Dems," he

said. "They made a promise before they went into coalition with the Tories and then they had to confess that being in power was very different and they couldn't do what they said they'd do."

"But at least they had the honesty to say it," Elspeth cut in.

"True," said Matthew. And then, turning to James, "So your godfather inspired you?"

"Yes. I've always been close to Uncle Joburg – ever since I was a little boy. He taught me how to play the pipes. And then one day he said, 'It's about time you learned how to make a clootie dumpling.' And that was that. I found that I really loved cooking."

"You're lucky to have a godfather like that," said Elspeth. "He's such fun."

"Yes," said James. "You know, I've never seen him looking unhappy. He's always cheerful. Except twice, that is. I remember just two occasions when he was pretty low."

They waited. James's smile had gone, to be replaced by a grave expression. "One time was when the Lord Lyon was after him, for claiming to be a duke when he wasn't. They really hounded him, you know. And then the other was when he heard that his cousin in America had died. She lived in a place called Columbus."

"Where's that?" asked Elspeth.

Matthew knew. "It's in Ohio, isn't it?"

"Yes," said James. "This cousin of his was called Barb. She owned a small country club just outside Columbus. Uncle Joburg said that it was quite a place – people went there to play tennis and sit about on the veranda. He said it was a really nice club."

"And then?" asked Matthew. He feared that the story would not end well; any tale that began in such a setting was bound to go wrong after a time.

"And then," James continued, "she was visiting the club one

weekend – it was a Saturday, I think – and she was watching a game of tennis when apparently she went up in flames – just like that. She caught fire."

Matthew caught his breath. *Spontaneous combustion!* He had read about this phenomenon, which he, at least, thought was a justified inference from what evidence there was. Others, he knew, were more sceptical, insisting that there always had to be an external source of heat before the human body could catch fire. But there were these apparently otherwise inexplicable cases in which people suddenly shot up in flames, sometimes with little more than their shoes remaining.

"She burned to a cinder," James continued. "They had a fire extinguisher in the club kitchens, but they couldn't get the pin out of the trigger. You know how they have those pins – just like hand grenades."

Matthew nodded.

"It had become all corroded," James said. "Kitchens can develop rather salty air. Things can corrode."

"How awful," said Elspeth. "For both of them."

"Yes," said James. "Uncle Joburg was really upset. He was very fond of his cousin. I met her too, when she came over once. She had flaming red hair."

Matthew frowned. Was that a portent, he wondered – or even a causal factor?

"How is he?" he asked. "The Duke? Have you seen him recently?"

James put down his Danish fork, or knife.

"I'm a bit worried, Matthew," he said. "You know that Gaelic-speaking driver of his? Padruig?"

"Yes."

"He's persuaded my uncle to finance him in a ridiculous project he has. And to help him – actually help him physically."

"Doing what?" asked Elspeth.

They listened, increasingly appalled, as James told them of

the kit that Padruig had bought for the building of a small, two-seater seaplane. "They're working on it in the byre at Single Malt House," James said. "And they're both having flying lessons out at East Fortune Airport. Once they've built it, they want to fly it from some sea loch over in Argyll."

"Oh my God," exclaimed Elspeth.

"Yes," agreed James. "OMG."

11

Merry Hart with Small Possessioun . . .

That Saturday, when Angus Lordie took Cyril out for his morning walk in Drummond Place Garden, he came across Bertie sitting on the stairs, directly outside the Pollocks' front door. That door was slightly ajar, and Angus could hear a radio playing music inside the flat, along with the sound of voices. Then a child began to cry.

"That's Ulysses, Mr Lordie," Bertie ventured. "My little brother."

"Of course," said Angus. "I've met Ulysses, Bertie. And a fine little chap he is, too."

Bertie looked doubtful. "He cries a lot, Mr Lordie. When Mummy was here he cried all the time. Now that she's in Aberdeen, he doesn't cry quite so much."

Angus said nothing, but thought: *post hoc, propter hoc.* He looked down on the small boy and smiled. He noticed that Bertie was wearing a freshly ironed shirt, and trousers with a well-pressed crease. The formality of his outfit was finished off by a small, clip-on tartan bow tie.

"Special occasion today, Bertie?" he asked.

Bertie took a few moments to answer. He stared down at the stone step on which he was sitting; he looked disconsolate. Eventually he said, "There's a party, Mr Lordie."

"Ah," said Angus. "And am I to assume that you don't want to go? Is that right?"

Bertie nodded mutely. Cyril, a good judge of human mood, nudged gently at his side – canine body language for *I understand.* Dogs understood misery.

"Whose party is it?" asked Angus. "Somebody at school?"

Bertie nodded again. "It's a girl called Olive," he said. "She's very bossy. When I went to her last birthday party, it was full of girls, Mr Lordie. Hundreds of them. I was the only boy."

"Oh, that's bad luck, Bertie."

"Yes. They played Jane Austen all the time – that's all that they wanted to do. And I had to be Mr Darcy for the whole afternoon."

Angus suppressed a smile. "That can't be easy, Bertie." And added, "Even for Mr Darcy himself, I imagine." He paused. "Do you have to go, Bertie? You could always send your apologies."

Bertie sighed. "My granny says I have to go. She said I had accepted the invitation, and we must always keep our promises."

"Did you accept?" asked Angus.

Bertie sighed again. "Only because Olive made me," he replied. "She said that if I didn't accept she'd tell everybody never to talk to me again."

Angus frowned. "That's very bad, Bertie. But I can see why you felt you had to say yes."

"So now I have to go. At least Ranald will be there this time."

Angus remembered Ranald Braveheart Macpherson, whom he had met, with Bertie, after that remarkable rugby match when Scotland trounced New Zealand at Murrayfield. "Well, that's something. Maybe Olive's party won't be so bad after all."

Bertie looked unconvinced. Once again, Cyril nudged at him with his sympathetic, wet, dog's nose.

"Cyril doesn't want you to be sad, Bertie," said Angus. "He wants you to cheer up."

"I'll try, Mr Lordie," said Bertie. "But I wish I could . . . I wish I could go and live in Glasgow, Mr Lordie. That's what I'd really like."

Angus lowered himself on to the stair beside Bertie. "Listen," he said, "the world often isn't quite as we'd like it to be, Bertie. But it's a mistake, you know, to think that things will be better somewhere else. It's an old mistake." He paused. Things were better, he thought, for this little boy now that his mother had decamped to Aberdeen, but obviously not everything was perfect just yet.

"Have you heard of the town mouse and the country mouse, Bertie?"

Bertie shook his head.

"Well, it's a famous old Scottish poem by Robert Henryson. He got the story from Aesop. They both lived quite a long time ago."

Bertie was listening.

"And the story's quite simple really," Angus continued. "There was a mouse who lived in the country, you see, and she thought it would be a good idea to come into town and stay with her sister. She was told of all the fine food – the luxuries – that her sister had in the town. And the food was pretty good. But there was a cat, Bertie, and he gave the country mouse a real fright. He was called Gib, if I remember correctly."

"Did Gib eat her?"

"No, he threw her about a bit, but the country mouse managed to get away – just. But it made her think. And do you know what she thought?"

"No."

"She thought that it was a mistake to leave her simple life in the country. She thought it was a mistake to think that somebody else's life is better than your own."

Angus waited. Cyril looked at Bertie, who continued to stare at the stone beneath his feet.

"I don't remember many of the lines," Angus said. "But I do remember these. Henryson – he was the poet, Bertie – said: *Thairfor, best thing in eird, I say for me / Is merry hart with small possessioun.* That's in old Scots, Bertie, but I rather think you'll understand it. Have a merry heart even if you don't have much else."

He watched the small boy struggle. And as he did so, he felt that urge we all feel when we see the young in their unhappiness. We want to reassure them, *This will not last – it really won't. It will get better. It will.* But we don't say that, and even if we did, the young would not listen, for the simple reason that they have not lived long enough to know what we, for our part, have learned.

Angus rose to his feet. "There's another poem about a mouse, Bertie."

He did not have time to tell him. "'To a mouse'," said Bertie. "Mr Burns wrote it, Mr Lordie. He disturbed a mouse when he was ploughing a field. He felt very sorry for it."

"He did indeed, Bertie," said Angus.

Bertie stood up. "I have to go," he said.

"Feeling better?" asked Angus.

Bertie was silent, but his nod gave the answer.

"And some time soon I must tell you about a plan I've hatched."

Bertie looked up enquiringly.

"I'm going to build a shed," said Angus. "I'm going to build a shed in Drummond Place Garden."

Bertie drew in his breath. A shed! He looked up at Angus, who knew immediately what the look meant.

"Of course you can," said Angus. "Of course you can use my shed."

Olive's party, and all the dread it entailed, receded. A shed would change everything. But then Bertie thought: what possible use could an adult have for a shed? Was Mr Lordie planning something?

12

Olive's Party

Olive received her guests at the front door. This was not so much out of courtesy as to ensure that all presents were scrutinised before being stored in such a way as to prevent their repossession by the donor. This precaution was necessary, Olive felt, after an incident at Lakshmi's party, where one of the guests had taken back her present after a spat with the host. One could not be too careful when it came to presents, Olive thought.

"So, Bertie," said Olive, eyeing her guest with a certain triumph, "it's just as well you decided to come."

"But I told you I was coming, Olive," said Bertie. "I told you last week."

Olive pouted. "Oh, I knew you *said* you'd come, Bertie. I knew that. But if you believe everything everybody says – especially boys – then you're in for a big disappointment, aren't you?"

This last remark was addressed as much to Olive's lieutenant, Pansy, as it was to Bertie. Pansy was standing immediately behind Olive, ready to give as much support, physical as well as verbal, as was required.

Pansy was in full agreement. "That's right," she said. "All boys are well-known liars."

Bertie bit his tongue. There was no point in arguing with Olive, he felt – especially on her home territory.

He tried to pass through the hall and into the corridor beyond, but Olive prevented him.

"So, what have you brought me, Bertie? I hope you've got a present."

Bertie had, and he now passed over the neatly wrapped present that his grandmother, Nicola, had prepared for him. Olive took it suspiciously.

"I hope you like it," said Bertie. "Happy birthday, Olive."

Olive did not acknowledge this; she was busy tearing off the wrapping paper, which she handed to Pansy. The present was now revealed. It was a large plastic swan, its middle section padded in pink satin.

"What's this?" said Olive.

"It's a pincushion," said Bertie. "You put pins into it. It's a way of storing them."

Olive stared at him. "I haven't got any pins," she said coldly.

"You might get some," said Bertie. He wished that his grandmother had bought something more conventional. He knew that she cordially detested Olive, but he felt there was no point in provoking her unnecessarily.

Olive tossed the pincushion aside. Her attention had now returned to Bertie.

"So, why are you wearing that stupid bow tie, Bertie?" she asked.

"It's really stupid," chimed in Pansy.

"And gay," said Olive.

Bertie felt the back of his neck getting warm. He did not know what Olive meant, but he sensed she was not being complimentary. "It's not gay, Olive. It's my tartan. I've got a kilt just like it."

"A kilt!" exclaimed Olive. "I bet you look even more stupid in a kilt, Bertie."

"Ranald Braveheart Macpherson wears a kilt," said Pansy. "He looks stupid even without a kilt, but when he puts on a kilt it's even worse, with those spindly legs of his."

"Yes," agreed Olive. "I'd really hate to be Ranald Braveheart Macpherson. It'd be bad enough being you, Bertie, but a hundred times worse being Ranald."

"I can just imagine it," said Pansy.

"Anyway," Olive went on, "you're very welcome to my party, Bertie. Please go through into the living room and get yourself a helium balloon. And don't pop it, because there's only one per person."

In the living room, Bertie surveyed his fellow guests with sinking heart. There they all were – the people who made up Olive's circle of friends – Lakshmi, Priscilla, Chloe and Chardonnay. But then he saw Ranald Braveheart Macpherson, standing by himself in a corner, and his despair lifted slightly.

Ranald was relieved to see Bertie. "I'm really glad you're here, Bertie," he said. "You know what they're going to play?"

Bertie's heart sank. "Jane Austen?"

Ranald shook his head. "No. They've got a new game. They're going to play a game called *The Crown*. It's all about the Queen."

Bertie asked Ranald whether he had played it before.

"No," Ranald replied. "But Olive and Pansy have told me how it works. Olive's going to be the Queen and Pansy will be Princess Margaret."

"And what about us?" asked Bertie.

"I've got to be the Duke of Edinburgh," said Ranald. "I have to walk just behind Olive and say nothing. She warned me not to say anything at all."

"And what about me?" Bertie asked. "Did Olive tell you who I have to be?"

"You're going to have to be one of the Queen's dogs," said Ranald. He could tell from Bertie's expression that this news was not well received, and he tried to reassure his friend. "It won't be hard, Bertie. All you have to do is go down on your hands and knees and follow Olive wherever she goes."

"It sounds like a really stupid game, Ranald."

"I know," agreed Ranald. "But what can we do, Bertie? We're outnumbered."

Bertie could think of nothing that would relieve them of their predicament. He and Ranald made their way to the centre of the room where, on a small side table, several plates of macaroons and chocolates had been placed. Helping themselves to a macaroon each, they watched the girls on the other side of the room.

"You know something, Bertie?" said Ranald. "My dad hates Olive's dad. He says nobody trusts him and he has pinched a lot of people's money."

Bertie's eyes widened.

"Yes," Ranald continued. "Fortunately, we've got a safe, as you know, Bertie. So Olive's dad couldn't come and steal our money. I'm really glad about that."

"So am I, Ranald," said Bertie.

"Lots of adults hate other adults, you know, Bertie," Ranald said. "My mummy hates your mummy, you know."

Bertie said nothing.

"And she says your daddy hasn't got a backbone."

Bertie remained silent.

"Is that true, Bertie?" asked Ranald. "Can you be born without a backbone? Because it must make it quite hard to stand up straight, don't you think?"

"It's not true, Ranald," said Bertie. "My dad has got a backbone. It's connected to his ribs, I think. Maybe your mummy's thinking of somebody else."

"Possibly," said Ranald. He noticed that Olive was about to make an announcement. "I suppose we'd better listen. Olive's going to say something."

Olive stepped into the middle of the floor. "I've got something really important to say," she said. "So you'd all better shut up."

"I hate her," whispered Ranald. "I hate Olive so much."

Bertie looked down at the floor. Why did people dislike one another so much? Why was the world like this – so full of feelings that did not really need to be there?

"I heard you, Ranald Braveheart Macpherson," said Olive. "I heard what you said."

13

Olive Spells it Out

Olive stood in the middle of the floor and addressed her assembled guests.

"I know you're all really pleased to be at my birthday party," she said. "So, I'd like to thank you all for coming and also for the presents." She paused, acknowledging an encouraging smile from Pansy. "Most of the presents were quite nice – most, but not all." And here she sought out Bertie, and fixed him with an intense stare.

"But the whole point about a birthday is not to get presents," said Olive. "It's to share with your friends. Birthdays are about sharing, you know."

While this brought murmurs of agreement from the girls, Bertie and Ranald remained impassive.

"I want you all to enjoy yourselves," said Olive. "We've got a really good game to play, but before we do that you should have something to eat."

"There are plenty of cakes," said Pansy. "Although Bertie and Ranald have already had one and so they're going to have to wait until everybody else has had theirs."

"Yes," said Olive. "Don't think Pansy and I won't see you if you have more than your fair share. We will, won't we, Pansy?"

"Yes," said Pansy emphatically.

While her guests helped themselves to macaroons, Olive sought out Bertie and Ranald.

"There's something I meant to ask you, Bertie," she said. "You know how you and I are engaged? How you're going to marry me when we're twenty? You haven't forgotten that, I hope – because I haven't, you know."

Bertie opened his mouth to answer, but was cut short by Olive.

"I know what you're going to say, Bertie Pollock," she said. "But it's no use denying it. I've got it in writing."

"You made that up," protested Bertie. "I saw you copying my signature, Olive."

Olive pursed her lips. "How dare you accuse me of forgery, Bertie! And you know what? I'm not going to argue with you. There's no point in arguing with somebody who hasn't got a leg to stand on. All I wanted to do was to ask you whether you'd chosen your best man yet. That's all."

Bertie gasped. "We're not going to get married, Olive . . ."

Olive ignored this. "Because I think you should, Bertie. It may be a long time from now . . ."

"Thirteen years," said Pansy helpfully. "Twenty take away seven is thirteen."

Olive gave Pansy a dismissive glance before continuing, "You have to think of people's diaries, Bertie. People have a lot to do these days. You need to give them lots of notice. Even somebody like Ranald will have some commitments. It doesn't matter that he's got no friends, he'll still be busy doing *something*."

"I'm not going to—"

Olive cut him short. "So, I think you should ask Ranald right now to be your best man, Bertie."

Ranald looked up brightly. "Oh yes, Bertie. That's fine. I'll do it. I'll be your best man. Thank you very much."

"There," said Olive. "That's settled that." She fixed Bertie with a challenging stare, as if to dare him to contradict her. "And there's one other thing, Bertie. I am *not* having Tofu at our wedding. Definitely not. So, don't you go and invite him because there'll be real trouble if you do."

"Best not to," agreed Ranald.

"Yes," said Olive. "Ranald's right, Bertie. And, by the way, Bertie, how's your mother these days? Or should I say ex-mother, now that she's run away to Aberdeen."

Bertie looked down at the floor. Olive was unbearable, but he felt powerless to resist her. "She hasn't run away, Olive," he muttered.

It was as if Olive did not hear him. "My mummy says that your mother – I mean, your ex-mother – is having an affair, Bertie. I heard her talking to her friend about it. I know how to listen in on their phone, Bertie. You wouldn't know that sort of thing, but I do.

I listened to my mummy speaking to one of her friends, and she said that your mother had gone off to Aberdeen to be with her lover. With her lover, Bertie. But then she said that your ex-mummy's boyfriend has chucked her out of the house, Bertie, because he can't stand her. He's had enough, Bertie. That's what she said. And now she's found somebody else. A man who works on an oil rig."

Bertie started to protest. "That isn't true, Olive . . ."

"Oh, you can deny it all you like, Bertie," Olive interjected. "But you know something? Denying things doesn't make them not true."

And with that, Olive flounced away, leaving Bertie staring at Ranald Braveheart Macpherson in dismay.

"I'm really sorry about your ex-mummy," said Ranald. "It's really bad luck having a mother like that."

Bertie felt a wave of sorrow welling up within him. He wanted his mother back; no, he didn't want his mother back. He wanted . . . he was not sure what he wanted. He had always wanted a true friend, and he had thought that Ranald would be that friend, and yet here he was siding with Olive in the matter of his wedding – encouraging her, really, rather than standing by him in his programme of Gandhian civil disobedience to Olive's tyranny.

"You shouldn't have agreed to be my best man, Ranald," he muttered. "You shouldn't have said yes to Olive."

Ranald's eyes widened with dismay. "But I was only trying to help you, Bertie. Don't you want me to be your best man?" He searched Bertie's expression for some sign of understanding. This was awful for Ranald: he loved Bertie dearly; Bertie was definitely his best friend. He wanted to be his blood brother, if at all possible. They could prick each other's fingers with a pin and mingle the blood to make them blood brothers. He had heard that this is what you did with your best friends if you wanted to keep them for life. He would willingly do that with Bertie, but here was his friend, his dear, dear friend, accusing him of treason – and with Olive, of all people – Olive, the ultimate enemy.

Ranald Braveheart Macpherson started to cry.

"Oh, Ranald," said Bertie. "Don't cry, Ranald."

And then Bertie started to cry too.

Olive and Pansy were quick to notice this. Olive came skipping across the room and peered into the faces of the two boys.

"Why are you two crying?" she demanded. "You really shouldn't cry on somebody's birthday, you know. It's jolly selfish of you."

"Typically selfish boys," echoed Pansy, who had now joined Olive. "Just thinking of themselves. Crying all over the place like that."

"Really!" exclaimed Olive. "How can one even begin to understand boys?"

"I have no idea," said Pansy.

14

A Stendhal Syndrome Survivor

Antonia Collie had now settled into her new flat in Drummond Place, just round the corner from Scotland Street. Finding it had been a stroke of luck – the flat had belonged to an old friend who had happened to mention to Antonia that she was moving to Melrose. She would prefer, she said, to sell the flat without having to put it on the market, as that would entail her getting it into a fit state for sale and also putting up with all the inconvenience of showing it to prospective purchasers. Sensing an opportunity, Antonia offered her friend the valuation price, and this offer was rapidly accepted. It was at the upper limit of what Antonia could afford, but she thought it was well worth what she had to pay. The flat was on the first floor, and had the high ceilings and elegance of a Georgian drawing room flat. Not only that, but it had a view of the gardens in the centre of the square and, most importantly, the owner had the right to use those gardens. It was summer, and a good one too, and Antonia looked forward to sitting in the gardens, reading, and thinking about her great project on the Scottish saints.

Antonia had lived in the area before. She had originally been Domenica's neighbour in Scotland Street, but that was before that fateful trip to Italy. It was in Florence that she had been struck down in the Uffizi Gallery with a serious case of Stendhal Syndrome, a rare psychiatric condition afflicting those who become overwhelmed by beauty, whether of art or architecture or both. The syndrome involves an acute state of anxiety, and most cases end up in a psychiatric hospital.

A closely connected condition is Jerusalem Syndrome, which affects those who become overwhelmed by the fact that they are in Jerusalem, with all that that signifies spiritually and aesthetically. Again, this may lead to a spell in hospital, although the patient usually recovers quite quickly.

In Antonia's case, while her initial treatment was in a psychiatric hospital, she was taken in for recuperation by an order of nuns. In the care of these nuns she was gradually able to recover, spending her days in the grounds of their well-appointed convent in the Sienese hills. The life suited her, and she ended up staying far longer than was required by her original misfortune. She liked the nuns, and they liked her, referring to her as "our Scottish sister". Rather unwisely, she sold the flat in Scotland Street, and it was acquired by Domenica, who had long needed a bit more space. Through the removal of a wall, that goal was achieved, and Domenica and Angus now enjoyed the use of several extra rooms.

Antonia eventually returned to Scotland in the company of one of the nuns, Sister Maria-Fiore dei Fiori di Montagna, an aphorist whose observations on a wide range of subjects had both dazzled and impressed much of Edinburgh. Sister Maria-Fiore also proved to be something of a social success, and was soon seen at parties, surrounded by a growing band of acolytes. It was convenient for both Antonia and Sister Maria-Fiore to share a flat, and their short time in Dundonald Street had thrown up no disagreeable surprises, so the nun had now moved into the new flat in Drummond Place, occupying the spare bedroom at the back that Antonia described as her *cell*.

"Not in the prison sense," Antonia joked. "I was thinking more of convents."

"I require little," Sister Maria-Fiore assured her. "Those who require little can make do with even less than they have."

This was typical of the nun's aphorisms, and, like many of them, prompted analysis at several different levels. Even a simple observation on the weather could, when delivered by Sister Maria-Fiore dei Fiori di Montagna, assume extraordinary significance. "If there is rain today," she might say, "then rain will surely follow." That could mean that any rain is likely to be prolonged, with shower following shower, or it could be a comment on the inevitability of the weather. Or it could mean something altogether different. Whatever the real meaning might be, the remark would be greeted with nods of agreement and comments of "Yes, I suppose that's right" or "How very true!"

The two women lived together in satisfying amity. Sister Maria-Fiore both paid her way and undertook her share of the domestic chores. Antonia would have been willing to accommodate her for nothing, but the nun insisted on paying the going rent for a room in a New Town flat. She had, she explained, a flow of ready income from a shop that had been given to her by her uncle, who ran extensive protection rackets in Naples, Cosenza and Messina. "My uncle is a sinner," Sister Maria-Fiore told Antonia. "But we must love sinners, mustn't we? The love we give to sinners is the same as the love they give to us."

Antonia was unsure what to make of this. So she nodded, which she had found was the best response to much of what Sister Maria-Fiore said.

"Yes, he is a sinner," Sister Maria-Fiore continued. "But he is nonetheless a man of great piety. He attends Mass every day without fail – without fail."

Antonia raised an eyebrow. That sounded like hypocrisy to her, but she was not sure whether she could say it.

"Some might call that hypocrisy," said Sister Maria-Fiore.

"Yes, I can see . . ."

Sister Maria-Fiore cut her short. "But I would not call it that. Piety can exist in the deepest chambers of the heart. And who can fathom those chambers, Antonia? Not I. Nor you, I suspect."

Antonia nodded.

"My dear uncle will have to give an account of himself in the next world," Sister Maria-Fiore continued. "And I am sure that he will be treated with mercy – because of his piety. I expect to meet him on the other side."

"That will be nice," said Antonia. "Will you introduce us?"

"Of course. I shall be happy to do that," said Sister Maria-Fiore.

Rent was negotiated, and Sister Maria-Fiore dei Fiori di Montagna paid it regularly, by a standing order on a Neapolitan branch of the Banco dello Spirito Sancto.

"The Holy Ghost's bank," quipped Antonia.

"We never joke about banks in Italy," Sister Maria-Fiore admonished her. "It is considered bad luck."

And with that she crossed herself and, simultaneously, made a sign against the evil eye.

15

Garden Governance Issues

Shortly after she had moved in, Antonia invited Domenica to visit her in her new flat. That visit took place one Friday morning, when Sister Maria-Fiore dei Fiori di Montagna was at her Pilates course.

"Dear Sister Maria-Fiore dei Fiori di Montagna loves her Pilates," Antonia said.

"We are very unfit," said Domenica. "Angus and I barely raise a finger from day to day."

"But I see him walking about so purposefully," said Antonia. "One would never know he had nothing to do."

Domenica bristled. The remark was typical of Antonia, she thought. She has never forgiven me over that blue Spode teacup issue, she said to herself.

"Angus is actually rather busy," she pointed out.

"Of course," said Antonia, in such a tone as to imply that nothing could be further from the truth.

"He has several commissions at present," said Domenica. "Including one from the Scottish Government."

Antonia sniffed. "I'm not sure that I agree with spending government funds on art," she said. "But I imagine there are those who take a different view."

Domenica gritted her teeth. "It's so nice to see you, Antonia," she said. "Are you still writing that book of yours? What's it about again? Irish saints?"

Antonia corrected her sharply. "Scottish saints, Domenica."

"Of course. Though the distinction, surely, was slight in those early days. Would you consider Columba to be an Irish saint or a Scottish saint?"

"He was Scottish," said Antonia firmly.

Antonia had taken Domenica into the drawing room, and Domenica was looking about critically. "It'll be much nicer once you've decorated it," she said.

"But I already have," said Antonia.

"Ah. I see. Oh well, what I was thinking of was your stuff – your own furniture. I just can't believe the bad taste of some people."

"But this is my stuff," said Antonia.

"Ah. I see," said Domenica breezily. "Nice old stuff is always best. It doesn't matter that it's cheap. You can get used to anything, they say."

They progressed to tea, which was served in blue Spode teacups. As she saw them being produced, Domenica caught her breath: obviously Antonia was more than happy to rake over old coals.

"Blue Spode," said Antonia. "My favourite."

"Very nice," muttered Domenica. She would not be drawn on that one. The past was the past and it was hardly helpful to revisit things that had happened some years ago.

"I used to have more cups than I currently do," said Antonia. "I'm down to two now. I used to have three."

"I know how you feel," said Domenica. "My Minton breakfast cups are both chipped – one so badly we can't really use it. I have my name down for one with those china search people, but nothing has turned up."

"I'm at a loss to explain how I could lose a teacup," said Antonia. "But there we are."

"Yes, indeed. There we are."

"It's almost as if somebody *stole* it," Antonia continued. "But who would steal a teacup?"

"Who indeed?" said Domenica.

There was an awkward silence. I would, thought Domenica

guiltily. She had taken the teacup from Antonia's kitchen in the belief that it was hers, wrongly held by Antonia. But then she had discovered her original teacup – the one she thought had gone missing – which meant that she must have taken a teacup to which Antonia was actually entitled. She should have restored it to its owner, but she did not. She could not admit that she had removed a teacup in the first place, as it would be tantamount to admitting to house-breaking.

"But let's not dwell on theft," said Antonia. "There is so much to talk about." She looked out of the window. "I do love the gardens," she said. "I'm so looking forward to being on the committee."

Domenica drew in her breath. The gardens committee wielded considerable power and it did not bode well that Antonia was insinuating herself onto it.

Antonia was aware that Domenica was now on her guard. She smiled as she delivered the next piece of news. "Yes," she said, "both Sister Maria-Fiore and I decided to offer our services. We were co-opted at the last meeting of the committee."

Domenica remained silent. This was dangerous news, because there had been talk of the committee flexing its muscles in a way that could be very much to the disadvantage of Angus and herself – indeed of any of those on Scotland Street who used the gardens. According to the original charter, the only people entitled to a key were those who lived on Drummond Place itself. In a historical concession, the privilege of key ownership had been given to a few residents of Scotland Street, but only to those who had windows overlooking the gardens. That brought Domenica into the category of those who were entitled to have a key, but it excluded others. And the window concession, as it was called, was vulnerable. It did not appear in the charter, and every so often there had been talk of withdrawing it. She and Angus, then, used the gardens on sufferance – and now that sufferance was controlled, in part at least, by Domenica's old rival.

"Not very democratic," sniffed Domenica. "Co-opting people, that is."

"Oh, I don't know," Antonia said. "It's rather like the House of Lords, isn't it? One can recruit a broad range of talents."

"Oh, I wouldn't compare the gardens committee to the House of Lords," said Domenica. "And, frankly, with all due respect to Sister Maria-Fiore dei . . ."

"Dei Fiori di Montagna."

"Yes, with all due respect to her, what can she possibly bring to the table? She's an Italian nun, after all. Do Italian nuns have particular insights into the needs of Scottish gardens?"

Antonia was not prepared to let that rest. "As a matter of fact, she does. She's very good at botanical names. She knows them all. I am constantly astonished at her knowledge of such things."

"But we all know the names of the trees in the gardens," said Domenica. "I could identify every one of them for you if you need assistance in that department. I wouldn't want you to be in the dark, so to speak, about any of our trees."

"That's very kind of you," said Antonia. "But I am quite cognisant of them, you know."

Domenica looked out of the window. Outside, the very trees under discussion were caught by a breeze, making their branches sway gently. This was very dangerous territory because of Angus's ambition to build a shed. He had several allies on the gardens committee who had assured him that they would allow a shed, provided it was open to all. Now it was possible that the balance of power would shift, and she could imagine Antonia delighting in the chance to veto a shed.

The branches of the trees moved once again in the wind. *The winds must come from somewhere when they blow* . . . The line of poetry came to her unbidden. It was so beautiful. But who had written it? *The winds must come from somewhere when they blow* . . .

16

Wee Moupie

Big Lou had changed the opening hours of her coffee bar. A piece of laminated paper, stuck to the front door, announced that the premises would shut at four in the afternoon. It made no real difference to the business – the two hours between then and the old closing time of six were never particularly busy. The notice announcing this change had been couched in tactful terms. *After extensive consultation with customers, it has been decided to close the coffee bar at 4pm each day rather than 6pm.* It was true that there had been consultation, but it had hardly been extensive. In fact, it had consisted of no more than a brief conversation with Matthew, who had said, "Sure, why not?" and one with Angus Lordie, who had said, "I didn't know you were open after four anyway." In Big Lou's view, these two regular customers could be taken as speaking for the entire public, and the decision was taken.

The reason for this change had nothing to do with any laziness on Big Lou's part. She had been used to working long hours all her life; even as a small girl, she had put in lengthy periods working on the family farm, helping with the lambing, rounding up sheep, mucking out the byre – all the tasks that a farm-child takes in her stride. And she came from a part of the world where hard work was taken for granted, where people accepted responsibility for themselves and their families, and where leisure was a rare treat. There was always something to do on a farm, there was always something to be cleaned, or painted, or put away. That was the way it had always been, from the days when the hay was scythed by hand, the cattle were driven to market along drove roads, and everybody retired to bed by eight at the latest, tired to the bone from the day's work.

The reason for the change in opening hours was connected with Big Lou's foster son, Finlay. She had taken this little boy, Bertie's contemporary, into her home after he had had a bad start in life with parents who, for various reasons, were unable to give him the love and attention he deserved. That was what he needed above all other things, and that was what Lou, in the bigness of her heart, gave him unconditionally. From being shy and withdrawn, uncertain as to where he stood in the face of confusing life events, Finlay had blossomed into a secure and happy child, safely settled at Flora Stevenson primary school in Stockbridge, and now a promising member of a small ballet class.

At the end of each school day, Finlay was picked up by a woman with whom Big Lou had an arrangement. This woman looked after three children after school, keeping them in her flat in Stockbridge until a parent collected them at the end of the working day. This small after-school club suited all parties: the woman earned a bit of money and the parents were secure in the knowledge that their children would be well looked after.

This arrangement might have continued unchanged had it not been for Finlay's suddenly expressed desire to go to ballet classes. This had happened when Lou's eye was caught by a television showing of *The Red Shoes*. It was on an evening when Finlay was up late, having been unable to settle because of a gastric upset. He was lying on a couch with her, enjoying the joint treat of more time with Lou and late-night television. When *The Red Shoes* started, Lou assumed that Finlay would at last doze off, allowing her to transfer him to his bed. The opposite, though, was the case, and Finlay, from being somnolent, rapidly became alert.

He watched the film intently, and at the end said, "Lou, can I do that? Do you think I can do that?"

"Do what, Wee Moupie?" Wee Moupie was her pet name for Finlay – a name that he appeared to accept quite happily. The name just came to Big Lou, as fond names for children so often can. A *moup* was a Scottish rabbit, and that might have been the inspiration – Big Lou was not quite sure. But it suited him, as such names usually do.

"Dance."

She looked at him quizzically. "You liked it? You liked the dancing?"

Finlay nodded vigorously. "Very much, Lou. I really want to do it myself. Could I, do you think?"

The request was made with earnestness and urgency. Even so, Lou was hesitant. "You haven't tried it yet," she said. "It's one thing watching people dancing on television – it's another, you know, to actually dance yourself. It's a lot of hard work."

"I don't care," said Finlay. "I'd still like to do it."

Big Lou smiled indulgently. "Not many boys do ballet," she said. "It's mostly girls, I think."

It was a difficult subject to deal with. Where she came from – the rural hinterland – there would have been no doubt about how boys, among themselves, viewed ballet. She doubted whether those attitudes would have changed all that much. But this was Edinburgh, of course, and things might be expected to be different, especially in Stockbridge where boys were probably encouraged to be in touch with their balletic side. Or was it altogether wrong to regard ballet as a feminine interest? There was a widespread tendency to do that, but was that now considered outdated if not actually impermissible? Big Lou was not sure: the problem with the *Zeitgeist*, she felt, was that it was not always easy to tell if you were in touch with it quite as closely as you were meant to be.

"I don't care," said Finlay. "I bet I'd be good at it."

He smiled at her, and her heart gave a lurch. Finlay's arrival in her life had been a miracle, she thought, and that original miracle had been compounded time and time again as she witnessed the occasions of the small boy's happiness. She could scarcely believe how easy it had been to bring him joy; how much he had appreciated the attention she gave him; how much he valued the fact that in her flat in Canonmills he had a room of his own, filled with his things, and decorated according to his taste. For there on the walls were his framed picture of the Hearts football team, the players lined up and smiling as if victory in all their endeavours was all but assured; there, hanging from the ceiling, were his model planes, painstakingly assembled from balsa wood kits; and there, on the dresser, was his stuffed Pluto the dog, faithful companion of Mickey Mouse, which he had brought with him from the children's home.

"You really want to try it?"

He nodded eagerly. "Really, really, really."

"Then I'll find out where there's a class."

Finlay flung himself into her arms and kissed her. He smelled of freckles, and untidy hair, and boy. She let her cheek linger against his. She said, "Oh, Wee Moupie . . ."

He looked at her, and smiled again.

17

A Worrying Prospect

With her changed hours, Big Lou was able to collect Finlay at four-thirty from his after-school club and take him directly to his ballet class in St Stephen Street. This class took place in a converted church, now a yoga and dance studio, where the instructor, a woman in her thirties, who wore her hair tied back, almost painfully so, in the manner of ballet dancers, coached children through the grammar of dance, the ballet positions that they would practise repetitively day after day. A dapper pianist, seated at an old upright, played medleys with the beat of which the pupils synchronised, like marionettes, their movements – their *pliés*, *tendus* and so on – at the barre.

Big Lou had expected Finlay to lose interest after a few lessons, as his teacher at Flora Stevenson, in her last report, had mentioned a lack of persistence. The novelty of ballet lessons, she felt, with all their demands, would soon pall, particularly since he was the only boy in the class of ten. That this had not happened after five lessons caused her mild surprise; that it had not happened after twelve was even more significant.

"You're really enjoying ballet, aren't you, Wee Moupie?" she said one evening as she walked him back to the flat in Canonmills.

Finlay nodded. "Yes, Lou. I really like it."

"So I see."

He was silent for a while. They were now rounding the corner at the old St Stephen's Church, where the road dipped down towards Fettes Row. She looked down at him as he walked beside her. His hand, still damp after the exertions of the lesson, clasped her own hand tightly. It was so small, and yet he held on to her so – perhaps because he was frightened of losing her, as he had lost other things in his life.

"I'm always going to look after you, Wee Moupie," she said, her voice lowered, as if she were telling him a secret. She did not know why she should suddenly say that, but she said it nonetheless.

"Thanks." His voice was almost inaudible, but he said, "Thanks." Then he went on, "She says I'm really good at it."

"She?" asked Big Lou. "She who?"

"Her," said Finlay. "The ballet teacher. Miss Murray."

"She said that, did she?"

"Yes. She said that she's going to talk to you about it. She said I can really dance."

Big Lou smiled. "Well, that's good to know."

And the following Friday, when Big Lou went to collect Finlay, Miss Murray indicated that she wanted to speak to her. "You sit down over there, Finlay, while I speak to Mummy about something."

Big Lou said, "I'm not actually his mother. I'm a foster parent."

Miss Murray frowned. "I'm sorry. It's just that . . ."

"It makes no difference," said Big Lou. "I just thought you should know."

"Thanks. And of course it makes no difference." Miss Murray paused. "Well, maybe it does."

Big Lou looked surprised. "In what way?" she asked.

Miss Murray led Lou over to the other side of the studio, where there were two bent-pine chairs, both uncomfortable-looking. "I'm sorry we don't have anything better," she apologised. "We use as much of the space as possible for the actual classes."

As she sat down, Big Lou looked at the wall behind her. A framed photograph showed several adults – the studio's staff, by the look of things – standing to the side of a small group of young girls, one of whom was proudly holding a trophy. Next to that photograph, in a cheap gilt frame, was a black and white photographic studio portrait of a male dancer, wide-eyed, with high cheekbones; a Slavic face, thought Big Lou. At the foot of the photograph was an indecipherable signature, scrawled in fading ink.

"I'll come straight to the point," said Miss Murray. "Your wee boy, Finlay, is . . . well, I don't know any other word for it – he's exceptional."

Big Lou said nothing. She waited for the teacher to continue.

"No, I mean it," Miss Murray continued. "I wouldn't say it if I didn't mean it. He's the most gifted pupil I've ever had. Ever. In eight years of teaching here."

Big Lou laughed. "Well, who would have thought?"

"Yes, who would have thought? I suppose that's what everybody says when they come across something that they really weren't prepared for. And I wasn't prepared for this. He's a bit of a prodigy, I think."

"You mean . . ."

Miss Murray sounded even more convinced. "Yes, a prodigy. He's just got it . . . in him. It's there, in him. He dances like an angel."

Big Lou smiled. "He's a great wee boy."

"Oh, he's that all right," Miss Murray agreed. "But this boy, Mrs . . ."

"Call me Big Lou. Everybody does."

Miss Murray blushed. "Lou?"

"If that's what you want. Others call me Big Lou – it's my name, you see."

Miss Murray thought she could never use such a ridiculous name. She could not.

"The point is, Lou," she said, "is that we need to get Finlay to a ballet school. Or you could consider it. I'd just like to get that possibility onto the table."

"But he *is* at ballet school," said Big Lou. "He comes here – to you."

Miss Murray shook her head. "No, I don't mean that. I mean a proper, full-time ballet school. There are places, you know, where they take children and school them while at the same time giving them all the tuition they need to dance."

Big Lou's gaze returned to the photograph of the male ballet dancer. "Aye, I've heard of those places."

"Well, I think he could get in. He would have to audition, of course, and he might not get a place, although I'm pretty sure he would." She paused. "I don't see how they could refuse somebody like him. He really is . . ." She searched for the right word, and decided on *special.*

Big Lou was silent for a few moments. Then she said, "But have we got one of these schools in Edinburgh?"

Miss Murray shook her head. "No, we haven't – unfortunately. I wish we did."

"So . . ."

"No, don't worry," said Miss Murray. "These places are boarding schools. The children go and stay there."

Big Lou averted her gaze. The little boy whom she had at long last found would be taken away from her. How could she even consider such a proposition?

Miss Murray was staring at her. "Well?"

"I'll think," said Big Lou.

18

She Would Do Anything for Him

That evening, after Finlay had finished the macaroni cheese she prepared for his supper, and following his bath, Big Lou tucked him up in his bed and began to read him the nightly story which they never missed and which, for both of them, had become an unmissable feature of the day. The story that night was about Babar the elephant, and the doings of his children, Pom, Flora, Alexander and Isabelle. It was the first book in the series, and it contained a section that Big Lou had been forewarned to omit – the death of Babar's mother, at the hands of a cruel hunter. It was this event that had propelled Babar to seek refuge in the city, where he benefited so obviously from French culture. As she read the saga of the kingdom of the elephants, Big Lou began to notice that Finlay was not paying as much attention as he normally did to the story.

"Have you had enough of Babar?" she asked.

The boy looked up at her. The space rocket counterpane, littered with stars and floating astronauts, was pulled up to his chin. "No," he said. "I don't mind Babar."

"You sure?"

He nodded. "I like elephants."

Big Lou continued to read. But then she saw him fidget. "I think you want another story," she said, closing the book. "Am I right? Are you too big for Babar now?"

Finlay shook his head. "No. I like Babar." And then, "What did she say to you?"

"Who?" But Big Lou knew whom he meant.

"Miss Murray."

Big Lou looked up at the ceiling. She did not know how she would answer this. You could not lie to children, but did you always have to tell them everything?

"She talked about your dancing. She said you were very good."

The answer seemed to please him.

"And?" he said.

"Well, she told me you were the best pupil she had ever had."

He looked thoughtful. "And did she tell you about this special school? Did she say anything about that?"

Big Lou was not prepared for this. It had not occurred to her that Miss Murray would have said anything about ballet school to Finlay. It was completely inappropriate, in her view, that the teacher should have done so.

"She did say something," she answered slowly.

"And can I go?" asked Finlay.

Big Lou hesitated. She felt a surge of anger, directed towards the teacher. Of course, a child would assume far too much. Of course Finlay would assume that the mention of a possibility was a promise that it would happen; that's how children viewed the world – possibility, probability, and certainty were all the same to them.

Big Lou reached out and took his hand. "Now listen, Wee Moupie," she said. "I'm really pleased that you're enjoying your dancing. Really pleased. But there are lots of other things in your life, you know."

The disappointment on Finlay's face was only too apparent.

"But she said . . ."

Big Lou stopped him. "I'll talk to Miss Murray," she said. "I don't think she promised anything, did she?"

Finlay shook his head. "She said I could go to a special school where you danced all the time. She said that."

"But that's not how it is," said Big Lou. "Yes, there are schools where there's a lot of dance. But you have to do other things, you know. Ordinary school work. Sums. Spelling. All that."

He was silent.

Big Lou pressed on. "And you're happy at Flora Stevenson, aren't you? You've got all your friends. You wouldn't want to leave them, would you?"

She knew this was a major card; children were bone-deep stick-in-the-muds, especially when it came to friends. They did not like change.

Finlay seemed to consider this. "I like Flora Stevenson," he began.

"Well, there you are," said Big Lou quickly. "You wouldn't want to leave, would you?"

"But I'll like the other school, too," he continued. "Especially all the dancing."

She nodded. "I see. And boarding? These schools are boarding schools. You have to stay away from home." She paused. "From here." A further pause, and then she said, "And from me."

She knew that she should not make that point. It was emotional blackmail, pure and simple. So she immediately retracted.

"Of course, I'd still see you. This would still be home. You'd come back in the holidays."

He smiled. "I could keep my room, couldn't I?"

Big Lou said that he could. Her heart, though, was cold within her. "Should we go back to Babar?" she asked.

Finlay nodded. "Poor Babar," he said. "The bit you didn't read – the bit where the hunter shoots his mother. I feel really sad for Babar."

Later, in the kitchen, as she prepared her own dinner, Big Lou rehearsed in her mind what she would say to the ballet

teacher. She would point out to her that it was nothing short
of cruelty to raise a child's hopes over something that she
knew might not be possible. And then, quite apart from that,
there was the issue of respecting the role of parents – or carers,
for that matter. She was only a foster parent, but she had
fostered Finlay for some time now and had started adoption
proceedings. She, more than anybody else, had the right to
decide where he would pursue his education. It was nothing
to do with Miss Murray, and she had no right to barge in and
interfere in this way.

This imaginary conversation with Miss Murray only
succeeded in fanning the flames of her anger. But, after a few
minutes, that anger was replaced by a hollow despair. Big
Lou had never been successful in her romantic life. Every
relationship she had had with a man had come to nothing.
There had been the Jacobite plasterer; there had been the Elvis
impersonator; there had been the chef who had gone off to
Texas; none of these had worked out. And this fostering of
Finlay had been the one area in which she had been the driver
of an important relationship. He was hers. She loved him. She
would do anything for him. And now, it seemed, she would
have to choose between allowing him to do what his heart
appeared to be set upon, or clipping his wings before he had
even had the chance to unfold them.

19
Bruce Reflects

Bruce Anderson – property surveyor, former boyfriend of the Australian extreme sports enthusiast Clare, graduate in land management and surveying (with a lower second), and *echt* narcissist – did not normally read horoscopes. Few people, of course, openly admit to reading what the stars have in store for them, and yet even serious newspapers, seemingly unabashed, continue to publish these vague prognostications. This is because in spite of the absurdity of the basic premise – that the influence of distant planets somehow affects human affairs – we still feel tempted to flirt with the soothsayer, whatever guise such a person takes. And this is nothing new: the Oracle at Delphi was never short of supplicants, and obliged those seeking her advice by doling it out in dactylic hexameters. The fact that this advice might be hard to interpret was perhaps no accident: Nostradamus, the Brahan Seer, and the casters of contemporary newspaper horoscopes all observe the same precaution: *Never give details, dates, or indeed anything specific.* In this way, vague statements capable of interpretation in any number of ways will, by the sheer law of chance, occasionally be right. So to say *You are in for a surprise today* is going to be proved accurate more often than not, for what day involves nothing unexpected? Similarly, the prediction *Romance is in the air* is at least sometimes going to be true – because that is the way things tend to be.

Bruce was the exception to the rule that most people will sneak a look at their horoscope in spite of their disbelief in astrology. He thought horoscopes silly, and not the sort of

thing that a man would read. In fact, Bruce had recently said
to somebody in the pub, when the subject of horoscopes
happened to come up, "That's girly rubbish." *Girly rubbish*
was a vague concept in Bruce's mind, embracing romantic
films and novels, sentimentalism of any sort, birthday cards,
mindfulness, and any talk about relationships. On the latter,
he had brisk views: "Look," he was in the habit of saying,
"boy meets girl. They click or they don't – where's the story?"

On that evening, though, Bruce found himself with a few
minutes to kill before going out, and happened to pick up a free
magazine that had been stuffed through his letterbox. There
was a short article on skin care for men, which he skimmed
through – a complimentary magazine would have nothing to
teach him about *that* – and he then found himself faced with
a monthly horoscope. *Your stars reveal the weeks ahead for
you*, ran the column's headline. Immediately underneath this
ran the boastful observation, *You read it here first!*

Alongside the predictions there was a box in which the main
characteristics of the signs of the Zodiac were set out. Bruce
had been born under Taurus, and was pleased to read that his
sign was governed by Venus. That meant that he was attractive
to the opposite sex and passionate by nature. He was also
likely to be solid and dependable, even if inclined to enjoy
being pampered. All of that, he thought, sounded accurate
enough, even if the whole thing was weak-minded nonsense.

He scanned the page to see what the month had in store for
Taureans. "You are at a crossroads," the Oracle pronounced.
"One way will lead to disappointment, possibly failure; the
other will lead to achievement and success. You are not alone
at these crossroads; there is a friend there who will show you
the way." In smaller text, a subsidiary prediction advised that
romance was in the air, but that one should always be careful.
"Your passionate nature means that the heart can sometimes
rule the head. Be wary!"

Bruce smiled. That could mean anything. Romance was in the air? Of course it was – there are any number of women in Edinburgh who have their sights set on me, he told himself. They wish! After that business with Clare he was determined to take a bit of a holiday in that department. The women could wait, hard though that might be for them. Tough. He was going to concentrate on himself for a month or two before dating anybody again.

He tossed the magazine aside and prepared to take a shower. It had been an unusually warm day. It was early summer, when temperatures might be expected to creep up, even in Scotland, but there was still a freshness to the days that was more spring-like than summery. Today, though, a surge of warm air from the south had changed things, and Bruce had found his shirt clinging to him. Standing under the blast of his shower, Bruce applied liberal quantities of shower gel. This was followed by His Secret shampoo, Hello Good-Looking conditioner and split-end therapy, and, once the shower was over, Afterwards post-shower skin balm. Bruce then dried his hair under his Mancare hairdryer, applied his clove-scented hair gel, and was ready to take a look at himself in the mirror.

He liked what he saw. Bruce was at an age – very late twenties – when the first signs of gravity's effect might be detected. As he looked in the full-length mirror on his bedroom wall, he was reassured. There was not an ounce of spare flesh in sight. And this was not just a subjective assessment – Bruce kept accurate scales in the bedroom and made careful calculations of his BMI. That was perfect – as was everything else.

He briefly flexed his muscles, adopting for a few moments the classic pose of body-builders – hands clasped together, pulling against one another, elbows raised. He smiled. Most body-builders looked ridiculous, with their oiled, over-developed muscles rippling impossibly. Women did not like that; Bruce knew what they wanted, and that was not it. Beefcake was the right word for it. Disgusting. He, by contrast, was lither, more slender, like Adonis or . . . he tried to remember the other one – the one who carried messages and had those useful winged sandals. Hermes. That was him. He was a bit like Hermes.

He dressed with care, as he always did: crushed strawberry chinos, the creases impressed by his electric trouser press, an Oxford blue-stripe shirt, opened to the third button, and a light blue linen jacket he had found in Stewart Christie on Queen Street. Loafers slipped on – no socks – he gave himself another quick glance in the mirror. He studied the face that looked back at him. I am very, very lucky, he thought. I could have looked like anybody else, but I got this. I suppose I have my dad to thank. He was the best-looking man in Crieff by far, people said; maybe even the best looking in all Perthshire. Pity that he sagged.

20

At the Wally Dug

A few weeks earlier, Bruce had started going to the Wally Dug. This was a pub in Northumberland Street, just round the corner from Big Lou's, and it was rather more convenient than the Cumberland Bar for his flat in Abercrombie Place. Angus had started dropping in there too, having initially been dragged in by Cyril, who had a strange affinity with the place.

"It's possibly something to do with the name," Angus remarked to Domenica. "Cyril must feel that a pub called after a dog is his sort of place."

Domenica was tolerant of what she regarded as Angus's tendency to anthropomorphise – at least when it came to Cyril. He endowed the dog with far too great a degree of understanding, she thought; Cyril might be intelligent by canine standards, but he was still a dog, with all the limitations that this implied. Ultimately, it was a question of neural matter: Cyril had a dog's brain, and that governed the extent of his abilities. Cyril would never have language; he would never have a command of logic; he would never have the ability to think out of the box that was *dogness*, or *canininity*: the state of being a dog. And yet, of course, he had emotions – and even Domenica, with all her doubts about dogs in general, had to admit that in the canine breast there were lodged the very deepest of emotions. Dogs suffered – they suffered daily; they felt the most awful pangs the moment their owner left their sight; they felt the most intense regret when they were in disgrace for doing any of the things that dogs find it so hard to refrain from doing; they pined when their routine was changed and the familiar was replaced with the unfamiliar.

But Domenica felt that any suggestion that Cyril might respond to a picture of a wally dug on a brewer's mirror was no more than the fondest of imaginings. Angus, she realised, wanted Cyril to be more human, and this ambition distorted his view of what Cyril might reasonably achieve, given the limitations of his species. Cyril was Angus's best friend: she understood that, and accepted it – to an extent. She would have preferred Angus to spend more time with other people, but understood that he was one of those men who seemed to get by without seeing friends regularly. Matthew was a regular friend, and Big Lou – up to a point; and there were four or five members of the Scottish Arts Club, but apart from that she would find it difficult to name many others whom he saw all that often.

Angus was on reasonable terms with Bruce, even if they had very little in common. If they met in the pub they would talk to one another, but Angus would quickly find himself irritated by Bruce's vanity and self-obsession. On that evening, as Bruce entered the Wally Dug, he did not expect to meet Angus, nor indeed Cyril. The person he intended to see, though, was already there, sitting on one of the bar stools, deep in conversation with Murray Campbell, one of the bar's owners.

Murray had business to attend to, and went off to do this while Bruce greeted his old friend, Gav. Gav had been at school with Bruce at Morrison's in Crieff, where they had been constant companions. They saw one another less frequently in their university years: while Bruce went off to study land management, Gav had enrolled for a course in product design at Napier University. Their meetings over the following few years had been irregular, but recently they had taken to getting together every couple of weeks, usually in the

Wally Dug.

Gav worked for a small manufacturing firm in Dalkeith, just outside Edinburgh. This firm designed silica-based pot holders, spatulas, and other kitchen implements. They also held the patent on a new method of getting recalcitrant lids off jars, and were hoping to put that into production in the not-too-distant future.

Bruce approached Gav and shook his hand warmly. They took evident pleasure in one another's company, reverting without difficulty to the easy-going relationship of their schooldays.

"So," said Bruce, "what's new, Gav?"

"Nothing, Bruce-o," said Gav. "Same old, same old. You know how it is."

This exchange of words had become a private tradition of their friendship, and never changed. Thereafter the real conversation began, which was seasonal. In winter, it was largely focused on rugby, and on the prospects of Scotland in the Six Nations and in various other organised stramashes. In the summer, the rugby conversation was briefer, being restricted to a quick review of the doings of the Australians and New Zealanders. Both Gav and Bruce had been at that significant event at Murrayfield when Scotland had trounced the All Blacks so convincingly. On this particular evening, at the bar in the Wally Dug, they relived those sacred minutes, as they had done so many times since the day, before they moved on to discussing affairs of the heart.

"How's that woman of yours?" asked Bruce.

"Sally? Oh, same old, same old." Gav paused. "And you? Breaking anybody's heart these days?"

"Fighting them off," replied Bruce. "You know how it is."

"Jeez!" said Gav. "Some guys have all the luck."

"You could say that," said Bruce. "Still, I do it all for Scotland!"

Gav took a swig of his beer. "Jeez, I needed that." He paused. "You know something, Bruce-o? I think I may have met somebody who's just right for you."

Bruce raised an eyebrow. "Oh yes? Italian fashion model? Drives a Lamborghini?"

Gav laughed. "No, not quite. But not too bad otherwise."

Bruce looked at his friend. "You don't think I need any help, do you? Because let me tell you, I really *am* fighting them off, you know."

"Oh, I'm well aware of that," said Gav. "It's just that . . . well, I think you're at a bit of a crossroads, Bruce-o."

Bruce was quiet. *You are at a crossroads.* He remembered the words of the horoscope he had read only half an hour earlier. *You are at a crossroads. One way will lead to disappointment, possibly failure; the other will lead to achievement and success.* And here was Gav, of all people, uttering exactly the same pronouncement. It was quite uncanny.

"Crossroads?" said Bruce.

'Yes," Gav replied. "I think you are. You have to decide, pal. You have to get yourself fixed up."

"Fixed up? Why?"

Gav made a gesture that was hard for Bruce to interpret. It might have signified acceptance, or it might have meant that a conclusion had been reached only reluctantly. "You don't want to be single for ever," he said. "Cooking your own dinner when you're forty. How sad is that?"

"I'm not forty. Far from it. I'm not even thirty yet."

"No, but you will be one day, mate. And then what?"

Bruce waited.

"Sally has this friend, see. And she saw you – this woman – she saw you at a party, and asked Sally whether she knew you."

"She asked Sally? This woman asked her if she knew me?"

"That's it. Apparently, she said, '*Who's the dead sexy guy with the hair?*' That's what she said, Sally told me."

Bruce shrugged. "So? That's what they all say."

"Yeah, sure. But let me tell you something about this woman. Something seriously interesting."

21

Where the Thickos Go

Seated at the bar in the Wally Dug, Bruce listened intently as his old friend from Morrison's Academy days, Gav Macfadzean, told him the news that he thought he would find "seriously interesting".

"Right, when Sally told me that this girl had been asking who you were, I said: so, who is she? Do you know her?" Gav paused. "You know what it's like at those parties? A bit of a scrum. You spend a lot of time talking to people you don't really know."

Bruce nodded. "You end up shouting. And the next day you're hoarse."

"Tell me about it," said Gav. He smiled. "You remember that cosmic party that Shuggie gave when we were students? Remember it? In Tollcross. Bob and Fridgie were there, I think, and we . . ."

Bruce rolled his eyes. "We broke things. Yes, I remember."

"That was some party," said Gav.

"And then, when we went on the rugby tour of Ireland," Bruce said. "Boy oh boy . . ."

"Who could forget that? Remember that guy down in Limerick who had that muckle great house and that pack of dogs? Chap with a great conk of a nose. Some sort of Irish earl or lord or something. Remember him? And he was the patron or chairman, or something, of the local rugby club and he invited us all out to his place after the game."

Bruce smiled at the memory. "And we played rugby in his library? We used that old globe as the ball? Remember?

Not that he minded. The Irish are like that. They don't really mind."

"Great people," said Gav. "And he had that Brazilian girl working in the kitchen. Remember her? She had come to Ireland to learn English and had ended up working in the kitchen and looking after their goats. Remember the goats? Johnny Ferguson tried to ride on one of the big ones and got butted in the stomach. Stupid git."

"He was a good prop, though," Bruce mused.

"Yeah, sure. But he was pretty thick, wasn't he? Went down to that university just outside Newcastle where they send all the thickos. Can you remember its name?"

Bruce shook his head. "Durham?"

"No, I don't think so," said Gav. "Durham's the place for debbie girls. This other place is just for thicko men. They do a lot of agriculture degrees. Sports sciences – that's another one for the thickos. You can actually study golf somewhere. Did you know that? You get a place on the course as long as you can count up to eighteen. The number of holes in a course, you see. Count up to nineteen and you get a scholarship. That's all they ask. No Highers or anything like that."

"Amazing," said Bruce. He took a swig of his beer. "But what about this girl?"

"Which girl?"

"The one Sally saw at the party you were talking about."

"Oh yes, that girl. Well, Sally actually knows her and told me all about her. Her name's Jenny, and she's a looker, I'm telling you."

Bruce waited. There were plenty of lookers. Edinburgh was crawling with lookers, he thought.

"Her old man's called Harry. He's got a place near Peebles. And one somewhere up in teuchter territory – Inverness-shire, I think. He's loaded."

Bruce listened.

"He has a whole stretch of some salmon river up north."

Bruce shrugged. "There are hardly any salmon these days. I was reading somewhere that on one of those rivers they caught just one last year. One fish."

"That's the Russians," said Gav. "The Russians and the Spanish. They're taking the fish out at sea. Anyway, this Jenny's old man is the real McCoy."

Bruce was cool. "Oh yes?"

"Yes. Seriously. Big time, I tell you."

Bruce explained that he was not sure.

"But she wants to meet you," said Gav. "How can you say no in these circumstances?"

For a short while Bruce said nothing. Then he asked about the place near Peebles. What was it like?

"It's an estate," Gav said. "Not far from Traquair – you know that place? Not far from there. They've got a big pheasant shoot, you know. And their place up in Inverness is massive. Twenty-eight thousand acres, somebody said."

Bruce took this in. "So why hasn't she got a boyfriend?" he asked.

"She did have one," said Gav. "He left her."

"Why?"

"Who can tell? People leave one another. They get fed up with somebody's face and they quit. You can't blame them sometimes." Gav paused. "But that isn't the point. The point, Bruce-o, is that she's seen you and likes the look of you. She wants to meet you. What have you got to lose?"

"Well, put that way – nothing, I suppose."

"And if you can't stand her, well, you make an excuse and leave it at that. No harm done. You must have dumped plenty of women in your time."

Bruce grinned. "My quota," he said.

Gav laughed at the joke. Some things never changed: they

were back at school together in their last year. *My quota.* Then he said, "And what about you? Have you ever been dumped?"

Bruce shook his head. "Me? No. I do the dumping, not them. You know how it is."

Gav looked doubtful. "Funny, that. I heard from Fridgie that that Australian dame had given you the old heave-ho. For some extreme sports guy up on Skye."

Bruce made a dismissive gesture. "We split up," he said. "Mutual consent."

"I see."

"She wanted me back," Bruce continued. "I said: 'You had your chance, girl. Too late.' Great gnashing of teeth. Sobs. Danced around me with no clothes on. The works. But no, I'd made up my mind."

"Her loss," said Gav.

Bruce drained his glass of the last of his beer. In the brewer's mirror on the wall behind him, he caught sight of himself. The light was just right, he thought; it made him look even better than usual. But then he thought: looks don't last for ever. When he looked in the mirror in five, ten years' time, what would he see? He would still be handsome, of course, but *handsome old.* And there was nothing more tragic, Bruce thought, than *handsome old.* You were reminded by *handsome old* of what had been, and was no more; *handsome old* spoke of the past, of loss, of what was now gone. *Handsome old* was the bitty glory of Calton Hill and the faded splendour of those old Edinburgh hotels, still dignified old matrons in spite of attempts to rejuvenate them with swanky new names. People and buildings, thought Bruce, are much the same, when it came down to it. The thought was a disturbing one. *You are at a crossroads . . .*

Gav had thought of something else. "And another thing," he said. "Her old man, Harry Whatever – he owns a distillery."

Bruce looked up sharply. "Owns it?"

"Yes. The whole lot. It's been in the family for yonks. They make a rather good single malt."

Bruce looked back at the mirror. A distillery. Single malt. These things opened doors. Good seats at Murrayfield. Drinks in the Scottish Rugby Union boardroom – with the players. *Highland Cathedral.* The works.

"Next week?" he said to Gav.

22

The Desperation of Dan

For Bertie, the realisation that his life was going to be better now that his mother had gone to Aberdeen came the second Saturday after her departure with a phone call from that northern quarter. Nicola took the call, but was listened in to by Bertie, who was in his room at the time reading *Scouting for Boys*. This book had been banned by Irene, who kept a list of off-limits publications almost as long as the infamous *Index Librorum Prohibitorum* maintained by the Vatican until only a few decades ago. That index, of course, not only contained *The Three Musketeers*, but also Flaubert's *Madame Bovary* and Victor Hugo's *The Hunchback of Notre-Dame*. Irene would not have sought to have such reach in her censorship of Bertie's reading matter, but her list certainly contained Baden-Powell's useful treatise on how to use tracking skills in the bush, how to light a camp fire, and how to send signals from hilltop to hilltop by means of heliograph. It also contained many of the publications emanating from the Dundee fastness of Messrs DC Thomson, whose nose for what people want to read had long been an unerring one.

So it was that Bertie had been told that both the *Beano* and the *Dandy* were unwelcome in the house, as were any of the Commando comics that emerged from Dundee – those breathless recreations of the Second World War, full of shouts of *Banzai!* and *Schweinhund!* and peopled by square-jawed, salt-of-the-earth British NCOs.

Bertie had brought home a copy of the *Dandy*, loaned to him by Tofu on payment of twenty pence. "And you'd better return it tomorrow, Bertie," Tofu had warned. "If you don't, it's fifty pence a day penalty. Every day, that is. Fifty pence. So you'd jolly well better remember."

He was enjoying the adventures of Desperate Dan when Irene had pounced.

"That, Bertie," she said, "is the most dreadful rubbish. What *are* those Thomson people thinking about?"

"But I love it, Mummy," said Bertie. "Everybody does. There's this man called Desperate Dan, you see, who eats cow pie and is really strong. Tofu says that he can tear telephone books in half with his bare hands."

Irene paged through the confiscated comic. "Desperate Dan indeed," she snorted. "A complete male stereotype. I ask you, Bertie! Really!" And underneath her breath she muttered, "Heteronormative, too."

"But he really is strong, Mummy. What's wrong with being strong?"

Irene sighed. "Physical strength is often accompanied by the wrong attitudes, Bertie. I don't expect you fully to understand that" – Irene was never one to split an infinitive – "but one day you will, Bertie, and you'll thank Mummy for it."

That was the end of the *Dandy*, and Bertie's reading of such literature was thereafter confined to the school playground, where Tofu allowed him, for five pence a time, to read the comics that he bought at the newsagent's in Bruntsfield. But now, with Irene's move, a new post-censorship era had opened in Scotland Street, and Bertie was able to read *Scouting for Boys* openly as well peruse copies of the *Beano* rented from Tofu.

Nicola, who had stepped into Irene's shoes on her departure, was perfectly relaxed about Bertie's reading matter. She had discreetly disposed of an entire shelf of the works of Carl Gustav Jung and Melanie Klein that Irene had stored in Bertie's room, and replaced them with the *Babar* books of Jean and Laurent de Brunhoff, the collected Secret Seven adventures in their original unbowdlerised editions, and the subtly anarchistic writings of Roald Dahl.

Bertie liked all of those, and when he asked after the fate of what had been there before, it was out of idle curiosity rather than regret.

"What did you do with all those books by Mr Jung?" he asked.

Nicola was evasive, but only slightly so. According to one way of looking at it, she had taken an unpardonable liberty in disposing of property that was quite clearly not her own, but according to another – the view that she took herself – she had simply uncluttered the room to make way for more pertinent content.

"I found a new home for those books, Bertie," she said. "I'm sure Mummy would be happy to know that they've gone to that big charity book sale we have. They like getting books like that, Bertie. My friend Mary Davidson collects them and then sells them up in George Street – all for a very good cause, Bertie."

"And that other friend of yours, Granny," said Bertie. "Mr Holloway. I've seen him carrying boxes of books round the corner. Were those books by Mr Jung too, do you think?"

"Possibly," said Nicola. "This part of Edinburgh is full of books by Jung, I think."

"What about Glasgow?" asked Bertie. "Is it full of books by Mr Jung too?"

"I doubt it," said Nicola.

Later, listening to Nicola speaking on the phone in the hall, Bertie realised that what was being said meant freedom for him. There had been talk of Irene's coming down from Aberdeen that weekend, but the one-sided conversation that Bertie now heard gave joyous warning that this visit would now not take place.

"I'm sorry to hear that," said Nicola. "But there we are. The boys will be disappointed, of course, but it gives them something to look forward to."

There was silence as Irene, on the other end of the line in Aberdeen, responded.

Then Nicola again. "Of course, I'll take him to yoga. Yes, yes. I know where it is."

A further silence, broken at length by, "I shall pass that message on to Stuart. I believe he's spoken to the psychotherapist."

Silence.

"Yes, carrots. Yes, definitely. I've puréed them and I did *not* put sugar in them. I never do."

The conversation did not last long after that, and Bertie withdrew from the door where he had been eavesdropping. The important thing was not psychotherapy or carrots – it was the fact that his mother would not be coming down for the weekend. Edinburgh now lay before Bertie like a fabled, golden city. He had the whole weekend to do what *he* wanted to do. His grandmother would allow that – she always did. So he would accept the invitation that Ranald Braveheart Macpherson had extended to spend the day with him. He knew that his grandmother wanted to go to Valvona & Crolla, but that could be done before he went up to Ranald's house. And she would get him *panforte di Siena* when they were there. She did not disapprove of *panforte*, nor of *panettone*. Oh, joy to be alive and to be free! Oh, joy! Oh, joy!

23

A Very Special Olive Oil

Nicola saw no reason why Bertie should not spend the day with Ranald Braveheart Macpherson. She liked Ranald every bit as much as she disliked Olive, whom she regarded as an incipient Irene. By contrast, in Nicola's view Ranald was an entirely suitable friend for Bertie, even if his parents, whom admittedly she did not know very well, seemed to be somewhat tiresome. Ranald's father drank a bit much, Nicola thought, and his mother was given to expostulating on all sorts of subjects of which she, in Nicola's opinion at least, had little or no grasp. She had also heard the occasional rumour about Ranald's father's business, Macpherson Securities and General Holdings, but she knew that comments of that sort were often motivated by envy and emanated from people who had no securities themselves and, indeed, no holdings either.

"It's a very good idea for you to go to Ranald's," Nicola told Bertie. "But first I think we should go to Valvona & Crolla. I need to get one or two things there."

Bertie was very happy to agree to that. Nicola phoned Ranald's mother and made the arrangements. After the trip to Valvona & Crolla, they would all travel up on the 23 bus, Bertie would be dropped, and then Nicola would take Ulysses for an ice cream at Luca's at Holy Corner. Ulysses had no social life of his own, and an ice cream at Luca's would, for him, count as a major socialising experience.

At Valvona & Crolla Nicola worked through her shopping list with Bertie's help. There was cheese to be bought – a wedge from a mouth-watering quarter-wheel of Parmesan; there were slices to be pared from a large Milanese salami; there were sun-dried tomatoes, Puglian olives, porcini mushrooms, and balsamic vinegar all to be acquired. Then there were egg-based tagliatelle, artichoke hearts, and a small jar of Simone Calugi's whole summer truffle to complete the list.

Bertie, who had been brought up on Italian food by the Italophile Irene, was completely at home in the delicatessen. He was able to point Nicola in the right direction for any of the things she needed, and to express a remarkably informed opinion on the choices available to her.

"You must get that olive oil over there," Bertie said to his grandmother, pointing to a bottle of rich green estate oil. "That's the one Mummy always bought."

Nicola suppressed the urge to reject the oil out of hand, saying instead, "Well, there's a lot to be said for continuity, Bertie."

"It's called Poggio Lamentano," said Bertie. "And it comes from Italy."

Nicola smiled. 'I'd noticed there's a fair amount of Italian produce here, Bertie."

"Mr Zyw makes it," said Bertie. "He grows the olives and then makes them into oil. He has somebody put the oil in bottles, and then Mrs Contini brings them to Edinburgh. That's the way it works, Granny."

Bertie reached out for one of the bottles, just within his reach. As he did so, though, he toppled, and snatching at the bottle for support, he brought it crashing down. There was a muted explosive sound as the glass shattered and the viscous green liquid spread across the floor. Bertie struggled to regain his balance and was almost on the point of falling over the fragmented glass when Nicola caught him by the arm, pulling him back on his feet.

"Oh, Bertie," she exclaimed. "Watch out!"

Bertie stood disconsolate, his shoes spattered with olive oil.

He looked up at his grandmother, an expression of horror on his face.

"Oh, Granny, I didn't mean to drop it. It sort of . . . sort of . . ." He could manage no more as tears sprang to his eyes.

Nicola embraced him. "Oh, Bertie, it doesn't matter. Olive oil's just olive oil. The important thing is that you didn't hurt yourself."

In his misery, Bertie just managed to get his words out. "I can pay for it, Granny. I've got some money in my piggy bank. I can pay for it. I've got enough."

"Oh, you don't need to pay for it, darling. I can do that. It wasn't your fault."

A voice came from behind them. "Of course it wasn't your fault, Bertie. It was nobody's fault, and it won't take us a moment to clean that up."

Nicola turned around, to see Mary Contini standing behind her. She had not met her before, but recognised her from photographs in her books.

"I'm terribly sorry," Nicola said. "He was reaching out and somehow lost his balance."

Mary produced a handkerchief and gave it to Bertie. "There, Bertie. You wipe your tears away and then we can have a bit of *panforte di Siena*. I seem to remember that you like that – and who doesn't?"

Bertie took the handkerchief and wiped his eyes.

"I'll get somebody to clear this up," said Mary Contini. "You go through to the café at the back and I'll come along and join you."

Nicola ushered Bertie round the pool of olive oil and along the corridor to the café. "Now, isn't that kind?" she said to Bertie. "An accident is an accident. Everybody understands that. You know that, don't you?"

Bertie nodded. "I didn't mean to do it," he said.

"Of course you didn't, Bertie." Her heart went out to

the little boy, to the little scrap of humanity that was her grandson; whose life so far, she felt, had been blighted by that shrill ideologue of a mother with her pressure and ambitions and consistent failure to understand what went on in a seven-year-old head – and a seven-year-old heart. She wanted to embrace him, to pick him up then and there, in the middle of the shop, among the salamis and the cheeses and the surviving bottles of Tuscan olive oil, and hug him to her and say *Don't worry, Bertie; don't worry about anything – anything at all.* In fact, at moments like this, she thought, she could only too easily fold her arms around *anybody* and say the same thing to them. Because the world was so full of anxiety and conflict and it was so unnecessary that this should be so, when all of us, in our heart of hearts, wanted the same thing, which was love and understanding and gentleness.

Mary Contini met them in the café. She had a freshly opened *panforte di Siena* and placed this on the table in front of Bertie. For Nicola, she had a fresh bottle of Poggio Lamentano extra-virgin olive oil, a tricolour Italian ribbon tied about its neck. "A gift from me," she said.

Bertie was eyeing the *panforte*. "Why wait, Bertie?" said Mary. "Tuck in."

24

Bonnie Charlie's Noo Awa . . .

Having picked up Ulysses from Stuart's care, Nicola was free to accompany Bertie and his small brother by bus to Ranald Braveheart Macpherson's house. Irene had always referred to this house as *la casa di Macpherson*, in a rather sarcastic, disapproving tone, as if the Macphersons themselves had given it a pretentious name. In fact, Irene frequently gave houses names that she thought the owners might apply to them in innocence of the mockery they would attract. A retired financier, for example, would live in a house called Dun Speculatin, while couples whom she considered hopelessly suburban would be described as occupying Mon Actual Repos. Others might live in Bourgeois Towers, or La Maison des Nouveaux Riches, or simply Nouveau Riche.

Nicola had heard her do this, and did not approve. It was only too easy to laugh at the aspirations of others and ignore one's own. But where did you start with somebody like Irene? Where could you possibly start? The Macpherson house was, in fact, a rather comfortable one, and not at all pretentious. It was typical of the sort of house built in the 1880s by speculative builders who had bought land to the south of Edinburgh, and were creating new suburbs for those wishing to migrate from the New Town and the reekiness of Auld Reekie. In this way Morningside had come into existence, providing families with the *rus in urbe* benefits of fresher air and a view of the Pentland Hills. That Morningside came, in due course, to be synonymous with a rather prissy respectability did not detract from the haven it provided for those keen to pursue the universal suburban dream – space, security, and, if you were lucky, just enough garden room, in the fleeting Scottish summer, to unfold a deck chair or grow a single row of beans.

The Macpherson house in Albert Terrace, perched on the crest of the hill that fell away down into Morningside, was fortunate in having a large walled garden in which there were several well-established trees. At the end of this garden was an area that Ranald's father had allowed to grow wild, and this had become overgrown with brambles, rhododendrons and a luxuriant and impenetrable stand of bamboo. From the perspective of a small boy, it was a jungle, every bit as full of possibility as a slice of real jungle in Africa or the Far East.

"I think there may be wild animals in my garden," Ranald once said to Bertie. "I think I've seen signs of them."

"You're jolly brave," said Bertie. "There are no wild animals in the Drummond Place Gardens."

"I'm not saying that there are zebras or anything like that," said Ranald. "But I think there may be one or two of those big cats – you know, jaguars, or panthers, or something like that. I've read that some of those have got loose and are hiding in people's gardens."

"Or wolves?" asked Bertie. "Do you think there might be wolves?"

Ranald was not sure. "Sometimes I've heard howling," he said. "But I think that might just have been a dog somewhere. But it might be a wolf for all I know."

"It's best to be careful," said Bertie.

When they arrived, it was Ranald who opened the front door to them.

"Well, well," exclaimed Nicola. "Look at Ranald, Bertie – he's wearing his kilt. Isn't that nice?"

"Why are you wearing your kilt, Ranald?" asked Bertie.

Ranald pointed over his shoulder into the house. "I always

do on Saturdays, Bertie. My dad has his Scottish country dance group. He likes me to wear the kilt when they're here."

"Isn't that nice?" said Nicola, peering beyond Ranald into the hall beyond. "To have Scottish country dancing on a Saturday afternoon . . . In Morningside . . ." She paused.

"Well, I'll come back for Bertie at six-thirty. I think that's what your mummy said, Ranald."

Ranald nodded. "She said that Bertie can have his tea here and then go back to Scotland Street. She said he'd get a better meal here."

"Did she now?" said Nicola.

She bent down and kissed the top of Bertie's head. Once she had gone, Bertie followed Ranald Braveheart Macpherson along a corridor to his room. He always enjoyed being in the Macpherson house, as the walls were lined with pictures of clan events – battles and gatherings, farewells and arrivals – all the things that made Scottish history so stirring. He paused at a large coloured engraving of Charles Edward Stuart, Bonnie Prince Charlie no less, about to embark on a rowing boat. The oarsmen, of whom there were four, were all obvious Highlanders, windswept and wild in their appearance, their brows set to the task in hand. In the background, towering above a range of Highland mountains, storm clouds signalled tricky weather ahead.

"That's Bonnie Prince Charlie," said Ranald. "My dad is a big fan of his. He says he's going to come back one of these days."

Bertie frowned. "I don't think so, Ranald. I think Prince Charlie's dead."

Ranald Braveheart Macpherson looked at Bertie with dismay. "Dead, Bertie? Since when?"

"Oh ages, Ranald. Months and months. Ages. That's why that song goes *Bonnie Charlie's noo awa* . . . You know the one? That means Bonnie Charlie's now away. That means he's dead, Ranald."

Ranald's lip quivered. "My dad's going to be really sad, Bertie."

Bertie looked sympathetic. 'Maybe someone else will come instead, Ranald. You never know."

Ranald shook his head. "I bet it was the Campbells. I bet they got rid of Prince Charlie."

"Very likely," said Bertie. "Campbells are very wicked people, Ranald. Everybody knows that."

They moved on to Ranald's room. Drifting through from the drawing room came the first strains of "Mairi's Wedding" as interpreted by Jimmy Shand and his Band.

"My dad and his friends are going to start dancing," said Ranald. "They always play that tune when they're about to begin."

In the sitting room, unseen at that point by Bertie and Ranald Braveheart Macpherson, six couples, the men in kilts, the women in long tartan skirts and white tops, took their places for the first dance. This was a regular meeting, brought about after Ranald's father's conviction by Edinburgh Sheriff Court for a regulatory financial offence connected with his company. It was not an offence of dishonesty, but it did involve disregard of the law, and for that the sheriff deemed it appropriate to impose a community service order. The resulting sentence was two hundred hours of Scottish country dancing, the first forty of which had already been danced, and the remaining one hundred and sixty were yet to be completed.

25
The Reel of the 51st

It did not take long for Bertie and Ranald Braveheart Macpherson to get bored with the Scottish country dancing that was taking place in the Macphersons' large sitting room. Jimmy Shand, played on an expensive stereo system, wheezed his way through the repertoire, bringing Auchtermuchty into the heart of Morningside. Close one's eyes and one might be in Oban, in the bar of the Royal Hotel, or in Tobermory, at a ceilidh in the Western Isles Hotel; open them and one was back in Edinburgh, watching six couples work their way through the intricacies of increasingly obscure traditional dances. Some of these dances had no discernible beginning, nor middle, nor indeed end, and just went on and on until the accordionist and his colleagues succumbed to fatigue or, as in the case of one famous regular ceilidh in an Argyll village hall, until the accordionist, being too drunk to continue playing, fell backwards off his chair, thereby signalling an end to the evening of polite and couthie entertainment.

"Have you had enough of this, Bertie?" whispered Ranald as the dancers prepared for the third Gay Gordons of the afternoon.

Bertie nodded. "I wouldn't mind doing something else, Ranald," he replied. "But it's your house – you decide."

Ranald leaned closer to his friend. "I've had an idea, Bertie. Would you like to hear what it is?"

Bertie said that he would.

"Then we'll need to go to my room," said Ranald. "I'll tell you there."

They left just as the music started. On the first bar, several of the dancers let out a whoop of delight – that signal, familiar to all practitioners of Scottish country dancing, that at least somebody is enjoying himself.

In his bedroom, the door closed firmly against the music, Ranald told Bertie of his plan.

"I saw something in the *Evening News*," he said. "It was an advertisement for a circus, Bertie. I asked my Mummy to read it to me . . ."

"You should learn how to read, Ranald," said Bertie. "It's really useful, you know."

"I know that," said Ranald. "I'm planning to learn next week. I've been a bit busy, you see."

"And write too," said Bertie. "That's useful too."

"I will," said Ranald. "But do you want to hear about my idea?"

"Yes."

Ranald lowered his voice. 'There's a circus on the Meadows – just down the road, Bertie. It's a proper circus, with clowns and a trapeze and everything. A real circus."

Bertie's eyes widened. "A trapeze?"

Ranald nodded. "Yes. And some performing dogs too, I think. There was a picture of them in the paper."

"I wish I could go," said Bertie. "I can mention it to my grandmother, Ranald. Then maybe you could come too, if she took us."

"But I think we should go right now," said Ranald. "There's going to be an afternoon show today – a matinée. We could easily go."

Bertie stared at his friend. Was he suggesting what Bertie thought he might be? Was he actually proposing to go unaccompanied? The idea, so bold and dangerous, nonetheless appealed.

"By bus?" Bertie asked.

"Yes," said Ranald. "There's one that goes from the end of the road."

A practical issue occurred to Bertie. "But how are we going to pay, Ranald? I haven't got any money with me."

Ranald did not think this would be a problem. "I've got stacks of money in my piggy bank, Bertie. Dollars, euros, the lot. Dad gives them to me. I'll pay."

"I'll pay you back, Ranald. One of these days I'll pay you back."

Ranald was generous. "No need, Bertie. You can be my slave, if you like. That could do instead."

Bertie was hesitant. The last person whose slave he agreed to be was Tofu, in return for two back numbers of the *Beano*. It had not been a good bargain, as Tofu had extracted his pound of flesh – and more – remorselessly until Bertie had stood up to him and said that his period of voluntary servitude was at an end. Ranald was a more reasonable master, though, and suggested that if Bertie carried his books in and out of the classroom for a week and did his arithmetic homework for him, that would be more than adequate.

They set off, slipping out of the house unnoticed by the adults, who were halfway through a three-couple longwise set of the Reel of the 51st Division. Catching a 23 bus before it lumbered down the brae towards Holy Corner, Ranald and Bertie barely had time to find their seats on the top deck before they reached their stop at Tollcross. Thereafter it was a ten-minute walk to the Meadows and to the sight of a striped big top, pitched amongst the trees of the park, the saltire flying proudly from the top of the protruding central pole.

Ranald nudged Bertie. "That's it, Bertie. That's the circus I told you about. You see, I was right."

Bertie was almost too excited to speak. "Yes," he said. "You were right, Ranald."

They ran across the grass to the ticket office, a small tent pitched near the entrance to the big top. Behind a counter, smoking a cigarette and talking on a mobile phone, a woman with a prominent neck tattoo looked down on the two boys.

"Are youses under ten?" she asked.

"Yes," said Bertie.

"No," said Ranald.

"Make up your minds," said the woman curtly. And then into the phone, "There are some weans here who dinnae ken their own age."

Something was said at the other end of the line, and the woman laughed.

"Half price," she said to Ranald, who had extracted a Royal Bank of Scotland twenty-pound note from his pocket.

Ranald paid, and then he and Bertie made their way towards the entrance.

"So, boys," said the attendant to whom Ranald handed the tickets. "You look like a couple of likely lads."

Ranald and Bertie looked up at the man. They could not help but notice that he had one good eye and one that was clouded and opaque. His teeth were blackened and his lips seemed stained yellow with nicotine. He had only one complete arm, the other terminating in a stainless steel hook to which a cigarette holder had been attached.

As they found their way to two empty seats, Ranald said to Bertie, "That man, Bertie . . ."

"The one with the funny eye?"

"Yes," said Ranald. "Do you think he's English? I think he looks it."

Bertie nodded. "Maybe, Ranald."

Ranald Braveheart Macpherson lowered his voice. "My dad says you have to watch out for the English. The English and Campbells." He paused. "Perhaps we should be ready to run, Bertie."

"I don't think so," said Bertie, adding, "And you know something, Ranald: people can't help it if they're English. And Campbells can't either. It's not nice to blame people who can't help it."

Ranald looked doubtful. "Are you sure, Bertie?"

"Yes," said Bertie. "I'm very sure, Ranald."

26
Price on Application

At the same time that Bertie and Ranald Braveheart Macpherson were being admitted to the afternoon performance of the Grand Glasgow and Greater Clyde Circus, in its temporary site on the Meadows, Pat Macgregor was accompanying her part-time employer to a sale of Scottish art. This was taking place in the Lyon & Turnbull auction rooms in Broughton Place, where Matthew had spent a large part of that Friday afternoon viewing the lots. From his perspective it was an unusually exciting sale: at least two of the paintings on offer were, he thought, being put up at an attractively low estimate, and several others, he felt, could benefit from upgraded attributions. These were all attractive propositions to any dealer who might wish to sell them on, and he had decided that he would make every effort to get at least two paintings, or even possibly three, at this sale.

For Pat, participation in a sale was a new experience. Although she had worked at Matthew's gallery for some years now, and although she had an undergraduate degree in the history of art, her responsibilities had mostly revolved around dealing with customers who dropped into the gallery from the street – passing trade, as Matthew referred to them. This she did as a back-up to Matthew if he was otherwise engaged, or on her own at such times as Matthew was out of the gallery, at coffee or lunch, or on some errand dictated by Elspeth. Living out at Nine Mile Burn and being responsible for triplets meant that Elspeth rarely had the chance to come into town unencumbered. It was then left to Matthew to go to Valvona

& Crolla or, more prosaically, the dry cleaner's or chemist's.

Matthew had recently made a trip to London with a friend to visit an art fair. This friend, who had been an art dealer for considerably longer than had Matthew, had generously instructed him in the ways of art fairs, and in the specific language that, like some ancient shibboleth, distinguished the art trade's insiders from those merely seeking admission. It was important, for instance, to say that a painting was *with* a gallery rather than to say that the gallery *had* the painting. Similarly, there were conventions as to the appropriate circumstances in which price could be mentioned. If advertising in one of the glossier magazines, for example in *Country Life*, it was in distinctly bad taste to mention the price at which a painting was being offered. This suggested that the sort of person who might want to buy it might actually need to know the price in advance, and in respect of some paintings that was simply not the case. Rather, the painting should be represented as just being there, as if it had descended from somewhere; yes, it was for sale, but that was only as an act of generosity – an act of sharing – rather than as part of a commercial transaction.

The use of the acronym *POA* was similarly a matter of some delicacy. If a gallery inserted a price list into a catalogue – an important courtesy – then even if most prices were given, there were some that should not, and the term *Price on Application* should be used. This conveyed the important message: *This is really expensive.* It also said: *We are a bit embarrassed about this, but there we are.* Some things are indecently expensive, and saying *POA* shows people that you, the seller, are conscious of how these high prices may look a bit bad, even greedy. So to say *POA* means that the prospective purchaser will understand that you would love to give it to them for less, but cannot. Incidentally, it also allows the enquirer to show the seller that he or she is the sort of person who is unperturbed by the letters *POA*.

Of course there is the additional implication – that the seller of the painting does not want anyone to know how much he has received for it. This may be because he does not want people to think that the painting went for what might seem a rather low sum, or that he does not want others, including the person he is currently divorcing, to know how much he has raised by the sale.

"It's a messy business at times, the art trade," Matthew's friend had said. "Basically, Matthew, we're all car salesmen, aren't we? Everybody is. We're all selling cars."

"There's nothing wrong with selling cars," Matthew responded. "I have some very good friends who sell cars – and where would we be without them?"

"Oh, I agree," said the friend. "And at least car salesmen don't say *POA*, do they? They're up-front about it. They say things like *Price on the road*. How much more direct can you get than that?"

"And we should say *Price on the wall*?" suggested Matthew.

"Ha," said his friend. "Very funny."

In the plane on the way back from London, Matthew had picked up a business magazine from the back of the seat in front and had paged, without much interest, through the articles on MBA courses and so on (POA). He thought these magazines insufferably dull, but on this occasion he found himself reading an article that really did engage his attention. This was by somebody described as a "motivational enabler", and it was about how you, as an employer, might do more for the development of your staff. "Don't take your staff for granted," the article warned. "Skills atrophy – remember that: skills atrophy unless developed. Skills are like muscles: use them or lose them."

Matthew had heard that advice before, and it always made him feel – rather nervously – his biceps, to see whether they were quite as firm as they used to be. And he did this now, in the plane, before continuing to read the article. As he read, he realised that he had done nothing to help Pat develop her skills. He had never so much as lent her a book or drawn her attention to some article in the *Burlington Magazine*. Nothing. He had taken her for granted.

And so he had decided that at the next opportunity he would take her to an auction and let her see how things operated there. He would even let her bid – under supervision, of course, and while he was at her side, but hers would be the hand that was raised. The thought made him feel warm inside, as any benevolent act might do.

"Pat," he said, "I want talk to you about auction catalogue attribution."

Pat looked at him expectantly.

"Do you know the difference," Matthew asked, "between *attributed to*, *school of*, *circle of* and *follower of*?"

Pat stared at him. "Of course I do," she snapped. "I wasn't born yesterday, Matthew."

27

Scottish Art and Goose Pimples

They arrived early enough at Lyon & Turnbull's to be able to spend ten minutes or so inspecting each of the paintings in which Matthew was interested. There were four of these, and they were all displayed in the main body of the auction hall, the lesser pictures being relegated to the upper gallery. A few people were still up there, trawling through the rural scenes, the portraits of Highland cattle, the School-of-Park floral pictures of formal roses, and the ubiquitous sub-MacTaggart studies of children playing on a windswept beach. "Such a common theme in Scottish art," Matthew commented drily to Pat. "Children paddling on an East Lothian beach, looking so cold. In fact, that's one way of determining the authenticity of any Scottish figurative painting: do the people look cold? If they do, then the painting's authentic."

Pat laughed. "Are you sure?"

"Of course I'm sure," said Matthew. He had only just invented the theory, but it seemed to him it was immediately and obviously true. If you considered Italian figurative painting, it was full of unclothed models, often lazing about in sylvan settings, oblivious of their state of undress. This was for climatic reasons: you could do that sort of thing in Italy – and in much of France and Spain as well. In Northern European painting this was less common, although it did occur. He had seen a charming little painting by one of the Breughels, an unclothed Judgement of Paris painted on copper, in which flesh was on display with little sign of goose pimples or frostbite, but that, of course, was the artistic imagination at work. A painter's experience of a Dutch summer might easily enable such a scene at least to be envisaged, but to a Scottish painter that leap of the imagination simply would not be possible, so deep-rooted would be the feeling that the requirements of naturalism entailed plenty of heavy wool clothing.

Matthew warmed to the theme. "Look at Raeburn," he said.

"Yes, what about him?"

"Look at the sitters. They are, pretty much without exception, warmly wrapped up. In fact, in some of them – particularly those portraits of people in Highland dress – they have vast swathes of plaid draped about them. That picture of The Macnab, for instance, or the portrait of MacGregor of MacGregor – just look at them. The Macnab looks really freezing – his jaw is set in such a determined way because he is absolutely frozen stiff. And lots of his other paintings are the same – everybody looks a bit chilly."

"Did he heat his studio?" asked Pat.

"He must have," said Matthew. "Most rooms had fires in those days, but the fire wouldn't make all that much difference unless you were huddled about it. I'd be prepared to bet that the vast majority of people who sat for portraits by Raeburn were feeling cold at the time. And that shows – that's half the charm. The people look alive because they're cold."

Pat looked thoughtful. "You know, Matthew, I think you may have something there. I'd never thought about it, but you may be right."

Matthew smiled. "Perhaps a little article in one of the art reviews? *The influence of ambient temperature on Scottish painting*. We could write it together."

"We could," said Pat. She wondered who would be the first-named author – a major issue in academic publishing.

His name would be first, she imagined, because that was the way it worked. The senior people put their names before those of their co-authors . . . because they were the senior people. It did not matter who did the work, it was the senior person who went first. Mind you, this had been Matthew's idea, and he would deserve to be the first-named author, but it was galling nonetheless to think that one would never be named first in an article.

Pat's train of thought was interrupted. Matthew had stopped speculating on temperature and was pointing out to her one of the paintings he intended to bid for.

"Adam Bruce Thomson," he said. "See. Isn't it lovely?"

It was. The picture was one of a woman engaged in a kitchen task. A small pile of vegetables lay on a table while she chopped something, a handful of kale perhaps, with a large-bladed knife. It was a scene of quiet domesticity, not dissimilar to a seventeenth-century Dutch painting in which somebody goes about their daily business in an interior.

"He was the closest we got to the Nashes or to Bawden," said Matthew. "Or Ravilious. The English had all those in the nineteen-twenties and -thirties. And I love their work so much. But we had Adam Bruce Thomson."

"I love it," said Pat. "It's so sad. She looks so . . . so resigned."

Matthew nodded. "That's what makes it true." And as he spoke, and looked at the quiet painting of the woman in her kitchen, another theory occurred to him: expressions of resignation in Scottish art. Did people look resigned in Scottish painting? Perhaps they did, because there was so much that people had to be resigned about in Scottish history. There was the weather (see theory above) and then there was the sheer burden of a life pinched by poverty and struggle. Life was hard in Scotland in the past, and it would be surprising were this fact not to be represented in Scottish art.

He was distracted by Pat. "And what else? What else shall we go for?"

"That one over there," answered Matthew. "You see that picture of a man with a dog at his feet?"

Pat moved closer to the painting to get a better view. She leaned forward and examined it more closely. "Who is it by?" she asked.

"Well, that's the thing," said Matthew. "There's no attribution. They just say *Scottish School*. That's it. Nothing more."

Pat stepped back. "It's rather good," she said.

"Oh yes," agreed Matthew. "It's a fine painting – beautifully done. Look at the man's hands. Look how natural they look."

"And it's so calm," said Pat. "Have you any idea?"

Matthew looked about him, as if to detect the presence of eavesdroppers. "I think it might be a Raeburn."

Pat frowned. "But surely somebody would have picked that up?"

"Not necessarily," said Matthew.

"And what about the experts? They look at the sale catalogues. They wouldn't let anything slip through."

Matthew shook his head. "You're wrong there, Pat. Plenty of pictures slip through the net. Sometimes massively valuable, obvious paintings. What about that da Vinci that somebody bought at an auction not all that many years ago for ten thousand dollars or something? Now it's over a hundred million, or whatever."

"But . . ."

"But it happens, Pat. It happens."

Pat leaned forward again and peered at the painting. "It certainly has a Raeburny feel to it. That relaxed, fluid sweep . . ."

"It does," said Matthew.

"So, what's the estimate?"

"Four hundred pounds," said Matthew.

Pat drew in her breath. She had noticed something that pointed to authenticity: the man looked cold.

28
Do Angels Cook?

"Well?" Matthew said to Pat as they left Lyon & Turnbull's auction rooms that Saturday. "What did you think?"

It was a clear day, and the sky above them had that washed, thin tone that is typical of summer in Scotland, a sky devoid of heat or glare, or the murky pall by which industrious humanity asphyxiates itself elsewhere. High above them, a jet traced an arc of vapour trail on its way westwards, a thin line that stretched out and then dissolved, white into blue. Pat pointed at the plane, a tiny, silver speck, and said, "I wonder where they're going?"

He looked up. He imagined the protected capsule of people hurtling through the sky; and here they were, bound to the stone of the pavement, standing, doing their earthbound things, and he was just Matthew, and she was just Pat, and they were not terribly important in the scheme of things.

"Who knows? America, I should think. Or Canada. Maybe coming from Paris or Amsterdam and shooting over Scotland without noticing it."

"And they don't know about us, standing far below them, thinking about them."

Matthew laughed. "No. They don't know about us."

"Quite a thought, isn't it?" said Pat.

Matthew looked at her. "You're coming over all philosophical, Pat."

She smiled back at him. "Am I? Well, maybe." She shrugged. "It's just that I find – at the moment, that is – that I'm thinking a bit about where I am, so to speak."

"You're here. You're in Edinburgh. And we've just stepped out of Lyon & Turnbull and . . ."

She cut him short. "Oh, I know, I know. Existentialism. I know all that."

"Well, then . . ."

"It's just that I feel that something's about to happen to me."

He hesitated. "You're not feeling dread, are you?"

She seemed surprised. "Dread? Why should I feel dread?"

He explained that sometimes that was what people felt. They experienced a sudden moment of dread when they thought of just how helpless they were in the face of . . . in the face of what? The world? The ultimate pointlessness of human existence?

But Pat was not feeling dread; nor fear; nor trembling. It was something else, and she could not explain it to Matthew because she was not sure that she understood it herself. So she looked at her watch instead and said, "Well, I think I'll get back to my flat."

"But what did you think? Did you enjoy that?"

She nodded. "I found it a bit scary. When you went up to a thousand for that . . ."

"Scottish School painting? The man and the dog?"

"Yes. Because you don't know, do you, and it could be . . . well, it could be nothing."

Matthew looked self-satisfied. "Yes, but I wasn't alone, was I? There was somebody else after it. He must have thought the same as me."

"Maybe. But then you don't know whether he just liked it because he liked pictures with dogs in them? Something like that?"

Matthew was prepared to concede that possibility, but he had no buyer's regret. "It's one thousand well spent, Pat – I bet you anything."

She said that she hoped this was the case. "But I really should get going."

"Because?"

"Why because?"

He did not want her to go. "Because you're going out to dinner this evening? Or cooking for somebody and have to get the stuff?"

She shook her head. "I'm not going out. I was just going to make something for myself."

"You could have dinner at our place. Elspeth would love to see you." He had not thought about the invitation and he had no idea what Elspeth had planned, but she liked Pat and he could always offer to do the cooking himself. Or James could, although he had cooked for the last three nights in a row.

Pat hesitated. "Elspeth might have other plans."

Matthew shook his head. "I could phone her. Should I do that?"

Pat looked up at the sky. The vapour trail had almost disappeared. "All right."

Matthew's pleasure showed. "Do you want to go home first?" he said. "You could come out to our place by bus. There's a bus that goes to West Linton and Biggar. You could get that. It's pretty regular. Just remember to get off at Nine Mile Burn. We had somebody come out to see us who was reading the paper and next thing he noticed he was in Carlops."

They agreed that Pat would catch a bus that would get her to Nine Mile Burn at six. "I'll bring the boys up the drive to meet you," said Matthew. "They'll think it's a big adventure."

"Good. I can't wait to see them. They must be growing up so fast."

"Average speed," said Matthew. "They're talking now, although it's mostly nonsense. And they're covered in bumps and bruises because they run everywhere and fall off things.

They're boys, you see."

"Oh dear."

"But they recover." Matthew paused. "And James? Have you met James yet? He's our au pair."

Pat shook her head. "I didn't know they made male au pairs."

"They do. And we've got one. He's amazing. He cooks like an angel."

Pat frowned. "Why do people say that? Cooks like an angel. Do angels cook?"

"I haven't really looked at the iconography," Matthew replied. "They're usually depicted hanging about in choirs. But I suppose some of them cook."

"And James can?"

"Yes. And he's really good at other things. He's fantastic with the boys. You should see him – they worship the ground he walks on."

"That must be useful."

Matthew nodded. "I think you'll like him."

Pat said nothing. *Cooks like an angel.* She was thinking of what it would be like to have somebody in the kitchen – a man, yes, a *man* in the kitchen – cooking for you. And then when the man had finished cooking he would serve you whatever it was that he had cooked for you and you would taste it and say, *This is divine!* And perhaps add, *You cook like an angel, you know.* And he would smile, and say, *I love cooking for you.* And then he would put on some music and say, *I know this is really corny, but couldn't we dance?* And you would say, *Why not?* And he would take your hand and you would dance right there, in the kitchen, and it wouldn't matter that your flatmates had left the washing up in the sink and there was a cup with lipstick stains round the rim and the food waste bin needed emptying . . .

Matthew was looking at her. "Are you all right?"

"Yes, I was just thinking." And then, quite casually, "This James . . . why is he your au pair? I mean, what's he doing? Learning English?"

"His English is fine," said Matthew, smiling.

"So?"

"So, he's on a gap year."

Pat sighed. Too young. Cooks like an angel, but is still a cherub . . .

"But he's amazingly mature," said Matthew.

29
Time, Poetry, Triplets, Life

Out at Nine Mile Burn, Elspeth sat in the kitchen, looking out over the lawn towards the Moorfoot Hills. She glanced at her watch, and saw that one of the hands had fallen off. Trapped underneath the glass, the tiny metal finger, the minute hand, had been caught up on the sweep of the hour hand and was now lodged in such a way as to bring the entire mechanism to a halt. This impasse had been reached shortly before three. *At ten to three* . . . An old memory was triggered, of an aunt who liked poetry, and had read to her when she was a girl. *Stands the church clock at ten to three? And is there honey still for tea?* Her aunt had considered these lines poignant, but Elspeth had not understood why this should be so. Surely there was nothing special about a clock that stopped at ten to three, and honey was . . . well, honey was all right, but one would not want to have it for tea every day. Was it nostalgia that lay behind that poem, or irritation perhaps? Clocks had to stop somewhere if nobody wound them up, or if their minute hand broke off, and the fact that it was at ten to three was neither here nor there. What might be irritating, though, was if nobody bothered to fix them, and then did nothing about variety in what was offered for tea. Honey again? Oh really . . .

And then another line came to her – something about five in the afternoon. *A las cinco de la tarde* . . . At five in the afternoon, at that terrible five in the afternoon. And she was back at school, a little bit older than she had been when it had been church clocks and honey, and in a very different register. Lorca, that was it. The death of a bullfighter. Elspeth was at school again, on a warm afternoon in the summer, and studying for her Higher English and they were looking at Lorca. And she found herself wondering what was so special about five in the afternoon. Why should five in the afternoon be so terrible and require to be repeated time and time again before the poem came to an end? And she had voiced those thoughts and the English teacher had looked at her and smiled before saying, "That's not the point, Elspeth; that's just not the point." And had then returned to Lorca and the drum-like repetition of *a las cinco de la tarde*, at five in the afternoon.

Bullfighting . . . that was a terrible thing, Elspeth thought, and the people who did it should be thoroughly ashamed of themselves. To dress up for the slaughter of an animal, in terror; to accompany it with music and cheering and all the accoutrements of a popular spectacle while before you, trapped in a ring, a poor creature was stabbed and cut to its death. What sort of mentality revelled in that?

Her thoughts drifted. Of course, there were other people who dressed up to slaughter animals, particularly foxes. Elspeth had lived in the countryside long enough to know that foxes and farmers were not the closest of allies, but did you have to dress up to do what you felt needed to be done to protect your chickens and lambs?

She looked at her watch again. It was a pity, as Matthew had given it to her shortly after they had become engaged, and she had chosen it at Hamilton & Inches. Would they be able to fix it? They probably could, but she would have to go into town or give it to Matthew to drop off on George Street, and Matthew seemed to be so busy now and did not like to be burdened with errands, and . . . She stopped, and looked out towards the Moorfoots once more. Everything was so empty here. The land was empty; the sky was empty; there was nowhere for her to go for a cup of coffee with friends, or to read the newspaper or her e-mails. And there were so few e-mails to be read, anyway, as she never saw her friends any longer, now that she was stuck out here with the triplets. Every minute of the day was taken up with attending to the needs of the three small boys, except for those spells, as now, when James took them and entertained them. Without him, life would be utterly impossible, but even with him here and working in such an obliging manner and without complaint it seemed somehow to be so empty, like the sky, and the land, and . . .

Elspeth started to cry. I love my husband, she thought. I love my boys. I love this house. And yet I feel so miserable and alone and trapped. Yes, trapped *is* the word. I'm trapped. Caught. Pinned down. I wanted to be something, to have a career, to have a life of my own. I wanted to travel and see the world and get caught up in adventures with interesting people. I wanted to have those interesting people about me, saying interesting things and sending me interesting e-mails. But where are they? Not here in Nine Mile Burn. Not in my life.

There was a burst of sound – a banging of doors and the clatter of high-pitched young voices. This meant that James had brought in the boys from outside, and there would be mud on their boots – there always was – and that mud would be transferred to the carpets – it always was – and then onto the sofa, which had covers that did not detach easily and were impossibly light-coloured, anyway, for a household with male triplets on the rampage. And then there was Matthew's dog, Henderson, who was also always covered in mud and regarded the sofa as his territory when he could get away with it, and who had the irritating habit of grinding his teeth, which the vet had said dogs just did not do. The vet had offered pills, but Matthew had turned them down.

"You shouldn't tranquillise dogs," he had said. "It's not natural."

"But do we have to live with it?" Elspeth had asked.

"It's a stage," said Matthew. "Henderson's young. He'll get over it."

"But what if he doesn't? What then?"

Matthew had looked at her in the way in which men sometimes look at women. As if to imply that she did not *know*. But she did. She knew, and had always known.

And then, just as she was trying to compose herself, and not let the boys see her crying, the telephone rang and it was Matthew and he said that he had invited Pat round for dinner that night and he hoped she didn't mind. And Elspeth closed her eyes and was unable to stop herself sobbing, more volubly now, so that Matthew thought there was a problem with reception and rang off with a jaunty, "That's fine then. Bad line. See you later, sweetheart."

30

Weegie Dugs

Ushered into the tent of the Grand Glasgow and Greater Clyde Circus and armed with two packets of popcorn purchased at the door, Bertie and Ranald Braveheart Macpherson took their seats and waited for the show to begin. The man with the wall eye and the hook for a hand had disappeared but now came back sporting a red tailcoat and a battered top hat. He was the ringmaster, and announced himself as such to the audience, which now more or less filled the tent. As he introduced the first act a small band – a keyboard player and a guitarist – provided background music: a hotch-potch of Harry Lauder, the Proclaimers and Bach's Suite No. 1 in G major for solo cello. This was perhaps a little bit loud, as the ringmaster had difficulty in making himself heard. He threw several reproachful glances at the musicians, but they did not seem to notice, and, if anything, played slightly louder than before.

Bertie and Ranald watched with rapt attention as the first act began – a juggler who doubled up as a fire-eater.

"They have special inflammable toothpaste," said Ranald. "I know how it works."

Bertie was impressed. He had always admired Ranald's independence, but the organising of this trip, along with his apparent familiarity with the ways of circuses, raised Bertie's respect for him to a new level. How lucky Ranald was, Bertie thought, to have the parents he had: parents who drank and did Scottish country dancing. How lucky he was to have avoided psychotherapy and yoga, and all the other clouds that had hung over Bertie's life for as long as he could remember, even if now, with his mother in Aberdeen, his situation had improved so dramatically. Perhaps from now on, he said to himself, my life will be more like Ranald's; perhaps now I shall be able to do the things I've longed to do all these years.

The juggler finished with a flourish and a final exhalation of volatile fluid and flame. There was thunderous applause, even as every parent in the tent mentally rehearsed the warning they would give to their impressionable offspring after the show: do *not* try that at home, darling.

Now came the clowns, two knockabout endomorphs in loud tweed jackets, tartan trousers, and outsize glengarry bonnets. These were Chuck and Chick, and in broad Glaswegian they assailed one another with comic accusations while attempting to make bread in a large mixing bowl. The resulting dough-fight brought squeals of delight from the audience, some of whom were spattered with lumps of dough in the process.

Then, with the band playing a valiant, Wagnerian fanfare, into the ring came Wee MacTavish and his Brainy Dugs. Wee MacTavish, a Glaswegian dwarf, was assisted by his wife, Ma MacTavish, also of limited stature, and their friend Sammy Cameron, a Gaelic-speaking dwarf from Mallaig.

"Sammy here's a teuchter," Wee MacTavish shouted to the audience. "He canna tell a banana frae an apple. You dinnae get either up in Mallaig!"

(Loud laughter. Cries of "Donald, where's your troosers?" More laughter.)

Sammy then said something in Gaelic, which brought hoots from the audience and a cry of "Aye, mine will be a double, Sammy!"

"Ladies and gentlemen, boys and girls," shouted Wee MacTavish. "Kindly shut yer gobs. Thank you. It's time for ma brainy dugs, every one of them with a degree frae Strathclyde University!"

Into the ring now ran four Highland terriers, each sporting a large tartan bow around its neck. These dogs sat down in a line and looked expectantly at Wee MacTavish.

"Right," said Wee MacTavish. "These dugs, ladies and gentlemen, are able to do mathematics. Aye, I'm no making this up. I shall show you if you kindly sit down on your bahookies and let me continue uninterrupted."

"Is that how they talk in Glasgow?" asked Ranald Braveheart Macpherson, his voice lowered.

Bertie nodded. "Yes," he whispered. "I can understand quite a bit of it, Ranald. I could translate if you like."

"No," said Ranald. "That's all right, Bertie. I think I'll understand a bit too."

Wee MacTavish now stood on a stool and faced his brainy dugs. "Right, boys," he said, wagging an admonitory finger at the dogs. "Noo then, what's two plus two?"

One of the dogs raised a paw.

"Yes, Hamish?" said Wee MacTavish.

Hamish barked four times.

"See?" said Wee MacTavish. "That's Hamish for you. Two plus two equals four. Nae flies on that dug!"

There was loud applause.

"Now something harder," said Wee MacTavish, pointing to another dog. "What's eight minus six, Jeanie?"

The dog barked twice.

"Is that the right answer?" Ranald asked Bertie.

"Yes," said Bertie. "It's amazing, Ranald. These dogs are really clever."

Wee MacTavish turned back to the audience and took a bow, as did Ma MacTavish and Sammy Cameron.

"Now," announced Wee MacTavish, "here's a good question for ma clever dugs: which is better – Edinburgh or Glasgow? One bark for Edinburgh; two for Glasgow."

Without hesitating, the dogs, in unison, gave voice to two

barks. This brought immediate laughter, and hissing, from the audience.

"Weegies!" shouted a voice from the back. "Weegie dugs!"

"Aye," said Wee MacTavish. "Good Weegie dugs!"

The dogs performed a few more tricks and then, to uproarious applause, they left the ring.

"That's the best show I've ever seen in my life," said Bertie.

"It was amazing," said Ranald Braveheart Macpherson. "Those dogs are very clever, Bertie. They may come from Glasgow, but they're very clever."

The dogs were followed by acrobats and by the reappearance of the clowns. Then there was a strongman, who tore the Glasgow telephone directory in half with his bare hands, a trapeze artist, a pair of female tango dancers, who danced together for ten minutes, and finally a man who sang "Flower of Scotland" in Japanese while riding round the ring on a unicycle.

It ended far too early for Bertie and Ranald Braveheart Macpherson, and only too soon they found themselves leaving the tent with the rest of the audience. They were not quite as pushy as others, and so were out last, coming face to face with Wee MacTavish, who was smoking a cigarette outside a small caravan parked near the big top.

"Hey, youse boys," he shouted. "You want tae see something?"

"It's Mr MacTavish," said Ranald Braveheart Macpherson, digging Bertie in the ribs. "What do you think he wants, Bertie?"

31

A Gift from Glasgow

Wee MacTavish stubbed his cigarette out under the heel of his shoe and beckoned to Bertie and Ranald Braveheart Macpherson.

"Youse boys," he called out. "Did you like the dugs?"

Ranald Braveheart Macpherson nudged Bertie. "We ought to go and talk to him, Bertie," he said.

Bertie nodded and led his friend over to the MacTavish caravan, where the diminutive showman was waiting for them. There was a light on in the caravan and he could see Ma MacTavish and Sammy Cameron sitting inside, a teapot and mugs on the table in front of them.

It was an unusual experience for the boys to be talking to an adult who was more or less the same height as they were, but if they felt that, neither Bertie nor Ranald showed it. It had been stressed to Bertie and the others in his class at school that physical difference was not something that should be remarked upon, and that tact and courtesy should be shown when confronted with it. Wee MacTavish was a dwarf – they knew that – but they knew that this should make no difference.

And as for Wee MacTavish, a lifetime's experience of being stared at, of being the object of surprise, embarrassment, and sometimes sheer unkindness had inured him to the reactions of others. He had reached the point of not caring too much; he was a showman, and as such he knew that the last laugh was often his own. Nor did he care much for elaborate efforts to find words for who he was. *Dwarf* was the word that everybody understood and that many of the people who spoke on behalf of dwarfs said should be used. *Midget* was different: that rubbed it in, he thought, and had a derogatory ring to it.

"If you're wondering what to call me," he had said to the proprietor of the circus when he had first joined it, "how about my name?"

The proprietor had shifted his feet awkwardly. "I didn't want you to . . ."

Wee MacTavish cut him short. "Like everybody else," he said, "I have a name. That's the important bit."

"Very well," said the proprietor. "But do you really want me to bill your act as *Wee MacTavish*?"

"Well that's what I've always been called, pal," said Wee MacTavish. "And I'm no big, am I? If you called me something like Big MacTavish it would be a bit odd, don't you think?"

Now Wee MacTavish surveyed the two small boys who had been in his audience and wondered. He did not really like Edinburgh, which he thought a stuck-up place that thought itself better than Glasgow, where he had been born and brought up, in Possilpark. These two boys had that Edinburgh look about them, although they were only weans, for heaven's sake. He did not hold that against them, of course – children were children wherever you went – but he could just imagine their parents. And he smiled as he thought of what they would think. You could just see it? He gave you *what*? You *accepted* it? That would be one in the eye for Edinburgh, with all its smugness. That would be Glasgow saying, "Here you are, then, here's a wee present from Glasgow! You know, we're the other place just over there, the place you're so sniffy about! Here's a wee present!"

"Do you like dugs?" Wee MacTavish asked.

Bertie had no hesitation in answering. "Yes, Mr MacTavish. We both like dogs, don't we, Ranald?"

Ranald nodded. He was still a bit in awe of Wee MacTavish, and his voice was not very loud as he answered. "Yes, I like dogs too, Mr MacTavish."

Wee MacTavish was surveying the two boys. "So, you're called Ranald," he said. "And you, young man? What's your name?"

"I'm called Bertie Pollock," said Bertie.

Wee MacTavish smiled. "Bertie Pollock. That's a good name. I know a couple of Pollocks over in Glasgow. Both of them in Barlinnie, but you boys wouldnae know much aboot that."

Bertie gestured to Ranald. "His full name is Ranald Braveheart Macpherson, Mr MacTavish."

Wee MacTavish grinned. "Now there's a name and a half. Braveheart? That'll put the fear of God into one or two people. Good for you, Ranald Braveheart Macpherson!"

"Thank you," said Ranald.

Wee MacTavish pointed into the caravan. "We've got a dug in there that's had puppies. Six of them."

"That's a lot of puppies, Mr MacTavish," said Bertie.

"Aye, you're right there, Bertie," said Wee MacTavish. "Too many for one maw to deal with, I'd say. And I can't give all of them a job in the act, can I? It takes a lot of training to get a dog up to scratch in mathematics."

Bertie nodded politely. "Your dogs are very clever, Mr MacTavish."

"So that's why I'd like to give you one of the puppies," Wee MacTavish continued. "As a present, mind. I'm not going to ask you to pay for it."

Bertie drew in his breath. "But . . ." He trailed off. A puppy?

"That's really kind, Mr MacTavish," said Ranald. "Bertie loves dogs, don't you, Bertie? There's that dog called Cyril."

"Cyril?" asked Wee MacTavish. "That's a good name for an Edinburgh dug."

"He's got a gold tooth," said Ranald Braveheart Macpherson. "He has, hasn't he, Bertie?"

Bertie confirmed this, and Wee MacTavish whistled in admiration. "A gold tooth? Well, well, that's a good class of dug you have over here, I must say. A gold tooth? Well, well." He paused. "But you come in, boys, and we'll get Ma to help you choose a puppy. One hundred per cent free, as I said."

Bertie hesitated. What would his father say if he came home with a dog? Or his granny? Or – although he hardly dared think it – his mother? What if Irene came back from Aberdeen some weekend and found that they had a dog? She was always so rude about dogs. She called them middle-class. She hated dogs. Bertie was sure of that.

But Ranald Braveheart Macpherson was whispering to Bertie now. "We can share it, Bertie. We can take it back to my house to begin with and keep it in the garden. Then you can have a shot of it and take it over to your house."

Bertie swallowed. The temptation was just too great, and the solution that Ranald proposed would be bound to work – there was plenty of room for dogs in Morningside.

"So, it's all agreed," said Wee MacTavish. "You come in and choose. Ma will help."

"You're very kind, Mr MacTavish," said Bertie.

Wee MacTavish laughed. "Well, so I am, now that you come to mention it."

32

A Free Man Thinks

With Bertie on the other side of town safely under the eye, Stuart assumed, of Ranald Braveheart Macpherson's parents, and with Ulysses in the charge of Nicola, who, having taken him for an ice cream at Luca's Holy Corner Ice-Cream Parlour, had then gone on to the museum in Chambers Street, Stuart was left with time on his hands. The flat at 44 Scotland Street was uncharacteristically quiet, and he felt vaguely ill at ease. For years his Saturdays had been given over to the demands of fatherhood; suddenly not having any child-related duties unsettled him. It was the same feeling he had had in his student days, when he had always felt that there was something he should be doing, some book he should be reading for a future exam, some essay or assignment that needed attention before the deadline for submission crept up. Now he realised that the whole afternoon was his, and his alone; that he could do as the spirit moved him rather than what duty required.

Like most of us, Stuart had rarely given more than cursory thought to freedom. He understood, of course, that he lived in a country where certain freedoms were protected – where he could not be arbitrarily arrested at the whim of some malicious official, nor indicted for some non-existent crime, nor thrown into prison or even shot. He understood that if he so desired he could walk up the hill to Waverley Station, purchase a ticket – even if at astonishing cost – board a train, and travel down to London, or even further afield. He could travel to Paris, or Rome, or wherever he decided to go, and nobody would do anything to stop him. In that respect he was fortunate in a way in which so many others were not. There were so many whose lives were led under bombardment or threat, who could not go anywhere because nobody wanted them or because it was too dangerous to make the attempt; who clung to life by their fingernails, and could do nothing about it. Stuart knew all that and understood that none of it applied to him. He was free.

But, of course, that freedom, although a big thing when viewed from the perspective of those unfortunates who could do nothing to change their lot, was a small thing in practice. Stuart had two small boys who depended on him. He had a flat with a mortgage that required to be paid at the end of each month. He was bound, in short, by the ordinary arithmetic of life, which required the totting up and reconciliation of income and expenditure columns. He had to work, and he had to be in the same place at the start of every day and at its ending. Those were the real limits of our freedom, he thought, and it was within the narrow confines of those boundaries that we had to exercise such freedom as we had.

There, in the flat in Scotland Street, on that particular afternoon, Stuart stood in a beam of light falling at an angle from a skylight window, took a deep breath, and closed his eyes. Hours were at his disposal – whole, gloriously empty hours. The boys would be back at seven, and he would help Nicola with bathtime and the story that each child would expect: a chapter or two for Bertie and a short, almost wordless story for Ulysses about a family of pigs that did very little, as far as Stuart could ascertain. Yet it was reassuring, he reflected, that there were pigs leading these blameless and uneventful lives, smaller, by far, than his own, and not wanting, it seemed, to do anything other than that which they were accustomed to do; which perhaps was the secret to contentment: not to want anything other than that which somehow comes to you.

He stood there, under the warm beam of sunlight, and

thought: I want somebody to love me. And then he thought: I want that thrilling, unmistakable, unbeatable feeling of being wanted by somebody. And as he thought this, he opened his eyes and made his decision. He would walk out of the flat, lock the door behind him, and make the fifteen-minute journey by foot to Howe Street. Once there, he knew which door he would seek out, which stair he would climb, and which bell he would ring. And it did not matter if there was no reply, nor indeed if he was turned away. He would have made a consciously free decision. He would have *acted*. He would have done something that was authentically his.

That thought angered him. For years he had danced to a tune written by somebody else. He had wasted his life, his precious, irreplaceable life, by not doing with it that which he wanted to do. He had submitted. He had agreed to a contract of subservience, the terms of which had been dictated by Irene. Now she was not here – she was just not here – and he could act without thought as to what she would make of what he did. She no longer mattered.

He almost gasped at the thought, at its sheer effrontery. Irene did not matter. She could disapprove of him as much as she wished; she could disparage his views, his choices, his attitude, as she had done, subtly and unsubtly, for years and years – but it did not matter. He no longer had to think about her.

He took a deep breath. Now, this moment, he thought, I am going to do something that is *mine*. And then he took the first step, and made his way, light-headed, down the stair and out into the street. Round the corner, in Drummond Place and in Dundonald Street, there were people going about their business: a woman walking a dog, a man polishing a car, a teenage couple hand in hand and giggling over some silly, private secret. Stuart looked at them and felt a surge of affection, a feeling of *agape*, brought about by his own decision to act. Love what you're doing, he thought. Do what you want to do. He wanted the woman to revel in the companionship of the small dog; he wanted the man to be proud of his much-loved car, with all its pointless, shiny surfaces; he wanted the boy and girl to savour every moment of their togetherness because sooner rather than later life would close in on them.

And then he was in Howe Street, looking up at that window on the third floor, at the Georgian windows with their perfect proportions, the Golden Ratio expressed in stone and wood and glass, behind which lived a young woman who had been forbidden to him by Irene but whom now, as a free man at last, he would visit, and confide in, and to whom he would address that request we all put to the world: *Please love me as I am prepared to love you.*

33

In Howe Street

Stuart climbed the curving stairs slowly, the mahogany rail smooth to his touch, the tread of stone uneven beneath his feet, worn by generations of householders. The stairway, shared by six flats, had that smell so typical of Edinburgh common stairs – a dry, slightly dusty smell; not dank or malodorous in any way, or redolent of hardship or poverty, but rather the smell of . . . He stopped and thought. What was it? The smell of what? Of Edinburgh? A classical smell? Was that it? The smell of old stone, still used; the smell of human habitation in a cold climate, where the wind came in from the North Sea and met the tang of brewing and cloth and money?

On the first landing he saw, on the door of one of the flats, a small brass plaque that he remembered from when he was last there. This proclaimed the name of the owner of the flat. *Colquhoun.* It was one of those Scottish names pronounced in a way that was different from the way it was written: *Cahoon.* So Mr Colquhoun, or Mrs or Ms Colquhoun, was still there, as was the Finlayson family (*No Junk Mail Please*) next door. Stuart smiled. It was all very well to put *No Junk Mail* on one's door, but did it work? Did the Post Office pay any attention to this plea, given they were paid so much to push advertisements for pizza or delivery or Indian meal takeaways through people's doors? And how was junk mail defined, given that there must be grades of junk in the shady world of unsolicited post? Well-written junk mail, grammatically correct and making proper use of semicolons, might, on literary grounds, escape the status of junk; whereas the crudely vocal variety, full of exclamation marks and intrusive misplaced apostrophes, might unhesitatingly be placed in that pejorative category. And then, one person's junk mail might be another's useful information: the inveterate consumer of home-delivered pizza might positively appreciate the tempting offers pushed through the letterbox. The Colquhouns obviously did not mind, or if they did mind, were too polite to register their preference, whereas the Finlaysons next door had no such compunction. One pushed junk mail through the Finlayson letterbox at one's peril, thought Stuart. In would go the advertisement for pizza, with fifteen possible toppings, and then out would come a Finlayson through the burst-open door, brimming with anger and threatening all sorts of retribution.

He moved further up the stairs, past two doors he did not remember, an anodyne Campbell and an anodyne Macdonald, although that made him stop for a moment and think: how far we've come in comity. And then, finally, he was on the landing that was his objective, and before the door, in particular, that he had hardly dared to envisage. Yet there it was, and he was standing in front of it, and reaching out to press the brass button which said *Press*, as if he could do anything else now but press, and hold his breath, and wait.

Stuart waited. A minute went past, and then another. He had not imagined that she would be out on a Saturday afternoon, but now the thought occurred to him, and he felt a bitter, crushing disappointment. But the door opened and he saw her standing in front of him, wearing jeans and a white muslin blouse, and nothing on her feet.

For a moment or two she looked confused, as one might on seeing somebody from one's past in an unexpected context. And then recognition dawned, and with it came signs of surprise. He noticed that she did not frown – that would undoubtedly have been a bad sign – instead, the surprise changed into something else, a look that told him she was pleased that he was there. That was always an unmistakable signal that people gave unwittingly, without knowing they were doing it, just as they signalled the opposite when they were confronted with somebody they did not want to see.

"Katie?" Of course it was her and it was unnecessary for him to utter her name.

And she replied, equally unnecessarily, but without the upwards inflection that made it a question, "Stuart."

"I was just . . ."

She did not let him finish. "Come in," she said. "Come in."

"I was just walking past . . ."

Again, she cut him short – perhaps, he thought, because she knew that he was *not* just walking past.

"It's such a nice afternoon," she said.

"Yes." He looked out of the window, as if to confirm his judgement.

"I love Edinburgh when it's like this," she said. "It makes you forget the times when it isn't . . . if you see what I mean."

He smiled, and with his smile the tension between them seemed to fade away. "I suppose it's the same with everything," he said. "Even if good things don't entirely cancel out bad things, at least they dull the memory of them."

"Wow!" she said.

"Did I say that?" asked Stuart, affecting diffidence. "An aphorism!"

Katie laughed. "I always thought you were capable of profound thoughts. Right from the first."

Their first meeting had been in Henderson's Salad Table on Hanover Street, when Stuart had ended up sitting opposite her, a complete stranger, and they had begun to talk. Their conversation had lasted through the meal, and beyond, and had led to a visit – innocent, of course – to her flat in Howe Street, and in retrospect that was where and when he had

fallen in love. For a short time thereafter, only too short, he had thought of little other than her, and this had lasted until Irene discovered that poem, pencilled on a scrap of paper, and had issued him with a stern warning and an interdiction. A hypocritical warning it had been too, because she was the one – it was she – who had been unfaithful, and with Bertie's psychotherapist too, but had never admitted it. Nor admitted that Ulysses looked the image of Dr Fairbairn and had even grabbed the psychiatrist when he had seen him in the coffee house and had refused to let go. Bertie had told him about that, and he believed him. Children could be inventive, and could misread situations, but in his account of that particular meeting Stuart thought that Bertie had been correct.

"We should go through there," she said. "We'll be more comfortable."

She had intended to gesture towards the open door of the sitting room, one of several rooms that gave off the flat's entrance hall. Instead, by mistake, she gestured to another open door – the door of a bedroom.

She saw Stuart's glance follow her gesture, and she realised her error. "I mean the sitting room," she said quickly. And blushed.

Stuart said nothing. According to Vienna, a mistake is rarely a mistake, but the tip of an iceberg of below-the-surface desire. He thought that, but was not sure whether he believed it.

34

Peppermint Tea

"Great view," said Stuart, peering out of the window of Katie's drawing room. "That's St Vincent Street down there, isn't it?"

Katie was standing immediately behind him. He had looked out of the window because that was always something you could do in a strained social situation, or in circumstances where, as now, your heart was beating at twice its normal rate, it seemed, because the adrenalin was flooding your system, because you were somewhere you should not be, perhaps, or contemplating doing something you should not be doing. I am still a married man, he thought; but then he reminded himself of the freedom that he had been thinking about only half an hour or so ago. He was free. Irene had left him and gone to Aberdeen. He had not asked her to go, but she had chosen to do so herself. They had not divorced – yet – and so he was still married, but not in any moral sense, he felt. If he wanted to see somebody else, then he was surely entitled to do so.

"I've always liked St Vincent Street," Katie said. "I like short streets that go nowhere in particular."

He turned to face her, and smiled. She returned the smile. He saw that her ears were small; he had not noticed that before. Don't we *see* other people's ears, he thought?

"There's a pub down there," he said. "The St Vincent. And a church – same name – next door – an Episcopalian church. They have an order, I think. Something to do with St Lazarus, with knights and so on; they wear rather nice green capes."

Katie had seen them. One Sunday she had walked past the church, she said, and people had come out dressed in green robes. "People love that sort of thing," she said. "And the clergyman who runs that place is called Maclean. He's a historian, and he knows all about clan matters. He likes having lots of other Macleans about the place. If you're called Maclean, then he'll rope you into a procession."

"Why not?" said Stuart. "If you're a Maclean or whatever you probably enjoy rubbing shoulders with a lot of other Macleans."

"I'm sure you do," said Katie. "And I must say I rather like living in a city where people dress up and process about the place. There's a lot of that going on in Edinburgh."

Stuart looked out of the window again, past the tops of the trees, the boughs caught in the breeze, swaying across the line of the buildings further down the hill. St Vincent Street descended rapidly to the corner of Cumberland Street; in a flat on that corner, he and Irene, with another couple, had been to dinner with a friend from his university days. He remembered it now. The friend had been a medical student and had married another medical student. Sitting in the kitchen before dinner, they had chatted while their host prepared *moules marinières* and had cut his thumb badly on the sharp edge of a mussel shell. There and then, at the kitchen table, he had unblinkingly sewed the wound closed with a few stitches while the horrified guests had looked everywhere but at the site of the casual human repair.

"I went to dinner in St Vincent Street once," he began to tell Katie.

"Oh yes?"

"And my friend cut his thumb on a mussel. Quite a bad gash." He was aware that the story sounded lame and he wondered whether she would think him boring. She was younger than he was. Ten years, at least. That made him anxious. Older people told long stories that younger people found dull. Everybody knew that, except for older people.

But Katie did not appear to find his story dull. She said,

"Ouch," with some feeling. And then she said, "I know somebody who lives on St Vincent Street. She collects old shawls. She has hundreds of them . . . or maybe not hundreds, but you know what I mean."

"People collect all sorts of things," said Stuart.

"Yes, they do."

And then there was a brief silence.

Stuart moved towards a chair. "May I sit down?"

"Of course. How rude of me. Please do." She smiled as she gestured at the room. "Anywhere you like."

Stuart sat down, as did Katie. She glanced at him, and smiled again.

He drew in his breath. "I'm very sorry about what happened," he began. "I wanted to tell you that."

He forced the words out. There were fewer of them than he had intended, but now he had said more or less what he had planned to say.

Katie looked uncomfortable. "You don't have to," she said. She turned away for a moment, as if in distaste.

"But I do," he pressed. "I didn't want to stop seeing you. I really didn't."

"No?"

"No. It was my wife, you see."

She closed her eyes, and he realised that what he had just said had been painful to her. That must be, he thought, because she did not like to be reminded that she had been involved with a married man. It was tactless of him, he felt, and he should not have mentioned Irene. But how else could he explain himself?

She opened her eyes. "I understand," she said. "And I don't think we should talk about it. Let's not."

"No?"

"No. Water under the bridge. Or . . . Choose your metaphor."

The reference to metaphor reminded him of what she did, and one of the reasons why he had been drawn to her. Katie was working on a PhD in Scottish poetry. That had thrilled Stuart when he had first met her. He had been surrounded by actuaries and here was somebody who was immersed in poetry.

"Your PhD," he said. "May I ask how it's going?"

"Of course you may," she said. "Why not?"

"Because people who are doing PhDs are often haunted by them. At least, that's my experience. They have these PhDs hanging over them like the sword of Damocles . . ."

She interrupted him. "Now *there's* a metaphor."

"Yes, I suppose it is. And then people come and say *How's your PhD going?* And that fills them with dread."

Katie laughed. "There are support groups for people doing PhDs. But I don't think I need to go to them – just yet."

"So, it's going well?"

"I'll finish next year. On time, even. Or I hope so."

"And then?" asked Stuart.

"Now that's the question you really shouldn't ask somebody who's doing a PhD. That's the really painful question." She paused. "But what about your little boy? What about little . . ."

"Bertie."

"Yes, Bertie. And his brother . . ."

"Ulysses."

"How are they doing?"

Stuart looked down at his feet. "They're doing really well. You see, their mother . . . my wife, Irene . . . she's gone to Aberdeen. She's started a PhD up there."

Katie did not react.

"She hasn't disappeared totally." Stuart continued. He knew she did not want to talk about Irene – she had said as much – but he felt he had to tell her something. "But she's more or less off the scene. She comes back for weekends, or is planning to. My mother's helping with the boys. She's moved into the flat."

Katie listened. Then she stood up. "What about coffee? Or tea? Would you prefer tea?"

"Tea," said Stuart. "If it's no trouble."

"Ordinary or peppermint? Or I think I've got lemon and ginger."

Toss caution to the winds, thought Stuart. "Peppermint," he replied.

35

Spinach for Strength

"Here's your peppermint tea," she said. "It's great for . . . well, for more or less everything, I think. Stomach. Nerves. Skin."

"These things make big promises, don't they?" said Stuart, taking the mug from her.

She nodded, and took a sip of her own tea. "I think people stop taking notice of a lot of these claims. We've got so used to being told we should eat this, that and the next thing – we can't take it all in."

Stuart smiled. "Perhaps more producers could start telling us that their products are positively *bad* for us. Then we'd take notice. *This won't do you any good, we're afraid.* That sort of thing."

"But they already do," said Katie. "Cigarette packets spell it out, I think."

"Yes, I suppose they do. And rightly so. I hate smoking." Stuart paused. He had assumed that Katie did not smoke, but suddenly he realised he did not know. He knew so little about her. So he quickly added, "I'm sorry – I don't know if you smoke."

She shook her head – quite vigorously. "I can't stand it either. One of the biggest, best things that's happened in my lifetime is the ban on smoking in public places." She took another sip of her peppermint tea. "My father used to travel a lot by plane. He was a plastic surgeon and he went to a lot of conferences because he was chairman of something or other in the College of Surgeons. He said that when he got off the plane his clothes stank of cigarette smoke, even when he was sitting in the non-smoking section."

"Shared air," said Stuart. "When you're on a plane you share the air."

"We all share the air," said Katie. "That's why pollution is something for all of us to worry about. China pollutes the air with its endless factories and we all feel it."

"We're not entirely innocent ourselves," Stuart pointed out.

"No, maybe not. But not everybody is equally guilty."

Stuart asked about her father. "Does he do facelifts – that sort of thing?"

She frowned. "He's retired now. But no, he was really opposed to cosmetic surgery. You know, the vanity variety. He looked after people who had burns or things like that. People who had been smashed up in accidents."

"I'm glad he didn't do cosmetic surgery," said Stuart. "I think that there's nothing worse than those awful stretched faces that you see after people have had their tightening operations. They look like the masked players in a Japanese Noh play. Ghastly."

"I think it's best to be content with the way you look," said Katie.

Stuart looked at her and thought yes, if you look like you. But what if you don't, and you're unhappy about your nose or your double chin or whatever?

Katie looked away, as if she were embarrassed. "I don't mean to be unkind," she said.

"No," he said quickly. "You weren't. You're right. We should be what we are. Maybe it's a great mistake to tell people they can be what they want themselves to be. I can't be an Olympic rower, for instance."

Katie laughed. "I don't know. If you drink enough peppermint tea . . ."

"No," said Stuart. "It's spinach you need for strength. Look at Popeye."

"Was Popeye happy, do you think?"

It was such an odd question. Was he? He sang a bit, and he seemed to have a smile on his face in most of the drawings. And he had a reasonably good relationship with Olive Oyl, it seemed. Yes, Popeye was happy enough and probably didn't want to be something other than what he was.

"I think Popeye was happy enough with his life," Stuart said. "I always rather liked him. And I liked Olive too. I liked her long legs and the way she tied her hair in a bun."

Katie agreed. "She was lovely. But a bit sad, I think. She seemed vulnerable, somehow."

There was silence. Stuart looked at his hands. I am not all that strong, he said to himself. I'm weak, in fact. You don't have to be strong to be a statistician. And then he thought: ridiculous thought. Ridiculous.

Katie thought: How am I going to tell him?

"I was trying to remember what your thesis is about," Stuart said suddenly. "I know it's Scottish poetry, but what . . ."

"It's changed a bit," she replied. "PhD theses can go through all sorts of changes. But I think I know what the final focus of mine is going to be. Place."

"Place?"

"Yes. The importance of place in Scottish poetry from 1930 until . . . well, until yesterday, I suppose."

He waited for her to explain further.

"A lot of poets write about place and how they feel about one place in particular. Remember MacDiarmid's lines about the rose of all the world, and about how that was not for him? He wanted only the little white rose of Scotland. I don't know if you know that poem, but it always gets to me. That bit about how Scotland's rose smells sharp and sweet and . . . well, then he says it breaks the heart."

Stuart said nothing. He listened. He could listen to her for hours, he thought. He loved what she said. It was so different from what Irene would say to him. He blushed. He was not disloyal by nature, and he did not want to compare, but this was so different. And imagine, he thought – just imagine living with *this*? With talk about roses and the breaking of the heart, and Popeye and Popeye's sweetheart, Olive Oyl. Imagine.

Katie glanced at her watch. "You know, I'm really glad you came, Stuart. I'm really pleased."

Stuart felt a wave of relief. He had not done the wrong thing. He had been worried about that, but he should not have been. It was the right thing to do – exactly the right thing.

"I'm really pleased," Katie continued. "But I have to go out quite soon, I'm afraid. I agreed to babysit for my professor and his wife. His mother lives in Dundee and has had an operation. They're going up there to get her out of Ninewells Hospital. One of their kids has got a cold and they don't want her to give it to his grandmother just when she comes out of hospital."

"Of course not."

"But I wondered if you'd like to come to dinner next week?"

Stuart beamed. "I'd love that."

"Tuesday evening?"

"Yes. Yes. That's fine."

Katie rose to her feet and took Stuart's mug. "I'd like you to meet George," she said. "I know that he's free on Tuesdays."

"George?" asked Stuart.

Two words to end a world. "My boyfriend."

36

Not Quite Scottish Enough

At about the time that Stuart was making his way back from Howe Street, filled with despair, but committed nonetheless to dinner at Katie's the following Tuesday, Bertie and Ranald Braveheart Macpherson were waiting to catch a 23 bus at a bus stop in Tollcross. In a robust supermarket bag made of green hessian lay the puppy given to the boys by Wee MacTavish, the performing dog trainer. This gift, mischievous in its intention and certainly self-interested – Wee MacTavish needed to reduce the size of the litter – had been received with enthusiasm by both boys, even if Bertie had felt considerable misgivings about taking on a dog without the consent of his father.

"Lots of boys have dogs without their parents' permission," Ranald reassured him. "It's perfectly normal, Bertie. Old people don't notice these things – particularly if they've been drinking."

Bertie expressed reservations. "I'm not sure that my dad drinks all that much," he said. "Statisticians don't, you know. I think your dad probably drinks much more than mine does."

"I'm sure that's right," said Ranald, a certain pride in his voice. "My dad really loves whisky, you know, Bertie. He can drink a big glass just like that. He says that he's doing it because it's a patriotic thing to do. My dad is really proud of being Scottish, Bertie. I think he thinks your dad isn't quite Scottish enough."

Bertie looked down at the ground. "That's not my fault, Ranald," he said.

"Never mind, Bertie," said Ranald. "There's always a chance your dad might become more Scottish. People can, you know."

"If they drink enough whisky?"

Ranald Braveheart Macpherson nodded. "That's one of the ways, I think, Bertie. But there are others. Fighting, I think. And playing lots of golf."

"And inventing things?" asked Bertie.

"Yes," said Ranald. "Scotsmen have invented bags of things, Bertie. All the time."

Bertie imagined what his mother might have made of that statement. Ranald needed correcting. "And Scottish ladies too, Ranald," he said.

"Oh yes," said Ranald, and then asked Bertie, "Such as?"

"Such as what, Ranald?"

"What things have Scottish ladies invented, Bertie? I just want to know, that's all."

As it happened, Bertie had been drilled by his mother to deal with subversive questions of this sort. She had told him about the many great strides taken by Scottish women over the centuries, including the role that Mary Queen of Scots had played in the development of shortbread. And then there was Mrs McLintock, who, in the first half of the eighteenth century, published the first printed recipe for the same delicacy. That was just a taster, Bertie said. "There are plenty of other things, apart from inventing shortbread, that Scottish ladies have done. I'll tell you about them one day, Ranald."

The conversation, which had taken this distinctly interesting turn, did not get any further, as a number 23 bus now hove into sight and the boys had to prepare to board it. Their puppy, snugly ensconced in its bag, now appeared to be sleeping soundly. As they made their way onto the bus and settled in their seats, the puppy gave a few half-hearted whimpers, and then lapsed back into sleep.

"What are we going to call him?" Ranald asked, as the bus picked up speed.

"Perhaps we could call him MacTavish," said Bertie. "After Mr MacTavish."

Ranald agreed this was a good idea. "We're very lucky to have a dog, Bertie," he said.

"Are you going to tell your parents?" Bertie asked.

Ranald hesitated. "Maybe not just yet. When he's a bit bigger I could, but not right now. It'll be a nice surprise for them."

The journey did not take long, and when they left the bus in Morningside near the Church Hill Theatre MacTavish was still soundly asleep. In this state they carried him back to Ranald's house, slipping round the side into his back garden. There, in the shed in which the gardening tools and lawnmower were kept, the puppy was installed, a bundle of old hessian sacking for his bed.

"He'll need food," said Bertie.

Ranald thought for a moment. "There's lots in our fridge," he said. "My mummy's always eating. She's got bags of food. She won't notice if we take some for MacTavish."

Inside the house, the reels afternoon was drawing to a close. A final Dashing White Sergeant, with the appropriate accompaniment from Jimmy Shand and his Band, marked the completion of three solid hours of Scottish country dancing.

"Enter that in the logbook," Ranald's father whispered to his wife. "One hundred and fifty-seven hours to go. The end's in sight."

Ranald's mother sighed. "Hardly. And quite frankly, I feel you should be more apologetic about this whole business."

Ranald's father raised a finger to his lips. "Hush, my dear. We wouldn't want everybody to know. It wasn't my fault that the accountants forgot to do what they were meant to do. And I'd remind you the sheriff accepted that there was no dishonesty on my part. I am *not* a criminal, my dear. It was an oversight – no more than that."

"Yet now we're having to do all this Scottish country dancing community service," his wife retorted. "Well, that's just grand, isn't it? You're negligent, and I have to suffer the consequences."

George spun round. "How much money did you have when I married you, Ishbel?" he asked, his voice lowered, but rising slightly in indignation.

"Oh, really! What a ridiculous question."

He was not deterred. "And how much do you have now? Rather more, I'd say. And who's responsible for that? Me. OK? Me."

She reached out and touched his arm. "Please, George. Ranald's watching us."

Ranald and Bertie were now in the hall, watching the adults in the living room. Ishbel went over to greet the boys.

"You were playing for a long time," she said. "Did you enjoy yourselves?"

"Yes," said Ranald, glancing conspiratorially at Bertie as he replied.

Ranald's mother was staring at something. "What's that lead for, Ranald?" she asked. "Did you find it somewhere?"

Ranald turned quickly to Bertie. "It's Bertie's," he said.

"I didn't know you had a dog, Bertie," said Ishbel.

Bertie looked up at Ranald's mother. He had always been truthful. *Scouting for Boys* was clear about that: you should never tell a lie. He lowered his eyes to the lead that Wee MacTavish had given Ranald.

An idea came to him. Some time ago, in one of his psychotherapy sessions with Dr Fairbairn, Bertie had told the therapist about Tofu. Dr Fairbairn had been intrigued; he thought that Tofu was an imaginary friend, and had quizzed Bertie along those lines. But Tofu was real – unfortunately very real.

"Imaginary," said Bertie.

Ranald's mother caught her husband's eye and they both smiled.

"Of course," she said. "Of course." She bent down to kiss Ranald on the tip of his head. Ranald blushed deep red.

After his mother had gone back to the guests, Ranald breathed a sigh of relief. "You're a very good liar, Bertie," she said.

"I didn't lie, Ranald!" Bertie protested. "I said imaginary, that's all. It's because your mother's so stupid, Ranald. Sorry to have to tell you that, but there are some things you just have to face."

"I know," said Ranald. "But it's not my fault she's so stupid, Bertie."

"I know that, Ranald," said Bertie, putting a comforting arm around his friend's shoulder. "Nobody's mother is their fault, you know." He was thinking of his own.

"Thanks, Bertie," said Ranald. "You're a real friend."

They went into the kitchen, where they found a large steak in the fridge.

"Just right for MacTavish," said Ranald.

Bertie nodded enthusiastically. Keeping a dog was easier than he had imagined. Grown-ups, he thought, made things sound much more difficult than they really were.

37

Men and Clothes

It was proving to be an eventful Saturday. For Stuart, it was a day of mixed emotions – of elation at his reunion with Katie, and of bleak disappointment at the discovery that she had acquired a new boyfriend. He understood, though, that there was no reason why she should not do this – after all, it was he who had brought their nascent affair to an abrupt end, and he had done so, he accepted, with rather less tact than might have been required. He had been craven – yes, that was the only word for it – in the face of a stern ultimatum from Irene. But then, how else could he have reacted to her threat to take the children away from him? Oh, the hypocrisy of it, the sheer, unadulterated hypocrisy. She and her psychotherapist friend; she with her cosy chats – very cosy – with Dr Fairbairn about Melanie Klein and Jung and all the rest of them, while all the time something else altogether was going on. And then to make him give up his friendship with Katie, because that's what it was: friendship, just friendship – well, with additional closeness, of course, although there was nothing sordid about it . . . And now it was all wrecked and he had nothing, nothing in his life.

That was Stuart's Saturday. For his mother, Nicola, it had been an altogether different sort of day. She had delivered Bertie to the house of his friend, Ranald Braveheart Macpherson – not without some misgivings about the quality of parental supervision in those latitudes: Scottish country dancing on a Saturday *afternoon*? There was something odd about that, she felt. People were entitled to dance reels if that was what they wanted to do, but on a Saturday afternoon? There was something vaguely suspicious about that, she thought – as odd as receiving an invitation, as she recently had, from a long-lost schoolfriend to join her and her husband at their house in Peebles for an afternoon of carpet bowls. That might be the sort of thing that went on in Peebles on a Saturday afternoon, but Nicola was having none of it. Carpet bowls in Peebles was a *symptom*, she said to herself, and I am not there quite yet.

After dropping off Bertie, Nicola had taken Ulysses to Luca's Ice-Cream Parlour at Holy Corner. Ulysses was on the young side to be given ice cream in public, and had succeeded in covering not only the table but the floor beneath it with vanilla and chocolate chip ice cream in equal measure. The young man on duty, however, was accustomed to this and even offered to replace the spilt and thrown ice cream with new supplies. Nicola declined, with thanks, but reflected, as he returned to his post, on his courtesy. We can still produce them, she told herself; we can still produce young men with manners, and decency, who are prepared to spend their Saturday afternoons working in ice-cream parlours and be pleasant to people like me, taking all the mess and stickiness in their stride.

She had then taken Ulysses to La Barantine, a coffee house and bakery in Bruntsfield, where, while she enjoyed a relaxed double-shot latte, he had thrown fragments of croissant over the floor and into the hair of a woman at a nearby table. Once again, decency and understanding had been the reaction of those affected, which left Nicola with an even greater appreciation of the civility of the city in which she lived. Was the rest of the world like Edinburgh, she wondered, or did she simply have the good fortune to live in one of the few remaining places where people treated one another with comity and enlightenment even as they were subjected to a barrage of croissants?

Back in Scotland Street itself, Domenica Macdonald had devoted herself to what she described as a day of necessary administration. Her husband, Angus, was used to this particular dedication of Saturday, and was content to spend the morning in his studio, lunchtime in the Scottish Arts Club in Rutland Square, and the afternoon back at his easel. He did not enquire too closely as to what Domenica did on Saturday, nor did she make enquiry of him. It was part of the secret of a successful marriage, he believed, that each person should have the space, emotional and physical, to follow at least some pursuits of his or her own.

It was perhaps just as well that Angus did not ask Domenica what she planned to do that day, as she had in mind a particularly delicate mission directly affecting him. Like most wives, Domenica had grave misgivings about her husband's clothes. It is a familiar truth, known to most women, that men have no dress sense. There are, admittedly, one or two men who dress with proper attention to colour co-ordination and such matters, but they are, of course, men who are in touch with their feminine side. For most men, clothes are more or less functional – mere cladding that serves to keep out the elements and disguise the shocking truth within. As long as clothes do that, then their colour, shape and texture are not of particular concern. And yet, in spite of this aesthetic blunting, men do have a strong sense of loyalty when it comes to clothes, and, unlike women, will not abandon a serviceable garment in favour of something newer or more fashionable. So it is that a man will keep a jacket, with pride, for twenty years or more if he possibly can. If it continues to fit, and if it is, to an extent, still in one piece, then why change it? In the view of most men, that question simply cannot be answered satisfactorily by women. Women just do not understand clothing loyalty. They do not get it.

Domenica had become increasingly exasperated by the

unwillingness of Angus to revitalise his wardrobe. Their marriage, a few years previously, had given her the opportunity to throw at least some of his clothes away, but she had discovered that he had not made a full and frank disclosure. It transpired that he had kept a cupboard of old, familiar clothes in his studio, and these had been reintroduced into his mainstream wardrobe. Now it was these old tweed jackets and corduroy trousers that were preferred to the few new outfits she had succeeded in buying for him. That they were becoming increasingly threadbare did not seem to exercise Angus in the slightest. That they were losing such vestiges of colour as they had once possessed seemed similarly irrelevant to him: if all your clothes were a faded brown, roughly the colour of a bracken-covered Scottish hillside in the winter, then all that meant was the colour co-ordination issue was resolved. And if your hair was brown, as Angus's was, then that further co-ordinated you.

But then Domenica had happened upon a passage in Walter Scott's *Guy Mannering*. One of the characters in the novel refuses to get new clothes. His wife, however, works out how to deal with the problem: replace them by stealth, while he is asleep. When he wakes up, he won't notice, and will get into the new clothes without realising it, as long as they are placed in the spot where he got out of the old clothes the previous night. Brilliant, thought Domenica. Can't go wrong.

And it was with Walter Scott in mind that she set out that afternoon for Stewart Christie & Co in Queen Street, tailors and stockists of just the sort of clothes that a well-dressed Angus Lordie might sport.

38

The Aphorist

A number of Angus's jackets and pairs of trousers had migrated from his studio and were now to be found blatantly hanging in his wardrobe. These would be thrown out in due course; in the meantime, all that Domenica required was a sample or two that could be used for sizing purposes. This was necessary as she had no idea of what size Angus took in various garments. Some months ago, when she had tried – unsuccessfully – to buy him a new shirt, she had resorted to slipping a tape measure round his neck while he was eating breakfast. He had shrugged the tape off, though, and had looked at her as if demanding an explanation. And she did find it rather difficult to explain why one should suddenly place a tape measure round one's husband's neck. Idle curiosity might explain many things, but this was not one of them. Absent-mindedness was similarly unconvincing, and so Domenica had simply said, "Oh, nothing," and changed the subject. Now, with a jacket, a pair of trousers, and a shirt tucked into a large shopping bag, she had all that would be needed by the experts up at Stewart Christie & Co. They could apply their own tape measures to the clothes and work out just what was required for Angus, even in his absence.

Scotland Street was deserted when Domenica shut the stair door behind her. It was a still afternoon, and the boughs of the trees in Drummond Place Garden, heavy with full summer leaf, were motionless. A cat prowled between parked cars, looked out over the setts, and then dashed out on some urgent errand of its own. A strident herring gull, having drifted up from Leith to scavenge amongst the pickings, noticed the cat and flapped up in the air *ex abundanti cautela*, mewing as it did so. And then another movement caught her eye, and she saw two female figures walking briskly along the pavement towards her.

Antonia Collie, Domenica's former neighbour in Scotland Street, was in the company, as she more often than not was, of her friend and flatmate, Sister Maria-Fiore dei Fiori di Montagna. Antonia, who dressed in a way that would previously have been described as blue-stockingish, was wearing a thick grey skirt and matching top – far too warm, Domenica thought, for mid-summer – while Sister Maria-Fiore dei Fiori di Montagna, who was altogether more stylish than her companion, was wearing a lightweight blue habit that looked as if it was made of soft linen.

When the two women saw Domenica, they waved in a friendly fashion, and increased their pace to catch up with her. Domenica, who would have preferred not to be distracted from her mission, nonetheless slowed down to accommodate them.

"Well, well," said Antonia. "Fancy seeing you."

Domenica smiled weakly. Why should it be considered in the slightest bit extraordinary that she should be walking on Drummond Place when she lived just around the corner? It really was a very banal greeting – almost, if not quite, as trite as *long time no see*. That was a particularly odd expression, reminiscent of the pidgin languages which Domenica, as an anthropologist with experience of Melanesia, had once mastered. And yet people who knew no other words of Tok Pisin still said *long time no see* like the denizens of a Chinese laundry in an old black-and-white film. Strange, she thought.

Then Antonia continued, "Long time no see, Domenica."

Domenica struggled to maintain her composure. "Well, actually, it was last week, wasn't it?"

"Perhaps," said Antonia, lightly. "Time passes so quickly these days, doesn't it?"

This was the signal for Sister Maria-Fiore dei Fiori di Montagna, who had said nothing until now but had smiled sweetly, as nuns are expected to do, to say, "The speed of time is the speed of our lives proceeding towards God."

Domenica looked at her. Sister Maria-Fiore dei Fiori di Montagna had become famous for her aphorisms, which had propelled her from obscurity to a near-central position in the society of Scotland's capital. It had been an astonishing phenomenon, thought Domenica: an Italian nun, of no particular distinction, had somehow made her mark in a country she barely knew by coining aphorisms of immense vapidity. These utterances had been seized upon by people who seemed, for quite unfathomable reasons, to be in need of such sustenance.

Domenica struggled with the temptation to say, "What on earth does that mean?" And succeeded in that struggle, because she simply said, "Well, that's one way of looking at it."

Sister Maria-Fiore dei Fiori di Montagna took this as a compliment, replying, with suitable modesty, "Thank you. You are very kind, dear Domenica."

Domenica bristled, firstly because she had not meant to be kind, and secondly, because there was something condescending about being called *dear Domenica*. Again, she let this pass: one cannot defeat an aphorist, she told herself. A trite aphorism will always win.

They walked together in silence for a few moments. Then Sister Maria-Fiore dei Fiori di Montagna observed, "The sunlight is upon the trees. Look."

Domenica looked at the trees. It was undoubtedly true: the sunlight was upon them. But why should that be a matter of remark? It would be odd, surely, were the sunlight to fall upon everything else but somehow miss out the trees.

"Well, it certainly is sunny today," she said.

"At the moment it is," cautioned Antonia. "But in Scotland, can one ever be sure? We get sunlight one moment and then the next, what? Rain. Or even snow. Our weather is so fickle."

"Of course, we have our micro-climates in Edinburgh," said Domenica. "It can be warm and sunny down here but go up to the Braids or Fairmilehead and it's a different story."

Sister Maria-Fiore dei Fiori di Montagna listened to this with interest. "It is always a different story," she said. "You get one story, and then you get another."

Domenica decided to move the conversation on. "And how's your work going, Antonia?"

Antonia answered briskly. "Very well. I am casting my net a bit wider and dealing now with more recent Scottish saints, along with the older ones. Light and shade, you know. The lives of the more recent saints illuminate the lives of the earlier ones. So I've been doing a bit of research into the Venerable Margaret Sinclair."

Domenica knew exactly who Margaret Sinclair was. There was to be seen, she had been told, a relic of this remarkable Edinburgh woman: her handbag – an item of considerable interest, and inspiration, to the devout. Relics often struck Domenica as macabre – fingers and so on, lodged in reliquaries, were a peculiar obsession for anyone to harbour – but a holy handbag, now there was something rather different.

39

The Contents of a Private Bag

Domenica did her best with Antonia Collie and Sister Maria-Fiore dei Fiori di Montagna. She had always found Antonia's manner hard to deal with, particularly since her erstwhile neighbour had suffered an attack of Stendhal Syndrome in the Uffizi Gallery. That was not Antonia's fault, of course: anybody could fall victim to Stendhal Syndrome, and if one of its sequelae was behavioural oddity, then that was something that should not be laid at one's door. So, if Antonia now tended to go on about the early Scottish saints, the subject of her long-awaited book, then the least one could do was to listen – even if some of the saints were not only apocryphal, but also themselves somewhat irritating.

The story of the Venerable Margaret Sinclair, though, and her holy handbag, was far from irritating. Margaret Sinclair was a good woman, born in humble circumstances in the Cowgate of Edinburgh and devoted, through her short life, to helping others. She deserved beatification, thought Domenica, irrespective of the necessary miracles that would be needed for her to complete the *cursus honorum* of a candidate saint. Domenica was happy to hear about her, but less interested in the wildly unlikely pursuits of some of the earlier Scottish saints, which took one, she felt, firmly into the territory of myth, credulity, and sheer nonsense.

As they walked together up Nelson Street and into Northumberland Street, Antonia told Domenica about a chapter she had recently completed on the minor saints of Whithorn, including one who was not only a saint himself but had married a saint and had several children, all of whom subsequently became saints.

"His local legend is really rather moving," said Antonia. "He was a sort of St Francis figure, actually – terribly good with animals."

"St Francis was a friend of animals," Sister Maria-Fiore dei Fiori di Montagna continued.

"So we have been told," said Domenica drily, adding, "Many times before."

"Indeed," said Sister Maria-Fiore dei Fiori di Montagna. "The animals trusted him."

"Was St Francis a vegetarian?" asked Domenica. "Or did he eat the animals who trusted him, I wonder."

Antonia shot her a sideways glance, but Sister Maria-Fiore dei Fiori di Montagna gave the question due thought. "History does not record that. I think it was rare in those days for people to be vegetarian." She paused. "Back in Tuscany, where my home convent is, we have bees that give us honey."

"How interesting," said Domenica.

"Yes," said Sister Maria-Fiore dei Fiori di Montagna. "Very."

They walked on in silence for a few minutes. Then Antonia pointed at Domenica's bag and said, "I see you're carrying a bag, Domenica."

"Yes," said Domenica. "I am." Noticing that Antonia was craning her neck slightly to see into the top of the bag, she adjusted its position slightly to prevent its contents being seen.

"It looks quite heavy," Antonia observed.

Domenica shrugged. "Not really. No, it's not all that heavy."

"No bag is ever heavy if the heart of the carrier is light," pronounced Sister Maria-Fiore dei Fiori di Montagna.

Domenica looked at her, and pursed her lips. From what wells of cliché sprang these observations, she wondered? And were those wells inexhaustible, like the magic water-barrel of

St Catherine of Siena that never ran dry?

"Yes," said Antonia. 'That's a really useful *aperçu*, Maria-Fiore, dear flower."

Domenica took a deep breath. Really, this was too much. *Aperçu! Dear flower!*

Antonia's curiosity now got too much for her. "What's in the bag, Domenica?"

Domenica sucked in her cheeks. "Which bag?"

Antonia pointed at the bag. "That bag. The one you're carrying."

Domenica chose her words carefully. "Oh, that bag . . . You mean, my *private* bag."

She put as much emphasis on the word *private* as she could, without being overtly rude. But it was not, as it happened, sufficient to deter Antonia.

"Yes, that bag."

Once again this brought forth an aphorism from Sister Maria-Fiore dei Fiori di Montagna. "The bag that is not heavy because of the lightness inside your heart," she added, helpfully.

"This and that," Domenica responded. "The sort of things you might expect to find in somebody's *private* bag."

"Books?" asked Antonia. "Are you heading up to the library?"

"No," answered Domenica. "I'm not going to the library."

There was a brief silence. "Where are you going, if you don't mind my asking?" said Antonia.

"Yes," said Sister Maria-Fiore dei Fiori di Montagna. "Where?"

Domenica stared studiously at the ground. She had decided she would simply ignore this question. It was none of Antonia's business, and even less of Sister Maria-Fiore dei Fiori di Montagna's, where she was going. You should *never* ask somebody where they are going because it might be somewhere very private – an assignation with a lover, for instance, or something of that sort. You might as well ask a friend, whom you met in the doctor's waiting room, why he or she was there.

Sorely tested, Domenica struggled with herself. Eventually she replied, "I'm going to see somebody."

This did not satisfy Antonia. "With a bag? With something for somebody – in your bag?"

"You could say that," said Domenica.

This spawned a further aphorism from Sister Maria-Fiore dei Fiori di Montagna. "There are so many things we could say," she said. "And yet we say so little. So much on one side, and so little on the other."

Something within Domenica snapped. "I don't know about that," she said abruptly. "You could argue – and I might be inclined to do so myself – that we have actually rather little to say – or some of us do – and yet we say an awful lot. You could argue that, you know."

"You could," conceded Sister Maria-Fiore dei Fiori di Montagna. "But to do so would be to fall into a trap. There are many traps set for the unwary. Traps are all about us."

"You could start by shutting yours!" muttered Domenica. This was *sotto voce*, but was it *sotto* enough?

Antonia frowned. "What was that, Domenica? Did you say something?"

Domenica immediately felt ashamed of herself. Being from Edinburgh, she was of course not given to vulgarity, but there were times . . . "There is so little we have to say," she said mildly.

"Precisely," said Sister Maria-Fiore dei Fiori di Montagna. "Dear Domenica puts it so well."

At the junction of Heriot Row and Dundas Street, Domenica was able to peel off from her two companions and make her solitary way to Stewart Christie at the far end of

Queen Street. She was not proud of herself; Sister Maria-Fiore dei Fiori di Montagna was a guest in Scotland and should be treated with all the courtesy that should be shown to any guest, while Antonia, for all her irritating ways, was a Stendhal Syndrome survivor, a former neighbour, and, underneath it all, a rather lonely woman, the sort of woman for whom it might be important to know what was in other people's bags. To understand everything was to forgive everything. Domenica remembered that, and resolved there and then, at the junction of Howe Street, to try harder with the two women when she next encountered them. But now an enjoyable task was at hand: the purchase of a new outfit for Angus, and buying clothes for men was always a pleasant task if you were a woman, because most women knew, at heart, that men really had no idea what to wear and could only benefit from this sort of loving attention.

40

Brogue Boots for Women, and Others

The premises of Stewart Christie & Co, Outfitters, were at the west end of Queen Street – the far end, as Domenica described it, since Scotland Street, and her world, were at the east end of the New Town. That geographical orientation was a matter of more than mere compass bearings: Domenica was sensitive to social geography, and in the eastern end of the New Town there had survived more of the original nature of Edinburgh's Georgian quarter. Edinburgh had always enjoyed a lively social mix, in which people of all backgrounds, or even none, lived cheek by jowl. This had also been the case in the Old Town, until its malodorous nature had caused flight to the other side of the Nor' Loch. But it was not just the gentry who fled the dank tenements, the winding closes and miasmic passages of the High Street and its neighbouring warrens; this flight involved others of more modest station in life, who found their own place in the interstices of the grander new quarters that sprang up on the other side of the city. Only much later did the social mix change, and the more prosperous streets of the New Town become the preserve of the well off. Scotland Street, and other streets in the east, continued to provide a roof for all sorts: it was no Moray Place, the grand, towering circle that cast its haughty frown over the Dean Valley below.

Now, as she stood before the tailor's window, her eye was drawn to a pair of fine brogue boots, displayed alongside a selection of green waxed jackets – the sort of jackets favoured by people who enjoyed standing about on expanses of moorland being buffeted by the wind. These boots had a small label under them, a card that said *Joseph Cheaney, for men and women (since 1886)*. Her eye lingered on them, and then fell to her own footwear, a pair of now rather ageing black shoes that were of no particular style, no particular provenance, and, she felt, no particular comfort. She tried to remember when she had last bought herself a pair of shoes. It was certainly not within the last year, and if she were to treat herself to a pair of Joseph Cheaney boots it would not be too much of a self-indulgence. And at that moment, she felt that extraordinary sense of excitement that comes with the decision to buy yourself a new pair of shoes. Of course, she was here for Angus, and she must not lose sight of the purpose of her visit, but that did not mean that she could not be here for herself too.

She went inside. Domenica had first been in the shop with Angus when she had brought him in for an adjustment to his kilt, but over the years she had got to know the staff. Now she saw Trevor and Andrew busy with customers while the owners, Daniel and Vixy, were conferring amongst the jackets and waistcoats to the rear. Vixy caught Domenica's eye and came over to greet her. As she did so, she spotted Domenica's bag. "Your husband's kilt?" she enquired.

Domenica shook her head. "No. That still fits."

"Kilts have such a distressing habit of shrinking as their owners go through life," said Vixy. "Or is it that men get a little bit . . . how should one put it? Stouter?"

They both laughed. "Angus is relatively low-carb these days," said Domenica. "His waistline remains unchanged. I have to watch him, though." She paused. "Those boots in the window?"

"The Joseph Cheaney ankle boots?"

"Yes."

"They're downstairs," said Vixy. "Would you like to . . ."

Domenica opened her bag. "Later. First, my real errand.

You know how men are with their clothes? You know how they like to keep them too long?"

Vixy nodded. "Men have their little ways."

"Well," continued Domenica. "I've decided that I simply have to get some new stuff for Angus. I could bring him in, but you know how he is. He spends so much time in his studio and I don't like to drag him out. Or he has to take Cyril for a walk. Or there are always excuses."

Vixy nodded again.

"So," Domenica went on, "I've brought in a pair of his trousers, a jacket, and one of his shirts. I apologise in advance for the state of these things, but I wondered if we could measure them and then choose something new."

"Of course," said Vixy. "Let's take a look."

A tape measure was produced and the measuring took place, the results being noted on sheet of paper. Angus, it transpired, had a forty-inch chest, a thirty-six inch waist, and a sixteen-inch neck. "Very nice measurements," said Vixy. "And let's start with the jacket. Something in tweed, I take it. Brown? Greenish?"

A selection of jackets was produced. This was followed by trousers, and finally a couple of shirts. Everything matched; everything sat perfectly with the garment with which it would be worn. The choice made, Vixy folded the clothing carefully and tucked it into Domenica's bag. As she did so, Domenica explained her plan to remove Angus's old clothes from the chair on which he placed them at night, and substitute the new ones. "The idea is that he won't notice," she said. "He'll simply get dressed in the morning, same as usual, but in the new clothes. I got it from a Walter Scott novel."

"What a brilliant idea," exclaimed Vixy.

Looking about her, Domenica noticed a display of colourful waistcoats. "Those are lovely," she said. "Look at that red. So many men would be improved by a red waistcoat. Just like that. Miraculous transformation."

Vixy smiled. "There are other colours. Distressed oatmeal is popular these days."

"Men need to be more colourful," said Domenica. "And look at those trousers."

She pointed to a section on the trouser rail devoted to trousers in varying shades of red, and even pink.

"Those pink ones look good," she said.

"They're very popular. Engaged strawberry," said Vixy. "Although you could call them pink, I suppose."

The clothing purchased, they went down to the lower floor, where Domenica chose a pair of Joseph Cheaney boots. She felt immediately at home in them, and decided to wear them out of the shop. It had been a most satisfactory outing in every respect.

She went out onto the street and took her first step in her new boots. The sensation was extraordinary. It was empowering. Good footwear somehow gave purpose. The steps we take in new shoes, or boots, thought Domenica, are somehow different. It was strange. But they were. They just were. And she thought: how is it that the things with which we clothe ourselves make such a difference to what is inside?

41

The Reading of Shoes

Well shod in her new pair of Joseph Cheaney boots, with all the security and assurance – not to mention support – that ankle-length footwear can give, Domenica made her way down Dundas Street. As she approached the corner of Heriot Row, she glanced down at her feet, conscious of the pristine look of the fine brown leather – so subtle and yet so strong, and brogue too. *Brogue boots to boot*, she thought, and smiled. There were some who thought of brogue as a statement, a political or social pinning of colours to the mast. But it was not that at all, Domenica felt, or not inevitably so. Some people might think brogue a bit . . . what? Old-fashioned? Domenica, though, knew several people who wore brogue shoes who were not in the slightest bit conservative in their outlook. Brogue shoes had nothing to do with how you viewed the world. Brogue was an aesthetic issue, and you should not judge people by their shoes' aesthetic qualities. Except sometimes . . .

She found herself thinking of two-tone black-and-white shoes – the sort of shoes once known as co-respondents' shoes, because they were the classic wear of those who went off with other men's wives. That was absurd, and old-fashioned too – the stuff of a Noel Coward song or a Somerset Maugham short story. Yet black-and-white shoes were relatively unusual and must clearly be a matter of deliberate choice. One would not just happen to have a pair of two-tone shoes – wearing such shoes involved the conscious embracing of shoes that were striking, were obvious: shoes that were the opposite of discreet or diffident. Shoes such as that said, with shamelessness, often with braggadocio: *Look at me.*

There were other shoes that made a statement. Sensible shoes – that odd, pejorative category of women's shoes – told you that their wearer was not concerned with fashion; that she preferred comfort to elegance. There was nothing wrong with that, of course, and yet there were limits. There was no reason why attractive shoes should not also be comfortable, even practical. Frumpish shoes, though, shoes that made no effort at all, signalled more than an attachment to comfort. They signalled a lack of interest in the whole idea of looking attractive.

Boots, thought Domenica, were a special case. One had to make distinctions when it came to boots, as there were different rules for men and women. And there were also different issues with ankle and calf-length boots, at least as far as men were concerned. Domenica had not given much thought to this in the past, but now, as she continued on her walk home, a taxonomy of boots came to mind.

Ankle boots for men raised no issues at all. Chelsea boots and the like were practical footgear for men who wanted to avoid sprained ankles. They were also useful for those who had a certain level of exposure to mud. They made no statement at all – about anything. Calf-length boots – when worn by men – involved more complex issues. These were very practical for those who lived on farms or in the country. They were good for use in fields and on hillsides, and on the banks of rivers. But could you wear them in an urban setting without making some sort of statement? The answer was probably no. Calf-length boots for men, worn where there was no practical need for them, were indicative of an authoritarian personality. Domenica was sure about that. A man in calf-length boots in a town or city would almost certainly be on his way to a meeting of like-minded authoritarians; the sort of people who drove Land Rovers without really needing to. In Domenica's mind, that was beyond doubt. She would never be comfortable in the presence of a man in calf-length boots unless he could come up with a good reason for wearing them.

Women could wear calf-length boots with impunity, and such boots signified nothing, whether worn in town or in the country. As long as they were calf-length; boots that went higher than that were a sign of . . . well, she did not need to spell that out to herself. Similarly, workmen's boots – rough, clunky boots with reinforced toecaps – when worn by a woman were intended to send a very clear signal that the wearer had no truck with femininity. The wearers of such boots would, in general, not wish to be misunderstood.

But these marvellous boots that Domenica was wearing – they went with everything, and spoke to nothing other than their wearer's good taste. And they made Domenica glow with pleasure, even as she thought: when did I last glow with pleasure?

She paused. She had drawn level with Big Lou's café, and she could see the light on inside, and a shadow against a blind that must have been Big Lou herself. Domenica hesitated – she did not really want a cup of coffee, but, slightly elated by the success of her mission, she thought that a conversation with Big Lou was just what she wanted to complete the day.

Big Lou, standing behind her stainless-steel counter, a cloth in her hand, noticed Domenica's boots immediately.

"Your boots!" she said, a strong note of admiration in her voice. "Those are definitely *the* boots, Domenica."

Domenica looked down, as if noticing them for the first time. "Oh, these? Yes, I must admit I rather like them."

"Like them?" said Big Lou, with mock incredulity. "Those are boots to die for, Domenica. Those are . . ." Big Lou searched for the right word. And it came to her – an old Scots word, the only one in the Scots lexicon, she thought, that could do justice to boots such as Domenica's.

"They're fantoosh," Big Lou continued. "Pure fantoosh."

Domenica beamed. "That's good of you, Lou. I do rather like them, I must say."

"I would have loved to have boots like that when I was back on the farm."

Domenica smiled. "They might be a bit too good for the farm, Lou."

"Oh, I know that," said Big Lou. "Everything was too good for our place. We just had the basics."

Domenica was struck by the note of wistfulness in Big Lou's voice. Big Lou was not one to engage in self-pity, but what she had just said sounded rather close to that.

"Are you all right, Lou?" she asked. "Is everything . . ."

She did not get the chance to finish. Big Lou was shaking her head. "It's not so good, Domenica," she said. "It was – or it used to be – all right, but no longer. Sorry."

Domenica stared at her friend. Everybody was so used to relying on Big Lou, to taking her cheerfulness and robustness to heart. This was something quite unusual – a sort of defeatism that she had never seen Big Lou display before.

"Tell me, Lou," said Domenica.

Big Lou sighed. "I'm selling the business. This is it. The end."

Domenica drew in her breath. "But, Lou, we all . . . we all love you. Nobody wants you to go. Nobody."

"Aye, well," said Lou. "That may be so, and it's good to hear it. But I've made up my mind. I need to raise some money and I've had an offer on this place. I'm going to take it."

42

Questions about Bags

"Well, well!" said Angus, when Domenica returned to the flat. "What have we here? Those boots . . ."

Domenica had not expected to find Angus in. He had told her that he would be spending the entire afternoon in his studio, and when he did that he never returned before six, which was the time that Cyril was given his late afternoon walk in Drummond Place Garden. A further reason why she would not have come home early was the fact that he had his current subject in for a sitting that afternoon, and that usually meant that he would be late.

"Like them?" asked Domenica.

Angus whistled. "Very fetching indeed."

"I know they're a bit of an indulgence," said Domenica. "But . . ."

He brushed her *apologia* aside. "Nonsense. If there were ever anybody who *deserved* boots like that, it's you."

Domenica smiled, and blew him a kiss; dear Angus, whose sense of when a compliment was needed was so pitch-perfect. Bless you, she thought; that I should find you at this stage in life, when there are so few people left to find – and hardly any of them men; bless you, for I have found myself in you.

But then she remembered what she was carrying. He had not noticed the large bag of clothing yet, and she did not want him to see it. "Would you mind putting the kettle on?" she asked. That would get him safely out of the hall and into the kitchen, giving her time to conceal her other purchases. But she was too late; Angus now spotted the bag and pointed at it quizzically.

"What's in the bag?" he asked.

It was the question that Antonia and Sister Maria-Fiore dei Fiori di Montagna had put so pointedly, but whereas they had no right to do so, Angus was perfectly entitled to ask the same thing. Were Angus to come into the flat with a bulging bag, she would naturally feel keen to find out what it contained. That, in a sense, was what marriage was all about: marry somebody and you lost the right to carry large bags about in private. You gained many other things, but you certainly lost that.

She played for time. "Bag?"

He pointed to the bag, with its impossible-to-miss *Stewart Christie* lettering emblazoned, gold on green. "That one."

And then he answered his own question, giving her time to recover. "Oh, of course," he said. "That's where you bought the boots."

She grasped the straw. "Yes. I bought them at Stewart Christie." And then, as quickly as she could, she added, "And be an angel, Angus, and make tea. I'm parched."

"Yes," he said. "I'll do that."

With that, he disappeared into the kitchen, giving Domenica the opportunity to go into their bedroom. There she took the new clothes out of their bag and stuffed them into her wardrobe. She knew that they would not be found, as Angus never looked in there. "I respect cupboards," he had once said to her. "It's something to do with being at boarding school."

Angus had been a boarder at a boys' school in Perthshire, a place tucked away in a glen, where he had, for the most part, been happy enough, but where privacy had been in short supply. "The only private place we had was our cupboard," he said. "Everything else was shared. Shared basins, baths, everything. Shared meals, shared studies, shared sports kit. Sometimes you found yourself wearing somebody else's socks because the labels had come off or names had been mixed up. You grew used to it. But your cupboard was always private."

Domenica, who had never had that experience, found it hard to imagine what it would be like.

"You don't mind too much," said Angus. "And I suppose it makes you more tolerant of others. It's difficult to be selfish if you've been brought up like that."

"You have a different sense of self," Domenica remarked. "The boundaries of the self are socially dictated. If you've been brought up cheek by jowl with a lot of others, then you're less likely to see yourself as separate from them. Radical individualism does not go well with the communal life."

"If you say so," said Angus.

"I do," she said. "Not that I want to be didactic, but I think we're losing sight of that. I've been reading a book about the Gorbals. Colin MacFarlane. About what it was like."

The Gorbals was a slum area of Glasgow, erased in the fit of construction that remade the city from the nineteen-sixties onwards. But before the cranes with their wrecking balls moved in, it had been a living, breathing hive of life. People shared their cludgies; they took their weekly baths in communal municipal bathhouses; there was little insulation from the ordinary sounds of life – the coughing, the yelling, the domestic battles, the moments of intimacy: there would be too many people sharing too few rooms for any of that to be private. And yet people knew one another, and loved one another, and nobody was anonymous. Later, filed vertically in tower blocks, living in the air, away from ordinary human landmarks, people sickened and grew sad, but had to live that disjointed life for decades, until the grossness of the original mistake could be admitted and these great towers of unhappiness began to be brought down, blown up in seconds, collapsing in clouds of dust. Squalor and deprivation had been exchanged for unhappiness and anomie – a complicated and double-edged bargain.

What people wanted was community, thought Domenica, and you did not have to be a social anthropologist, as she was, to work that out. They wanted to live somewhere definite, built on a human scale and with decency; they wanted to be relieved of want and uncertainty, in so far as was possible; they wanted to belong, to have an identity – to know who they were and where they were from. And throughout Scottish history there had been those who would take that away from them, or deny its possibility. There had been community, a long time ago, but land grabs and clearances had shattered that; then planners had disrupted people again, moving them to new towns; and now globalisation was doing its work to destroy our remaining sense of the local. She sighed. There were no answers, it seemed; or no easy ones, at any rate. Those who came up with easy answers, the panaceas to all our problems, were naïve or mendacious.

With the new clothes hidden, she returned to the kitchen, where Angus was making tea.

"I saw Big Lou," Domenica. "And there's bad news, I'm afraid."

Angus looked up sharply. Bad news meant cancer.

"Oh my God," he said.

"No, not a health thing," Domenica said quickly. "But she's sold the business."

Angus drew in his breath, aghast at what Domenica had said. Big Lou was a constant in everybody's life. They loved her and everything she stood for. This simply could not be.

43

Unearned Happiness

As he drove the car up the winding drive of his house at Nine Mile Burn, Matthew reflected on his good fortune. Here he was in his late twenties with a business of his own, an attractive wife, a house, and three boisterous, healthy sons – and he had earned it all by dint of . . . He stopped there. No, that was the whole point: he had not earned any of this, not really, with the exception, perhaps, of Elspeth and the boys, although he was not sure if it was appropriate to talk of earning, or deserving, one's family.

All you had to do to get a wife or a husband was to meet the other person, be reasonably nice to him or her, and then propose. For some, that might involve effort and concomitant achievement, but for others it was hardly a major battle. Effort would be most required, Matthew thought, if you had to work at being acceptable to the person you were hoping to marry; if you had major character defects, for instance, that you had to suppress in order to be thought suitable. You earned your partner in such circumstances by the effort of appearing to be nicer than you really were. But he had not had to do any of that – not that he was smug about how desirable he might be to anybody. He was nothing special – he knew that – but at least he was not unduly unpleasant in any conspicuous way. He was, he had always felt, pretty average.

It was luck, Matthew thought, that had brought him Elspeth. He had met her at a difficult point in her life, when she had been suspended from her teaching position for pinching the ear of a supremely irritating child, Olive. There was no excuse for pinching a child's ear, but in Elspeth's case it was possible to see why a teacher might be pushed into pinching that particular ear. Olive, who was in the same class as Bertie, was, Matthew believed, a supremely bossy little girl who had tormented the poor boy by diagnosing him with her Junior Nurse Kit. Olive had somehow added a real syringe to the kit's armamentarium, and had used this to take a blood sample from Bertie. It was on the basis of this blood sample that she had told him that he was suffering from leprosy.

Elspeth had told Olive that the old test for leprosy was to see whether a person had lost sensation in the ear lobe. And at that point, in her anger over Olive's sheer nastiness, she had pinched her ear to demonstrate the test. Her pleasure matched Olive's discomfort; some ears just ask to be pinched, and Olive's was one of them. But that was no excuse, of course, and the fact that Olive richly deserved this recrimination could not prevent the professional opprobrium into which Elspeth was plunged. Fortunately, Matthew was there to pick up the pieces – fortunately both for Elspeth and for him. They were happy together, and when the triplets arrived they were happier still, although busier, of course.

As for the business and the house, neither of these could possibly be considered the result of Matthew's own efforts. His father, who had extensive commercial interests, was a self-made man by any standards. He had started his career running a small building supplies firm and built it up through sheer hard work and business acumen. He could certainly say that he had earned everything, and would have preferred Matthew to be able to do the same. Unfortunately, Matthew's business instincts were less acute than his father's, and his earlier efforts had proved fruitless. Those failures had led to a resigned acceptance by his father that he should be given the chance to buy the gallery when it came on the market. To Matthew's father, the gallery would provide Matthew with something to do without risking too much capital and without stretching his son's very modest business talents too far. The result of this was that Matthew not only owned the business, but also the premises it occupied. There was, in addition, no debt, and a stash of working capital that made it possible to buy paintings at auction and sell them on at a suitable profit. It was not really a business model that could fail all that easily.

Then there was the house. Most young couples were burdened with mortgages, and these arrangements would remain round their necks for the first twenty-five years of their marriage. Inflation might reduce the proportion of monthly income that went towards house repayments, but in times of low inflation that effect would be barely discernible. Matthew and Elspeth had none of that to consider: his father's generosity had ensured that they owned the house at Nine Mile Burn outright. So here, once again, was something that Matthew could not say he had in any way earned.

Even the car he drove down the drive that evening was a gift from his father, and would have been out of reach of most young men in their late twenties. This was a British-racing-green Range Rover, complete with heated seats *and* heated steering wheel. It was ideal for transporting triplets and the impedimenta that triplets required, but it was far more luxurious than the cars driven by any of their friends, who made do with much more modest vehicles.

Matthew sighed. A less sensitive person might not have been bothered by any of this, but he was very much aware of the contrast between his life and the lives led by those without his advantages. He felt, too, that things you had not earned probably gave you less satisfaction than those for which you had needed to work hard. So he wondered whether there was something he had missed, and whether, in years to come, by not having had to scrimp and save he would feel that he had lost out on a valuable experience.

These thoughts were in his mind as he parked the car in front of the house, but he had dispelled them by the time he walked in through the front door. He was looking forward to the evening that lay ahead. He would see the boys for bathtime, which was always a riotous time of shouts and splashing, and afterwards he would read a story to them. That was always a good time for him, as the bottle of warmed milk which each boy nursed while they cuddled up to him seemed to induce calm. The boys smelled good too then – of soap, of Johnson & Johnson's Baby Shampoo, of warm milk and flannelette pyjamas – and the world, such a harsh and unhappy place at times, seemed somehow less so. The blessing of evening, thought Matthew; of home, and family, and the love that came with these things.

But when he went into the kitchen, he saw that Elspeth had been crying. She had evidently tried to conceal the fact, but there was smudged make-up, and smudged make-up spoke as eloquently as anything ever could of unhappiness beneath the veneer.

44

Being Simpatico

Matthew had always found it difficult to cope with tears. Others might be able to endure the visible dissolution that tears involved – the misting over of the eyes, the quivering of the lips, the display of weakness and vulnerability that was our real human lot, no matter how we covered ourselves with the clothing of certainty and conviction. We were, when all was said and done, children lost in the wood, and to break into tears was the most understandable of reactions, the most quintessentially human one too.

He went straight to Elspeth's side. "Darling, you've been crying."

She shook her head. "No."

"But you have . . . you have."

She turned away, wiping at her eyes with the sleeve of her blouse. On the white linen there were now streaks of mascara; she rubbed at those, making them worse.

Matthew put an arm about her. "Has something happened?"

"No," she said. And then, struggling to smile, she turned to face him. "And you? What about your day?"

He shrugged. He knew, from past experience, that he would not be able to get out of her what it was that had brought on her tears. Elspeth was stoic in these matters, and the most he could hope for would be some hint, obliquely put, that would throw light on the cause of her distress. He had a vague idea that it was something to do with being stuck out at Nine Mile Burn all by herself – or, if not entirely alone, with the company only of three toddlers and a young au-pair boy who, even if charismatic, was still only nineteen. Elspeth had always liked having somebody to talk to, but there were limits to the topics one could discuss with the triplets; James was another matter, of course. He was prepared to listen, and had an ability, rare in one of his age, to relate to somebody older. He was *simpatico*, Elspeth had decided. That was the simplest way of putting it: *simpatico*.

And Matthew was *simpatico*, too, she thought, even if not quite as *simpatico* as was James. Many men were completely non-*simpatico*, simply because they were masculine. Was that incompatible with being *simpatico*, she wondered; or was it unfair to men, who were inevitably masculine, to say that their basic classification, so to speak, was inherently non-*simpatico*? Why should masculinity be thoughtless or indifferent to the feelings of others? There were plenty of men, she felt, who did not want to be hard-hearted or unfeeling; there were plenty of men who felt the pain of others, who wanted to do something about it, who wanted to comfort those in need of comfort. Yet there were rather more, she suspected, who did not. Bruce Anderson, for example, with his preening and his view of women as playthings – he was definitely not *simpatico*. Nor was the man in the hardware store she sometimes went to, who spoke harshly to his wife; nor that man from Matthew's year at the Academy who had become a fund manager and could talk only of money and the stock exchange and expensive German cars with loud exhaust systems. She called him Porsche, because it seemed so much more fitting a name for him than his real name; Porsche was not *simpatico* in any sense. He was masculine in a turbo-charged, V8 sort of way – if V8 engines still existed, which Elspeth was not sure about. That was a question that no *simpatico* man could be expected to answer; a man who knew whether V8 engines still existed would, by the very fact of that knowledge, not be *simpatico*. But no, she told herself, that's not right – she had known a mechanic who was the most sympathetic of men, a faithful follower of Scottish Ballet who was as capable of being moved by the Dying Swan as he was by the sound of a finely tuned V8 engine – if such things still existed, of course.

Now, having composed herself, she looked at her watch. "What time was Pat . . ."

He did not allow her to complete her question. "I hope you don't . . ."

"Mind? Why should I mind?" Elspeth had read somewhere that you should never make your spouse feel guilty, as that would only exacerbate any underlying problems in the marriage.

"It's just that I thought you might . . . well, resent Pat in some way. You know how it is."

Elspeth looked away. "Why would I resent her?" Of course she resented Pat. What woman would not resent her husband's one-time girlfriend, especially when she continued to work for him? Matthew and Pat *talked*, about art and heaven knows what else, while she sat out there at Nine Mile Burn and looked at the hills in the distance and made mashed potatoes for the triplets. Of course she would resent her.

Matthew echoed her question. "Why would you resent her?" He shrugged. "I have no idea. It's just that when I mention her, you seem to breathe differently."

Elspeth spun round. "Breathe differently? What do you mean – breathe differently?"

"Your nostrils," said Matthew. "They seem to be pinched. You pull them in somehow."

Elspeth glared at him. "And how exactly do you pull in your nostrils? Perhaps you could show me."

Matthew took a deep breath, and felt his nostrils constrict and close. "Like that," he said.

For a few moments Elspeth said nothing. Then, turning away once more, she said, "Matthew, what about your own nose? What about it?"

He looked at her blankly. "My nose?"

"Yes," she said, clearly struggling to keep her voice even. "Your nose, Matthew. Have you ever stopped to consider it? I mean, really think about it?"

Matthew's hand went up to his nose. There had never been anything wrong with it, as far as he could tell. He had not thought about it very much, and now, for the first time, he felt doubts about it.

"You should tell me what you mean," he said. "You can't just say to somebody that there's something wrong with their nose and then leave it at that."

Elspeth shook her head. "But I didn't say there was anything wrong with it. All I said was that you should perhaps think about it. That's quite different, you know."

This conversation was interrupted by the sound of the doorbell. In the country, few people bothered with doorbells, and Matthew had even forgotten that they had one. So he said, "What's that bell?"

Elspeth dabbed again at her eyes with her handkerchief. "Your friend," she said. "Your dinner guest."

Matthew sighed. "Do you know something, Elspeth?" he said. "Sometimes I wonder why we got married."

He gasped at his own words, which were so completely unexpected, even by him; and immediately he wanted to snatch them back from the air, where it seemed to him they were hanging, in all their unkindness, like bursts of aerial flak. But it was too late; some words, and usually the wrong ones, seem chiselled in stone the moment they are uttered. Elspeth turned away. "Do you?" she muttered.

He pleaded with her. "No, my darling, no. No. I don't think that at all. I don't."

"Then why did you say it?"

"Because I'm . . . because I'm all over the place, and I don't think about what I'm saying and it just comes out. Just like that."

45

A Gift of Kiwis

There was no reason why Pat should have thought she was coming upon a scene of domestic disharmony when she arrived at the house in Nine Mile Burn. On the contrary, she was greeted at the door by a smiling Matthew, who ushered her into the rather untidy hall – it was, after all, a house inhabited by young triplets – where she hung her coat and put down the small holdall she had carried with her on the bus from Edinburgh.

"Kiwi fruit," she said, taking a brown paper bag out of the holdall. "I saw them in the greengrocer's near the King's Theatre. You know the one?"

"I've walked past it," said Matthew, peering into the bag.

"He has all sorts of exotic fruit there," said Pat. "And vegetables too – I mean, exotic vegetables – not that kiwi fruit are exotic any longer."

"We like them," said Matthew. "Thank you. Elspeth will be really pleased. She often has one for breakfast."

"You can eat them as you'd eat a boiled egg," said Pat. "You can take the top off and then use a spoon."

"I peel them," said Matthew. "I don't like the little hairs."

"Nobody likes hairy food," said Pat.

Matthew thought of globe artichokes. "What about artichokes – the above-ground ones? You know, the ones that look like thistles? They have all those hairs under the thick bit that you eat. Thousands of little hairs."

"But you're not meant to eat that bit," said Pat.

"No, of course not. I was just wondering whether you'd

describe them as hairy food, that's all."

Pat frowned. "Possibly. But what about pork? Sometimes pork is a bit hairy. You know – the crackling bit has hairs on it." She paused. "I used to love crackling. My father always gave me his, if we had pork for dinner. He would take his crackling and put it on my plate."

"Mine gave me his chicken skin," said Matthew. "He knew I loved it."

For a moment, both of them were silent at their respective memories. Pork, thought Pat, and, for his part, Matthew thought: the act of nourishment. That most simple transaction between parent and child, into which so much love was poured, so simply, so unquestioningly. And then he remembered what he had said to Elspeth, and he felt a sharp stab of remorse.

"I'll take these through to Elspeth," he said. "She's in the kitchen. Do you want to go along and see the kids? They're still up and about – somewhere down there." He waved in the direction of the corridor that led to the boys' rooms.

Pat went off, and Matthew made his way back into the kitchen. Elspeth was looking for something in a cupboard, and she turned round, looked briefly at Matthew, and then continued with her search.

"Have you seen the colander?" she said. And then added, "I haven't cooked anything. Nothing."

Matthew was surprised. Elspeth usually planned the day's meals each morning and had them more or less prepared by nine. She had always approached such tasks with an almost military precision, and to have nothing done about dinner at this point in the day was unusual.

"Couldn't we get James to do something?" he said. "You know how good he is at rustling something up."

Elspeth closed the cupboard door. "We could, I suppose," she sighed. "He does most of the cooking these days."

"He likes it," said Matthew. "He told me so. He said, 'I really enjoy cooking.' That's what he said, and I think he really meant it."

"Oh yes," said Elspeth. "Little Mr Perfection."

Matthew stared at her. "But he's . . ." His voice trailed off, as he wrestled with the idea that Elspeth resented James as well as Pat. He could understand if she had some grudge against Pat – not that Pat had done anything to deserve it – but James? Why would anybody resent a nineteen-year-old (just) young man – a boy really – who had the smile that James had, and the willing manner, and all the friendliness of a puppy dog? Who cycled to the supermarket in Penicuik and did the shopping, unbidden, and who had even been known to ride there all over again if there was something he had forgotten to buy? All without complaint? Who kept his shoes neatly under the bed and put his dirty washing in the washing basket – unlike any other teenager ever invented – and then took it upon himself to put *all* the washing in the washing machine? And who put the detergent in the correct side of the pull-out drawer?

Matthew expressed his astonishment. "Why call him that?"

Elspeth met his stare. She looked guilty. She knows she's in the wrong, thought Matthew. She knows that's a snide thing to say. And what about my nose? What did she say about my nose?

Elspeth suddenly moved forward and flung herself into Matthew's arms. "Oh, Matthew, I'm so sorry. I really am. I've been horrid to you, and what I said about . . ."

"About my nose?"

She shook her head. "There's nothing wrong with your nose. It's a fantastic nose."

"And yours is too," muttered Matthew, stroking her hair. "Your nose is really . . . well, it's just perfect. You couldn't have a nicer nose."

"Do you mean that?" Elspeth asked.

"Of course I do. What I said earlier on was just nonsense."

She turned her face up to his and kissed him. "Big kisses," she said.

"Really big kisses," Matthew replied. Then he added, "And poor James – you don't dislike him, do you?"

She did not hesitate. "Not in the least. He's sweet."

Matthew smiled. Of all the adjectives to annoy a young man, *sweet* was probably the best-chosen. *Cute* yes; *sweet* no. "I wonder what Pat will make of him."

Elspeth drew back. "Why?"

Matthew shrugged. "It's just that she had that thing for Bruce. I think it's over now, but it would do no harm for her to meet somebody who's nice, as opposed to Bruce-like, if you see what I mean."

Elspeth looked thoughtful. "But James is just a boy. He's . . ."

"Nineteen."

"Yes, but what age is Pat? Twenty-five?"

"Twenty-four."

"All right, twenty-four. That's five years between them."

Matthew felt that was not too large an age gap. "All I'm suggesting is that she might appreciate him."

"Appreciate as in . . ."

"As in appreciate. That's all."

Elspeth looked doubtful. "Five years at that stage is too much," she said. "And anyway, where is she?"

"She's with James and the boys. And she brought you some kiwi fruit."

He had put the paper bag down on the kitchen table, and now she opened it and took out a kiwi fruit. "Odd present," she said. "I wonder what this means."

"Oh really!" exclaimed Matthew. "Kiwi fruit means . . . kiwi fruit."

"Are you sure?"
"Positive, my little honeybunch. Positive."

46

An Upsetting Discovery

That Monday morning, Angus decided not to read the newspaper. It was an unusual decision for him, in as much as it was at variance with well-established personal custom. Like many men who married later than average, Angus had become set in his ways, preferring to lead his life each day in much the same way as he had led it the day before. In that respect, he had always felt some sympathy for members of monastic orders, whose every day was marked by the established and immutable liturgical hours. This routine should not be confined to monastic establishments, he told himself, but could be applied, *mutatis mutandis*, to those living in the non-monastic world. In this way one might progress from lauds (morning shower), to prime (breakfast), on to terce (morning coffee) and so on until the day was concluded with vespers (martini time) and compline (bedtime, and descent into the first of the sleep cycles). And those cycles, mused Angus, were the body's own equivalent to liturgical hours, though fewer in nature, more fretful, and less reliable.

Perusing the newspaper had become something of a ritual for Angus, carried out with punctiliousness and respect for order: the front page first, then the letters column, then the deaths, and back to the news. This ritual was deeply embedded in the day, so that not reading the paper in the morning gave rise to a very strange feeling, akin to that which might follow an act of deliberate defiance, of wantonness. So might one feel if one decided not to clean one's teeth, or not to shave, or to wear the same shirt for the second day running.

But there was more to it than that. Like so many, Angus felt that he had a duty to keep abreast of what was happening in the world. This meant that he was obliged to follow developments in current affairs, most of which were associated with political dysfunction of one sort or another. The world presented there was one of constant disagreement and conflict. Humanity, it seemed, was at odds with itself wherever one looked. Locked in perpetual enmity, the armed camps of the world exchanged threats and warnings; at more local level, politicians berated and condemned one another, refusing to acknowledge, it seemed, that there were different ways of seeing the public good. In this political universe, those who disagreed with you were grossly misguided, and, if not, then positively malevolent. Nobody said anything complimentary to anyone, energy being conserved for vituperation. And around the public generals in these battles flocked hordes of social media private soldiers – each, it seemed, intent on insulting and crowing in equal measure, flashing signals of virtue in every direction, and sniping, like all snipers, from the hiding places of anonymity.

Angus had little taste for the moral disaster that the public realm had become, and had come to the realisation that there was no essential merit in knowing what was going on in this fraught and distasteful arena. If he did not follow the parliamentary debates in the Scottish Parliament, did it make the slightest difference to anything? It did not, he decided. If he declined to read what the President of France had been up to, would this be noticed in Paris? Or anywhere else? He thought not.

And so, in search of inner peace, he had instituted a new custom: on one day each week he would neither read a newspaper nor listen to the news on the radio, nor watch it on television. Isolated from the world of events, he would give his attention to the world itself; he would inhabit *his* moment and *his* place, rather than the fevered world reflected in the news. And with that detachment he was delighted to discover a sense of peace and resolution that in the normal course of events eluded him, and eluded, too, he suspected, many of those who were enmeshed in the world of current events.

He had discussed it with Domenica, who had initially been doubtful. "The ostrich response," she had said. "Or something like it."

"You think I'm burying my head in the sand? Am I an ostrich?"

She was apologetic: few human-to-bird comparisons were flattering. Chickens, vultures, crows – these were all birds most people did not want to be. So she backtracked: "Not entirely. But isn't it a bit like that – just a tiny bit?"

Angus defended himself. "I'm not saying I'll ignore things all the time," he said. "It's like one of those five-two diets, where you have two fasting days a week, and then for the other five you eat what you want." He paused. "It's a sort of detox. One day a week without all the anxiety. Without all the intractable problems. Is that a selfish demand? Is that being irresponsible?"

Domenica looked thoughtful. "Put that way," she said, "what can one say but no, it's not."

"Well, there you are," said Angus. "And I feel better for it, you know. I find I have the room – the mental room – to think about things that I normally don't think about very much. About how I should lead my life, for example."

Domenica smiled. "The biggest of all questions: how am I to lead my life? That's big."

"Yes, it is."

She wondered what options Angus had alighted upon. If he *was* deliberating on that question, then she had not seen many signs that his life was changing very much as a result. Angus, she thought, did not like to do anything different from what he had always done, and in that respect she felt that his life led him, rather than being led *by* him. It was as if there was a pattern somewhere – a plan – that said: there will be a portrait painter called Angus Lordie, who will live in Scotland Street, in Edinburgh, and who will take his dog for a walk first thing in the morning, have a morning cup of coffee in Big Lou's, and then paint in his studio until it is time to lay aside his brushes and take his dog for another walk. Where was the room for moral improvement, or intellectual innovation, in such a life?

Yet Angus was making some changes in the shape of his daily life, and here he was, at a time when, under the old regime, he might have been reading the newspaper, taking Cyril for a walk in the Drummond Place Garden and *not* thinking about the world and its problems when, rounding a bend in the path, he and Cyril came across the body of a dead cat.

The cat was newly dead. Its eyes were open, staring up at the sky – the last thing it must have seen, Angus thought, in its tiny furry slice of this life. It was just a cat, and there were far more important things going on in the world, but for the cat this was the supreme tragedy – the loss of the only thing that it had, that it possessed, and that had any value for it.

47

Poor Fellow

When he came across the motionless cat on the path in front of him, Angus stopped in his tracks, uncertain what to do. Cyril, though, acted without hesitation. He was used to the wiles of cats and to their deceptive strategies. How many times had he fallen for the tricks of a particular cat, a resident of Northumberland Street, that would lie on a step as if asleep, presenting for any passing dog an impossibly tempting target? All the while, of course, that cat would not be asleep, but would be watching very carefully through a slit in its eyes, ready to leap out of reach – and then, triumphantly and provocatively, hiss its derision from its place of safety. As any dog would do, he fell for that every time, and, like any dog, he lived in hope that one day he would administer justice to that cat, paying it back for all the humiliation it had heaped on the canine world. Oh, there were scores to settle, all right . . .

So now, seeing this cat lying still on the path, Cyril uttered a low growl and began to inch forward, hackles raised, as a hunting dog might stalk its prey through the long grass. When the cat did not react and as he came within reach of it, it dawned on him that something was amiss. Looking back over his shoulder, he sought guidance from Angus. This was a very unusual situation and Cyril would naturally take his cue from his master.

"Stay, Cyril," ordered Angus, and stepped forward to take command of the situation. He leaned forward and reached out to touch the cat – a touch that confirmed what was so clearly the case: the cat was dead.

Cyril nosed at the body and then looked up at Angus. There was nothing here for them and they should move on – that was what Angus imagined Cyril was thinking. But Angus himself was of another view. He was disinclined to leave a dead cat in the gardens, in just the same way as he was disinclined to leave litter lying about. If, on his morning walk, he encountered – as he sometimes did – the remains of a fish supper tossed carelessly over the garden railings by some keelie, Angus would always pick it up and deposit it in the nearest bin. Discarded fish suppers encouraged gulls, who were noisy neighbours, or foxes, who were better off in the country than in the town. And quite apart from that, litter defaced and coarsened the urban environment, and if he did not pick it up, Angus reckoned, then nobody else would.

The same must surely apply to dead cats. If he walked past this cat, and everybody else did the same, then it would simply remain where it was and become a health hazard. There might be no vultures in Drummond Place, but presumably there were rats waiting in the wings, and these would make a mess of things. And then there was the question of sympathy for the cat itself. As a species, we buried our dead, but we also extended this consideration to the animals with whom we shared our lives. A domestic animal should not be left where it fell, but should be given a decent burial, thought Angus, and since he was the one who had found the poor creature, he should perform this service for it.

"I'm afraid that's the end of our walk," he said to Cyril. "We can't leave this poor chap here."

Cyril looked blank. None of the words that Angus had just uttered matched his small vocabulary of commands, with the exception of *walk*, which he thought he recognised. But they were already on a walk, so that hardly took matters any further.

While Cyril struggled with syntax, Angus bent down and gingerly lifted the cat from the ground. It was unexpectedly light, even though it appeared to be sizeable by the standards of domestic cats. The body was stiff, although not so rigid as to prevent the head from lolling slightly as Angus stood up. This meant that the eyes stared directly up at him, and he saw that they were green. He had not expected that – these green, sightless eyes; nor had he expected the pang of sorrow that came upon him.

"Poor fellow," said Angus. "Poor fellow."

Cyril was silent. He understood nothing of what was happening.

Carrying his burden, like a pall-bearer in some private obsequy, Angus, followed by Cyril, made his way back towards the gate. There was nobody to see them, but had there been, they might have stopped and watched this poignant procession of deceased, officiant, and chief mourner making its melancholy way down Scotland Street. And then seen the little procession disappear through the outer door of Number 44, where the next stage of proceedings – whatever that might be – would take place beyond the eyes of others.

That next stage involved Domenica, who watched as Angus laid the cat out on a newspaper spread across the kitchen table.

"I found him on a path," Angus told Domenica. "Do you recognise him?"

Domenica examined the cat. "No," she said. "He looks a little like that cat from Cumberland Street – the one that hangs about the bar – but that cat's eyes are . . ."

"Blue," said Angus. "He has Siamese in him, that cat. His eyes are blue."

Domenica peered more closely. "These are green. They're beautiful."

"Yes. Burmese cats have eyes like that. He must have Burmese somewhere in his background."

Domenica sighed. "Such a pity. Do you think he was run over?"

"Possibly."

"But does it matter now?" Domenica continued. "Somebody's going to miss him, I imagine." She paused. "What are you going to do, Angus?"

Angus made a gesture of uncertainty. "Bury him, I suppose."

"Where?"

He shrugged. "In Drummond Place Gardens? Where I found him?"

Domenica did not think that a good idea. "I'm not sure if the committee would approve. And I'm sure you need their permission for that sort of thing."

Angus frowned. "You're probably right. Remember that row over somebody planting some daffodil bulbs without permission. The committee sent out that notice saying that under no circumstances was anybody permitted to dig in the gardens. They were very explicit."

He looked to Domenica for guidance. "So, what do I do? Throw him out with the rubbish? Isn't that a bit heartless?"

She agreed that it was. But there must be some procedure for this, she thought – after all, there were plenty of dogs and cats that died in town – what did their owners do?

"I think it's a matter for the local council," said Angus. "There must be somebody up at the City Chambers who knows what to do."

"Phone them," said Domenica.

"Do you think they answer their phones?" asked Angus. "Or do they have a machine that gives you options?"

"They might," said Domenica. "Give it a try."

"And the machine will say *If you're calling about a dead cat, please press 179.*"

"It's not funny," Domenica scolded. "Have some respect."

48

On Being Escalated

Angus had not had much occasion to deal with the City Council. From time to time he exchanged greetings with members of the cleansing department as they emptied the bins – exchanges that were limited to observations on the weather and Cyril, whom Angus would be walking at the time. Then there were his visits to the Central Library on George IV Bridge, when he would become aware of what the council did in that regard, or the occasional function – the opening of an exhibition, or something of that sort – at which he would see the Lord Provost carrying out his formal duties. Beyond that, most people's dealings with the council took the form of complaints – about parking, lighting, air, water, roads, noise, drains, tourists, bagpipes, tennis courts, litter, people, buildings, and seagulls. These were the issues that brought people into contact with their councillors, those long-suffering representatives who fielded the moans of the populace on all of the above subjects and who were never thanked nor praised for what they did. Angus, not being a complainer by nature, never wrote to his councillor about anything, and indeed had no idea who his councillor was.

Now, faced with the need to speak to somebody in the council bureaucracy about the dead cat he had found in Drummond Street Garden, Angus was at a loss as to how to proceed. Domenica was similarly uncertain as to which branch of local government might be responsible for this sort of thing, and suggested that the best tactic would be to call the main council telephone number. From that number, one might be directed to the appropriate department.

"Tell them you've found a dead cat," she said. "Tell them that and then ask to be put through to the people who deal with . . . well, with dead cats."

Angus found the number. As he had feared, a machine answered, and gave him options. As the long list was recited, he began to doubt that he would be able to penetrate the electronic boundaries behind which authority now sequestered itself. But then, at last, a final option was presented. *If you are concerned with none of the above and wish to speak to an operative, please . . .* And at this point, the tape reached the end of the loop and the recital of the menu began again.

Angus decided that a random selection would at least get him into the system. Closing his eyes, he stabbed blindly at the keypad, to be immediately rewarded by the sound of ringing at the other end. A minute or two later, a voice came on the line.

"Trams," said this voice, and then added, "Good morning."

Angus's eyes lit up. "Trams?"

"Yes."

He drew in his breath. "So you're the people who built the trams?"

There was hesitation. "Well, we're in charge of them. We didn't actually . . . Well, let's not go there." And then the voice continued, "Is this a lost property enquiry?"

"It's about a dead cat," said Angus.

There was a further silence. Then, "Your cat's been run over by a tram? Is that what you're reporting?"

Angus laughed. "No, or at least I don't think it was a tram."

The voice was becoming short. Trams had been the front line of a long war between officialdom and its critics. This was a field in which guerrillas presumably operated. "Then what is it?"

"I found a dead cat," said Angus. "I want to speak to the department that deals with such matters. I've been put through to trams – obviously not the right place."

The voice relaxed. "Oh, I see. Well, you don't need us, do you?"

"No, I don't," said Angus. "But could you please put me through to the right place?"

This brought silence, before, "Dog Control, I think. I can transfer you."

"It's a cat," said Angus. "A cat."

"I heard what you said," the voice retorted. "It's just that we don't have a cat department. But we do have Dog Control. That's the closest I can think of. Would you like me to transfer you or not?"

"I suppose you don't have cat control because it's impossible to control cats."

The voice listened. Then came the response, "Hah! No, you're right about that. What do they say about herding cats?"

"That's it. It's impossible. You can't herd cats."

It had been a moment of real human contact, but now it came to an end. "Anyway, would you like to be transferred? They might be able to help you."

Angus opted to be transferred, and after a civil goodbye a ringing tone could be heard once again. As he waited for his call to be answered, he imagined the person to whom he had been speaking. It was a male voice, but not an assertive one. It was the voice of a tired official, one who probably did not like his job all that much, who might be counting the days to retirement, who had been stuck in trams for years, perhaps, answering public enquiries, fending off complaints about the impact of construction works, giving people details of fares and timetables, reuniting them with their lost umbrellas or briefcases, smoothing out the troubled relationship between *Homo sapiens edinburgensis* and the tram. Yet behind that official identity there would be a person – a person who knew what it was like to be in love, a person who had hopes, who wanted to go somewhere, who believed in something or other, who had ideas about how the world should be. And in spite of all that human hinterland, with its richness and its pathos, the person himself was stuck in trams, like a press-ganged oarsman in a galley.

Dog Control answered. This time it was a business-like voice – that of one accustomed to the exercise of authority. This was a voice that dogs would dread: if this voice said *Sit!* dogs sat.

Angus began to explain himself. "I know that you're in charge of dogs," he said.

"Yes we are," interrupted the voice. "Are you reporting a stray?"

"No," said Angus. "The fact of the matter is that I've found a dead cat."

For a few moments there was no response. Then, "This is a cat that's been killed by a dog?"

"I don't think so," said Angus. "I don't really know the cause of death. I just came across it in Drummond Place Gardens. It was lying there." He wanted to mention the green eyes, but he did not.

"I'm sorry to hear this," said the voice. "But I'm not sure that this is a matter for us."

"I only asked to speak to you because you deal with dogs . . ."

"Yes, dogs. We deal with dogs. Your matter is . . ."

"Yes, I know," said Angus. "I know it's about a cat. But I thought you might know who deals with cats. That's all. I'm not expecting *you* to deal with this. I just wanted . . ."

The voice interrupted him. "I see what you mean. Fair enough. But I don't think we have a department that deals with cats."

"Could you ask somebody?"

"I can transfer you up the line, so to speak," the voice suggested. "I can escalate your call."

Escalate my call! thought Angus. This was what every caller to any system most liked to hear. *You're being escalated.*

49

Constructive Mistruths

Stuart very much regretted his acceptance of Katie's invitation to dinner. He had done so, of course, before she had sprung on him the news that she had a boyfriend and that she wanted the two of them to meet. Having accepted, though, it would be difficult for him to get out of the commitment, and now the evening of the dinner party was upon him.

Nicola was happy to look after the boys. By now she was well established in the maternal role all but abandoned by Irene, and although she still maintained her flat in Northumberland Street, she frequently stayed overnight in Scotland Street. For Stuart, this was the perfect arrangement. He had the luxury of a constantly-at-hand babysitter, while his mother could still withdraw to the private space of her flat from time to time. Since her return to Scotland, she had re-established contact with her old friends from the Borders, some of whom had moved into Edinburgh from Kelso or Melrose and were now living barely a few minutes' walk away from Northumberland Street. It was a whole new second life – one blessed with friendship, regular bridge afternoons, and a role as grandmother. And being needed suited Nicola – the loss of that, above all, was what had distressed her in the collapse of her marriage to her Portuguese former husband, Abril Tavares de Lumiares. Abril had ceased to need her in his life, and that had hurt her to the quick.

"A dinner party?" Nicola asked.

"Yes," said Stuart. He was cagey. He had never liked discussing relationships with his mother. He understood why she should be interested, but this was an area of his life that he did not wish to share with her. That reticence went back a long time.

"Anybody I know?" asked Nicola.

"I don't think so," Stuart replied.

There was silence. Then Nicola remarked, "People don't have dinner parties all that much these days, do they?"

Stuart was non-committal. "Maybe not."

"In my day," Nicola continued, "people in Edinburgh had dinner parties virtually every week. Friday and Saturday were dinner party nights. You invited people to dinner and then they invited you back. You met the same people week after week."

"Somewhat tedious, surely?" said Stuart.

Nicola looked thoughtful. "Not really. I always found it rather reassuring. It created a sense of community." She paused. *Community, community, community*: it had become a bit of a mantra, and yet it did count for something, elusive and difficult to define though that something might be. "In fact, often I found myself hoping that there wouldn't be anybody I didn't know there. And I was relieved when I went into the room and there they all were. The usual crowd."

Was that the famous rut into which people fell, she wondered? Was that the mud in which they metaphorically stuck? Did this lead inexorably to the well-known slough in which they desponded? She imagined a map of such terrain. There was the unadventurous mud; there was the slough of despond – a Dantean morass of hopelessness; and there, glorious and shining, was the moral high ground – populated by the pharisaical – behind which, glimpsed through the clouds of confusion, were the peaks of achievement.

Stuart interrupted her reverie. "What happened?" he asked. "Why did things change?"

"People became busier," said Nicola. "That was one thing.

Social habits changed. Life became less formal."

Stuart nodded. He remembered a time when colleagues from work met in the pub on a Friday evening. That seemed to have stopped. Everybody was too tired.

Nicola had one more try. "Where is it?" she asked. "This dinner party of yours?"

Stuart told her. "Howe Street."

She waited, but there was nothing more. Nicola looked away.

"Darling," she said, her voice lowered. "You're a free man now, you know. And, frankly, I've considered you a free man for years. You did your best – you really did – and you put up with so much. Nobody – and I mean nobody – would reproach you if you tried to find happiness elsewhere."

For a few moments he said nothing. Then, turning to his mother, he confided, "Thanks, Ma. Thanks. And yes, I'd like to meet somebody. I thought I had, but I've found out that she's got somebody else now."

Nicola reached out to touch him gently on the forearm. "My darling . . ."

"She asked me to dinner and my hopes shot up, but then . . ."

"Oh my darling, my darling."

"It turned out that she only wanted to introduce me to this new man of hers. That's all."

Nicola's eyes narrowed. "That's what she said?"

"Yes. I went to see her and we got on really well. I thought I could resume what I'd started before, but then she mentioned this man and said that she would like me to meet him. I could hardly say no."

Nicola reflected on this. Her interpretation was different. "Are you sure that there's no hope? Don't you think it possible that she would prefer you? Otherwise, why would she invite you to dinner?"

"For old times' sake?"

Nicola shook her head vigorously. "Oh no, Stuart, that's not the way a woman looks at things. If she invites somebody to dinner in such circumstances, it's because she wants to achieve something."

"And what would that be?"

"One of two things," explained Nicola. "One possibility is that she wants to get the new man to pay her more attention. Bringing you to the table, so to speak, is intended to show him that there are always other possibilities if he fails to shape up. That's one possibility."

"And the other?"

"The other is that she wants you but would prefer it if the current boyfriend were the one to break off the relationship. She wants to provoke him into a show of jealousy, which will give her an excuse to end the relationship with him. It's called creating the *casus belli*."

Stuart was doubtful. "I don't think either of those is all that likely," he said. "I think she feels sorry for me."

"If that's the case," said Nicola, "then you should politely decline."

"Too late," said Stuart.

Nicola smiled. "People get flu," she said.

Stuart reproved her. "When I was a boy you told me never to lie."

Nicola defended herself. "You were too young to understand constructive mistruths," she said.

"Which are?"

"Lies that make things better."

"For whom? For the person uttering the lie, or the person to whom it's addressed?"

"Both," said Nicola.

"Too late," said Stuart. "I'm going. And I don't care any longer, Ma. I just don't care."

She moved forward and embraced him. "Don't say that, darling. Don't get all dried up inside." She looked at him. What had Irene done to her son? How had she managed to kill the spirit within him?

Nicola sighed. Throughout history, men had crushed women and any spirit that women might show. Now at last that was being confronted, but the necessary corrective had been interpreted by some women as licence to belittle men. Irene was one of those women. Irene had won. She had gone, but she had won.

50

Portuguese Shoes

And it was no better for Stuart as he stood at the door of Katie's flat in Howe Street. He looked down at his shoes – his brown suede shoes that Irene had been so disparaging about. In his view, there was nothing wrong with them, and they certainly did not deserve her scornful description of *Portuguese spiv footwear*. The shoes were Portuguese – as it happened – but the way that Irene put it suggested that they were suitable for wearing by Portuguese spivs, as if Portuguese spivs were worse than any other spivs. That was the trouble with Irene, Stuart thought: she went on about unacceptable attitudes in others, and yet her own views were every bit as arrogant as those of the people she disparaged.

Now, looking down on his shoes, he thought that they were perhaps a little bit too pointed at the toes. Was that why Irene had thought them spivvish? Would it have been better, he wondered, to wear his ordinary Oxford-cap black work shoes? The problem with those was that they seemed so dull, and he would not have wanted to be the only person at Katie's dinner party wearing Oxford-caps.

He took a deep breath and rang the bell. He could hear voices inside – laughter too – and when the door was not answered immediately he decided to ring the bell again, just in case it had not sounded. But it had, and the door was opened by a man wearing a blue sweater. He was younger than Stuart – about thirty, Stuart thought – and had a welcoming smile.

"You're Stuart, I assume." He held out a hand, and Stuart shook it. "I'm George."

George. Stuart registered the name. This was him. This was the man who had replaced him.

Stuart looked down at George's shoes. He did not do this deliberately, but his eyes seemed inexorably drawn in that direction. George was wearing trainers, the expensive leather sort, and Stuart immediately thought: my suede shoes are wrong. But George was now gesturing for him to come in so that he could close the door, and Stuart obeyed.

"I've heard a lot about you," said George.

Stuart nodded. "Oh yes." It was an embarrassing thing to say – in any circumstances. People did not want to hear that others had been talking about them. George, obviously, was a bit gauche in these matters. Surely Katie would see that. And then Stuart asked himself what Katie could possibly have told George about him. She hardly knew anything about him because they had spent very little time together and he did not recall talking much about himself. For the most part, they had talked about poetry and literature in general. So how could George know much about him?

Stuart now saw that George was looking at his shoes.

"Great shoes," said George.

Stuart felt the back of his neck becoming warm. This was not going to go well.

"Italian?" asked George. "Your shoes, I mean."

"Portuguese."

George raised an eyebrow. "Portuguese shoes?"

"Yes."

"I had a pair of Portuguese shoes once," said George. "They didn't last long. The heels fell off."

Stuart said nothing.

"I suppose I shouldn't have been surprised," George continued. "I didn't pay much for them."

Stuart decided to ignore this. He felt George's eyes upon him; he was being assessed, and it made him feel uncomfortable.

Then George said, "Katie said you were at Heriot's." This was a reference to the school Stuart had attended.

"I was," said Stuart, thinking: such an obvious, *echt*-Edinburgh remark – so typical. What did it matter where you went to school? What possible relevance did it have to anything? But, out of politeness, Stuart said, "And you?"

"Fettes."

Stuart looked away. Fettes was considerably above Heriot's in the social pecking order. He made an effort to smile, and said, "Poor you."

George laughed. "It wasn't too bad, actually."

"Not if you like cold showers."

George stopped laughing. "That all ended ages ago." He paused. "My father's time."

Stuart pretended not to register the point of this remark, which was: my father went there too. That, again, was typically Edinburgh, establishing . . . what was it establishing? Prior rights? Longer roots? Snobbery, thought Stuart. And how odd that somebody of George's age should play that particular game. This was out of the Ark. And he realised at that precise moment that he disliked George not for what he had done – taken his place in Katie's affections – but for what he *was*.

"Anyway," said George. "We shouldn't stay out here. Katie's in the kitchen. She'll be out in a sec."

They made their way into the drawing room – the room from which, a few days previously, Stuart had looked out over St Vincent Street. As they entered, though, the doorbell sounded.

"The other guests," said George. "I'll let them in."

Stuart was relieved that there were to be other people present. The evening promised to be difficult enough as it was – with others, George would be diluted.

He waited while George went off to open the door. He noticed that there was a small pile of books by the side of one of the chairs. He bent down to inspect this. On the top was an edition of Shakespeare's sonnets, complete with commentary. He picked this up and opened it at random. He read the first two lines of one of the sonnets, and then another couple of lines. These words, he thought, come from a long way away . . .

"The sonnets?"

He turned round. Katie had come into the room through a different door, on the far side.

Stuart replaced the book. "I shouldn't be snooping."

She smiled. "It's not snooping to look at somebody else's books. If books are private, they should be kept in a cupboard."

"Oh."

She gestured towards the book. "That has a fantastic commentary. Don Paterson. He's a poet himself. Professor of poetry at St Andrews. He's written a commentary to each of them. He really brings them to life."

Stuart sighed. "I know so little."

"What? About what?"

"About poetry. You know . . . well, you know so much. I don't. I haven't even read the sonnets. Not properly. One or two, I suppose – a few lines."

"You could take that book," she said, picking it up and giving it to him. "Yes, why not? Take that book and go through them. It's really one long poem, all about love. A love affair, or two, although it's difficult to disentangle. The one love affair shadows the other, if you see what I mean."

"I'm not sure I do."

"Read it, then. Read the commentary."

He suddenly noticed that she was looking at his shoes. Awkwardly, he shifted his feet and tried to draw her attention away.

"Was Shakespeare writing about himself?" he asked.

The question seemed to interest her, and her gaze left his

shoes. "Of course he was. All writers write about themselves – all the time." She smiled. "Or their mothers. Although that sounds a bit Freudian, which it is, I suppose."

Her eyes went back to his shoes.

"They're Portuguese," Stuart blurted out. "My shoes . . . they're Portuguese." And then he added, "I shouldn't have worn them. Sorry."

He sounded so miserable. And he was.

51

Nepalese Momos

Any further conversation about Portuguese shoes was forestalled by George's return to the room with three newly arrived guests. These were two women and a man, all of whom looked slightly older than Katie. The women were called Tina and Vicki, and the man was Graeme. "With an e," he said. "Graeme with an e." It was unusual, Stuart thought, to spell your name when you met somebody for the first time – unless it was to be written down for some reason. I could say Stuart with a u rather than an ew, he thought, but why should I?

The introductions made, they looked at one another discreetly. Stuart decided that Tina and Graeme were together; she brushed a hair off his jacket shortly after they entered the room, which was as reliable a sign of intimacy as one might find. It was also proprietorial; although sisters might groom brothers, and wives might groom husbands, beyond those close relationships the act of brushing another's shoulders was to be undertaken only with caution.

Stuart wondered where Vicki fitted in. If Katie intended to balance numbers, then she must be intended as a female counterpart to him, and that, of course, was suggestive of matchmaking. People insisted on matchmaking – they did so in spite of all the evidence that it often led to unhappiness. All sorts of things could go wrong: in extreme cases, people introduced their friends to their polar opposites – unwittingly, of course; they brought women together with men who would make their lives a misery; they matched the musical with the tone-deaf, the selfless with the selfish, meekness with braggadocio. And even if the result was not disaster, it could at least end in embarrassment.

His thoughts were interrupted by Katie. "Since we're all here," she said, "we might as well go straight to the table."

Graeme laughed. "Why not? I didn't have lunch."

Tina contradicted him. "You did," she said. "It's just that you don't call it lunch. A sandwich *is* lunch." She spotted another hair on his jacket, and reached forward to brush it off. Stuart glanced at his own shoulders. He did not suffer from dandruff, but there had been somebody at work who did and whose career, Stuart felt, had been blighted as a result. He was a talented economist who had never had the promotions he deserved, and Stuart had been sure that had something to do with his dandruff-covered shoulders. That was so unfair, and perhaps there should be protection against that sort of discrimination – specifically, by name, along with other conditions that already enjoyed protection.

"I had lunch in Henderson's," said Katie, looking at Stuart as she spoke. That was where she and Stuart had met, and now he wondered whether there was any significance in this remark. Was it a veiled invitation to go to Henderson's again, he wondered? And if it was, then why should she ask him? He looked at George. Was he good-looking? He was, and perhaps that was what attracted Katie to him. I can't compete, thought Stuart. It's too late.

He wondered what George did. Something to do with money, he decided. He had that look about him; there were plenty of people in Edinburgh just like George who made their living by handling money. They had a good conceit of themselves, for the most part, and paid themselves what they themselves felt they deserved – which was far more than the earnings of those who actually made things. Listen to me, Stuart thought. Am I a socialist? Yes, I am, and I shouldn't apologise for believing that we should share what we have and help our fellow-man;

nor for not believing that life is a struggle in which we should strive to come out on top of everybody else. And yet, and yet . . . Life *was* a struggle, and people had to be encouraged to pull their weight, and clever and resourceful people had to be rewarded so that they would do what they did and allow us all to benefit from their endeavours. So, he thought, I am a what? A *non*-socialist? A liberal? A conservative?

Perhaps I'm a bit of everything, he thought. I have some socialism in me, and yet I believe in individual endeavour. Am I a centrist, then? How dull that sounds, and how uninteresting it must be to women. Women were attracted to men who had about them a slight air of danger, and centrists were not like that at all. Centrists were sensible, balanced people, who said *On the one hand, and on the other*, who saw both sides of the argument, and who rarely spoke with passion. The centrist philosophy, for all its merits, was simply not sexy.

They filed into Katie's dining room, where a table had been laid for six. The tablecloth was a bright Indian print, and there were candles at either end of the table. A couple of bottles of Italian wine had been opened and placed at one end of the table, with a large bottle of Highland Spring mineral water at the other.

George told people where to sit. Katie held back – once the guests were settled she was ready to fetch the first course – but when George placed Stuart at the other end of the table from the end she was about to occupy, she threw a glance at him – not a friendly one, thought Stuart. Katie sat next to Graeme, and Stuart had Vicki on one side of him and Tina on the other.

As soon as they were seated, George reached for one of the bottles of wine and began to fill people's glasses. He started with Vicki, but she put a hand over her glass to indicate that she did not want any wine. "I don't drink," she began. "So please . . ."

The gesture, the universally recognised way of conveying abstinence, came too late. A thin stream of wine was already on its way, and it spilled across her fingers.

"Look out," exclaimed Katie. "Oh, George . . ."

He uttered an expletive. Katie looked at him sharply. Vicki drew her hand away and grimaced. Katie passed her a napkin to wipe the wine off her fingers.

"You could say sorry," muttered Katie. "Rather than swearing."

George turned his head to glare at her. "Not my fault," he snapped. "She put her hand in the way."

"You might at least have asked her," said Katie. She blushed, obviously embarrassed by this public spat between the two of them. She rose to her feet. "I'm going to fetch the first course."

George continued to pour wine. He looked angry. "She's made momos," he said.

"What?" asked Tina. "Mo-whats?"

"They're a Nepalese speciality," answered George. "Katie went to Nepal last year. She volunteered for a project and they had cooking lessons. Momos are seriously delicious. They're little dumplings that the Nepalis like to eat."

"My brother went to Nepal for his honeymoon," said Tina.

"He married somebody he met online," said Graeme. "She imports cashmere scarves."

"Just about everybody meets online," said Vicki. She looked at Stuart as she spoke, as if encouraging him to take part in the discussion. Stuart looked away. He had decided that he did not like Vicki. If Katie had been intent on matchmaking, then her efforts were going to be a failure. I want you, he thought. I don't want her, I want you. Can't you see it? Can't you?

52

An Albanian Story

"Is it really true that everybody meets on line?" asked Katie. "I wonder. George and I didn't. We met when . . ."

George gave her a discouraging look, intercepted by Stuart, who felt pleased. They don't get on all that well, he thought. And then he said to himself: she doesn't really like him. That possibility gave him considerable pleasure. Of course she didn't like him – she was interested in poetry and vegetarian cooking and he was interested in . . . in what? Money? Cars, probably. Rugby? Not poetry; definitely not poetry.

Graeme smiled.

"Something funny?" asked Tina.

"I was just thinking," said Graeme. "You remember that guy who went to Prague for the weekend? The one who used to work for the Bank of Scotland?"

Tina frowned. "The one with the ears?"

"No. He used to play rugby," explained Graeme. "In the scrum. He had a cauliflower ear. I don't mean him. He worked for that whisky company. This one was something to do with commercial mortgages. Anyway, him: he went to Prague on a stag weekend – somebody was getting married. And he came back with a Czech fiancée – that Monday, that actual Monday. He went on Friday and came back with her on Monday."

"He'd never met her before?" asked Vicki.

"Nope. Never."

"Did she speak English?" asked Katie.

"A bit. Not much, but a bit. Enough to say *I do*. And they were married a couple of weeks later. That was it."

Katie shook her head. "They're still together?"

"Yes. They're fine."

Stuart listened, and tackled his momos as he did so. "These are really delicious," he said. "And the sauce . . . boy, it's good."

Katie beamed. "I'm glad you like it."

"What's in it?" asked Stuart.

Katie was about to tell him, but Graeme had more to say. "There was this woman," he said. "She was called Sam, I seem to remember. Short for Samantha. She was related to somebody who worked for the BBC. I forget who. Anyway, this woman, Samantha Something-or-other, went to Albania. You can go there these days – it used to be closed, but now you can go there on holiday. It's still a bit grim, apparently, but bits of it are OK if you don't have great eyesight. Anyway, she went there with a girlfriend and they stayed in some beach resort. But they also went for drives up in the mountains, and apparently it's pretty primitive there. Dirt poor in places."

"They had bad luck," said George. "That ghastly dictator. What was his name?"

"Hoxha," said Graeme. "Sounded like a lung complaint."

"Never trust a politician who sounds like a lung complaint," said Tina.

George smiled. "And their last king was called King Zog, you know. King Zog of Albania. He had four or five sisters, I think, and he dressed them all in naval uniforms. They sat on sofas in their naval uniforms and had their photographs taken."

"Strange," said Vicki.

Graeme agreed. "Yes, strange. But anyway, these two women drove into some village somewhere in the sticks and they had a cup of coffee in the local café. It was pretty basic – run by a chap with a big moustache. Zorba type. And he had a brother who helped him in the café, who only had one leg.

"There was somebody in the café who spoke English – the local teacher. He struck up a conversation with them and explained to the others that the brother with one leg was too poor to get a proper artificial leg. He had been given a peg leg at the local clinic, but he hadn't got on too well with that and it irritated the stump. It was too heavy, I think. So he had to get by without.

"This woman – Sam – felt really sorry for him. She couldn't say anything to him because she had no Albanian and he didn't speak a word of English. But apparently she kissed him on the cheek, and he was pretty chuffed. Then the person who spoke English asked if they could take him back to their place down on the coast as there was an Italian doctor there who might be able to help him. They agreed."

"Is this going to end well?" asked Vicki. "I have a feeling that it won't."

"Wait and see," said Graeme. "They took him, and he went to this Italian doctor down at sea level. But the doctor said he couldn't do anything because Albanian artificial legs are pretty useless and imported ones cost thousands and have to be fitted by special technicians, and there were none of those left in Albania because they had all been persecuted for one reason or another. So the end result was that nobody could do much for him inside the country.

"In the meantime," Graeme continued, "this woman was falling in love with this character with one leg. After a few days she asked him whether he would come back to Coatbridge with her – she lived over there, you see, where her father had a pub.

"This Albanian guy with one leg didn't require much persuading. He knew a good deal when he saw it. Any Albanian who gets the chance of marrying an American or a Brit or somebody like that will jump at the chance. Albania's a dump, and Coatbridge would be a distinct improvement.

So this Albanian got ready for the trip to Scotland. He made arrangements pronto to settle his affairs in Albania and was there at the airport, balancing on his one leg and holding a walking stick in the other, ready to go off to Scotland for a new life."

"Good," said Katie. "That sounds like a happy ending. I was worried it was going to be rather different."

"Well," said Graeme. "Listen to this: they got back and the first thing she did was take him to an artificial limb maker and get him measured up. She had a legacy of seven thousand pounds from her grandmother, and she used this to order this Albanian a state-of-the-art new leg. It did everything, more or less, and he was pretty pleased. It took a month to make, but when it was ready it was obviously well worth it. He was really pleased and said to her, 'Me dancing now. Big time dancing.'

"So the moment he had mastered his new leg, he hopped on a bus and went to a dance in Glasgow. And because of the new leg being so well made and so responsive, he soon developed quite a following as a nifty ballroom dancer. And not long after, he met a new woman and ran off with her. On his new artificial leg that this Sam had bought for him."

There was silence. Then Vicki said, "I find that story really sad."

"For her?" asked Stuart.

"Yes," said Vicki. "She bought him a leg and he used it to run away from her. How sad is that?"

"Very sad," said Graeme. But he did not conceal his amusement.

Katie looked thoughtful. "The moral?"

Graeme shrugged. "Don't buy an artificial leg for somebody if there's the slightest chance of their running away from you on it."

Stuart raised an eyebrow. "It shows a lack of gratitude, if

you ask me." He looked at his empty plate and said to Katie, "Is that the end of the momos?"

She shook her head. "Come with me into the kitchen," she said. "Bring your plate. I'll help you."

He followed her into the kitchen. The conversation at the table swelled in volume. Graeme had said something amusing, and Tina had joined in with a story of her own.

In the kitchen, Katie turned to face him. "Well?" she said. "What do you think?"

"Of George?"

"No, of course not," Katie chided him. "Of Vicki."

Stuart frowned. "She's fine."

"I can tell she likes you," said Katie.

Stuart closed his eyes. This was entirely wrong. He opened his eyes and stared down mutely at his Portuguese shoes.

53

Innocents at Play

As a matter of general policy, Bertie and his friend, Ranald Braveheart Macpherson, tried to entertain themselves during the mid-morning play-break at the Steiner School. This was not out of any disinclination to socialise – both Bertie and Ranald were reasonably gregarious and enjoyed the company of others – but was prompted by the particular dynamics of the playground. This space was dominated by two camps, at odds with each other on most points, and both Bertie and Ranald had little taste for the machinations of the leaders of both these factions.

The dominant group was led by Olive, Bertie's nemesis in so many encounters, and holder of that controversial document relating to her proposed marriage to Bertie when they both reached the age of twenty. Olive claimed to have little interest in the doings of any of the boys in the class, but from behind this façade of indifference she watched the boys closely. She was convinced that boys somehow had more fun than girls, and devoted a great deal of her time to working out ways of making sure that this should not be the case. Olive had heard of systems of keeping track of dangerous offenders, and she took the view that a similar system should be introduced for boys. All boys should be obliged to sign up on reaching the age of seven, Olive said, so that girls would know exactly where boys lived. This system would also be a great help to the police, Olive thought, as if a crime were to be committed it would simply be a case of finding out where the nearest boy lived and dealing with him in as expeditious a manner as possible.

"I feel sorry for boys," Olive announced. "Boys may not know it, but they're history, Bertie. History."

The main opposition to Olive was headed by Tofu, a boy of Bertie's age but of a very different disposition. Tofu, who was the son of well-known vegan parents, ran several small-scale rackets in the playground. The most lucrative of these involved protection, with subscribers paying ten pence a week to ensure that nothing went wrong with any items of property they brought to school. Tofu's other source of income was a numbers racket, participation in which was virtually compulsory. Each participant was given a number between one and twenty, valid for a weekly draw, at which Tofu would announce the winning number. The profits that Tofu made through these enterprises were used mainly for the purchase of various salamis, which he bought from one of the senior students whose father ran a delicatessen. These he discreetly consumed in the school grounds each afternoon while waiting to be collected by his father. He had the time to do this, as his father's car, having been converted to run on olive oil, was very slow, usually arriving well after other parental cars had collected their charges and left.

Although there were occasional payments made to others, for the most part the prizes in the numbers racket were won either by Tofu himself or by his close ally, Larch, Tofu's all-purpose enforcer, known for his tendency to spit at anybody who disagreed with him. One of Larch's main targets was Olive. He tried, if at all possible, to sit behind her in the classroom, in order to be able to spit at the back of her head without her noticing. Other opportunities were seized where and when they arose, including during the performance of the school play when Larch, in his role as a Birnam Wood tree in *Macbeth*, was able to spit from the side of the stage at one of the three witches, played by Olive.

In the playground that Monday morning, Bertie and Ranald

Braveheart Macpherson were conferring about the puppy they had been given by Wee MacTavish, the well-known Glaswegian dwarf and circus performer. The puppy had been with Ranald since Saturday, when they had brought it home from the circus on the Meadows, and Bertie was eager to hear how it had settled in.

"He's fine," Ranald reassured his friend. "I'm keeping him in our shed. I've made him a bed and he's got a bowl of water."

"And food?" asked Bertie. "What has he had to eat? You have to feed dogs, you know, Ranald."

"I know that," said Ranald Braveheart Macpherson. "I gave him some smoked salmon and I found some lamb chops in the fridge. He ate everything. He really likes smoked salmon, Bertie."

It was while they were discussing their plans for the puppy that Olive and Pansy, flanked by two lesser acolytes of Olive's, Marigold and Hermione, approached the two boys.

"Look out," said Ranald Braveheart Macpherson. "Look out, Bertie – here comes Olive."

Bertie started to move away, but was too late.

"Don't try to avoid us," scolded Olive as she intercepted Bertie's attempt to escape. "You can't run away for ever, Bertie Pollock."

"I wasn't running away, Olive," said Bertie. "Ranald and I were just trying to have a private conversation, that's all."

Ranald Braveheart Macpherson was temporarily emboldened. "We don't want you sticking your nose in, Olive," he said. "Boys have rights too, you know."

Olive spun round and glared at Ranald. "*Used* to have rights, Ranald. And you'd better watch what you say, or you're going to get into serious trouble."

"Yes," said Pansy. "Really serious trouble, Ranald Braveheart Macpherson. You just wait and see."

Marigold stepped forward. "I know something about you

and Bertie," she said, coming up to Ranald and addressing him barely an inch from his nose.

Ranald drew back. "You don't know anything, Marigold," he said. He spoke as firmly as he could, but his voice lacked conviction.

"That's where you're wrong, Ranald," jeered Olive. "You tell him, Marigold."

Marigold grinned. "My cousin lives next door to you, Ranald. She's called Peggy Bogie. She goes to South Morningside School. She's the cleverest girl in the school. She has a certificate that says that."

"I know all that," said Ranald, affecting indifference. But his heart had already sunk. Peggy Bogie and he were not on the best of terms.

"She says that she saw you and Bertie in the garden the other day," Marigold continued. "She can see right into your garden, Ranald. She can see everything. And she says that if she stands on a stool she can see right into your mummy's bedroom."

Ranald blushed.

"Yes," continued Marigold. "And you know what she saw the other day? She saw you and Bertie putting a dog in your shed. She says that you and Bertie have a secret dog."

Bertie glanced at Ranald in dismay. This information, which needed to be kept as secret as possible, had fallen right into the worst possible hands.

"Well," Olive crowed. "Aren't you going to deny it, Ranald Braveheart Macpherson? Perhaps not – because it's true, isn't it?"

"It's none of your business, Olive," said Ranald. "Nor of yours, Marigold."

"Oh, but that's where you're wrong," said Olive. "You can't keep a dog in secret like that. If your parents knew, you'd get into real trouble, sure as anything." She paused. "The only reason we're telling you that we know, Ranald – and you, too, Bertie – the only reason is that we are concerned about the dog's welfare."

Bertie decided to appeal to Olive's better nature. "Please don't tell, Olive. Please."

Olive flounced. "I'm sorry," she said. "But I have to do my duty, Bertie. I know you're not as stupid as Ranald, but you shouldn't get involved in this sort of thing, you know. You should think about the consequences of what you do, Bertie – you really should."

54

A Matter of Mis-speaking

Olive's discovery was a disaster for Bertie and Ranald Braveheart Macpherson. Of all people to find out about the puppy, Olive was undoubtedly the worst. Bertie fully believed her threat to tell Ranald's parents that there was a dog in their garden shed, and he imagined that it would not be long before she did just that. Olive was as impatient as she was peremptory in manner, and that meant that if they were to forestall exposure they would have to act quickly.

"We're in real trouble, Ranald," Bertie said after Olive and Team Olive, as they called themselves, had left them.

Ranald's anxiety was palpable. "Do you think she'd really tell?" he asked.

Bertie nodded. "You know what she's like. She'd do anything to cause trouble for us."

Ranald knew that Bertie was right, and he knew, too, that indulgent as his parents were, they would never allow him to keep a dog. His father was mildly allergic to animal hair, and would certainly not tolerate a dog in the house. Ranald had thought that keeping the puppy in the shed would deal with that issue, as his father took very little interest in what happened in the garden, but he did not envisage a dog being allowed to stay officially, even on that out-of-doors basis.

"What can we do, Bertie?" asked Ranald. And then, in answer to his own question, and as an indication of his faith in Bertie, he went on, "I'm sure you'll sort it out."

Bertie's eyes widened. It was comforting to know that Ranald had confidence in him, but he could not think of any way in which in these dire circumstances exposure could be averted. Unless . . .

"If Olive's going to tell," he began, "then we need to move the puppy."

Ranald brightened. "That's a great idea, Bertie," he said. But then his face fell. "But where?"

"My house," said Bertie. "He can come to live in Scotland Street."

"But your mummy," Ranald blurted out. "I mean, your ex-mummy. What if she found out?"

"She's in Aberdeen, Ranald," said Bertie.

"And your dad?"

"He needn't find out," said Bertie. "If I keep the puppy in my room and remember to close the door, then he'll never know."

"That's a good idea," said Ranald. But he foresaw a problem. "Doesn't he come in to say goodnight when you go to bed? Parents like to do that sort of thing – at least mine do. They bring their drinks in with them."

"I can put the puppy under the bed," said Bertie. "Then, when my dad – or my granny – leaves the room, I can bring him out again."

"You're really clever," said Ranald Braveheart Macpherson. "You think of everything, Bertie."

"Thank you," said Bertie. He was pleased that Ranald approved of his plan, but he realised that there were still aspects of it that needed to be settled.

"How will we get him from your house to mine?" he asked.

Ranald thought for a moment before giving his response. It was simple. "By bus," he said. "There's one that goes past the end of Albert Terrace. We can catch that one, Bertie."

Bertie looked doubtful, but Ranald was confident his plan would work. "We'll tell your dad or your granny, or whoever your Named Person is, that you want to come and play at my place? Right?"

Bertie encouraged Ranald to continue. "And then?"

"Then, when you come, we get the puppy out of the shed and take it on the number 23 bus down to Dundas Street. Then we get off and take it to your house. See?"

"When?" asked Bertie.

"Today," said Ranald. "When your granny comes to fetch you, you tell her that you really want to come to my place." He paused. "You can tell her it's my birthday and that I'm having a party."

"But it isn't your birthday, Ranald."

Ranald laughed. "I know that, Bertie. But she won't."

Bertie's face fell. "Then it's a fib," he said.

Ranald looked at Bertie with pity. "Not if you cross your fingers when you say it," he said. "And anyway, if you don't want to tell her, then I will."

Bertie expressed further doubts. "I don't know, Ranald . . ."

Ranald Braveheart Macpherson cut him short. "This is an emergency, Bertie. Do you want Olive to get away with this?" He paused. "Well, do you?"

Bertie shook his head. "But I don't like telling lies."

Ranald had no time for such scruples. "But it's not telling lies, Bertie. These days it's called *mis-speaking*. If you say something that's not true, you're just *mis-speaking*. I heard all about it on the radio. It means that you're allowed to tell lies now – especially when you're dealing with somebody like Olive."

The plan was agreed, even if with some reservations on Bertie's part. Ranald Braveheart Macpherson, having urged Bertie on, offered to do the speaking – or the mis-speaking – and when Nicola arrived, with Ulysses, to collect Bertie from the school gate, she was greeted effusively by Ranald.

"It's my birthday, Mrs Tavares de Lumiares," he announced. "And Bertie would like to come to my party."

Nicola was surprised. "What, today?"

"Yes," said Ranald, unblushingly. "My party is at four o'clock." And then, as a precaution, he added, "Adults aren't invited, I'm afraid. Just Bertie and . . . a few others."

Bertie looked away. He was secretly appalled at the ease with which Ranald was lying. He was used to Tofu's mendacity, but it sat ill upon Ranald's shoulders, he felt, to tell such blatant mistruths. It was too late, though, to do anything about that, as Nicola, after only a brief moment of hesitation, agreed that she would allow Bertie to go home with Ranald.

"And my dad said he'd bring Bertie back," Ranald said.

Nicola was pleased to be spared another trip. "That's very kind of him," she said. "And I'm sure Bertie will enjoy the party, won't you, Bertie?"

Bertie kept his eyes on the ground. As his hands were firmly in his pockets, nobody saw the fingers he was crossing, desperate to avert the judgement that would undoubtedly come his way once his lies were discovered. Adults had a way of exposing the truth – that's what they did. But then he thought: I've said nothing – these are Ranald Braveheart Macpherson's lies, and if anybody is going to be punished it will be Ranald. That gave him some relief, but left him worried about what Ranald was doing. Was it a good sign to show such willingness to tell lies for a friend? He was not sure, but he felt that, on balance, Robert Baden-Powell, author of *Scouting for Boys*, would probably not approve. Boy Scouts, he more or less certainly said, should never mis-speak.

55

Für Elise

When he was told by a disembodied voice in the City Council's Dog Control department that his call was being escalated, Angus felt that gratitude that we all feel when somebody in officialdom takes us seriously. The term *escalation* has a soothing ring to it, and is suggestive of the smooth progress that an escalator makes in its ascent. *Height without effort* might be the mission statement of escalator manufacturers: *we carry you upwards*. Escalation of his query as to what to do with the dead cat he had found in the Drummond Street Garden was precisely what Angus felt he needed, as he thought that there must be, somewhere in the vast edifice of local government, some department that dealt with this particular issue. There must be, he told himself, or the city would be covered in dead cats. There must be someone, somewhere, whose job it was to deal with precisely this problem.

The man in Dog Control asked if he minded being put on hold. Angus assured him that he did not, and this led to a brief silence, followed by the playing of a looped recording of Beethoven's "Für Elise". The council was not the only body to use the key of A minor to entertain anybody who telephoned with an enquiry – numerous companies and government departments seem to share a belief that there is something in "Für Elise" that will pacify potentially impatient callers. Provided that it is interrupted from time to time with the assurance *Your call is important to us*, "Für Elise" appears to be capable of preventing people from hanging up or becoming irritated by lengthy delays. Other music is considerably less effective, although extensive research has revealed that the "Flower Duet" from *Lakmé* is not only capable of soothing callers through delays of up to twenty minutes, but also has remarkable qualities in combatting air-sickness. That piece of music, purloined by British Airways as its theme tune, is suggestive of the soaring of both the human spirit and of aircraft – a happy coincidence for the airline with which it is identified.

Angus did not have long to wait. After less than a minute of "Für Elise", the music stopped and he was switched through to another voice – that of a woman this time.

"Public health," she announced firmly, as if to discourage, through the mere annunciation of the name, any insanitary practices.

Angus cleared his throat. "I'm not sure if I'm through to the right person," he said.

"Public health," the woman repeated.

"Yes," said Angus, "but this is actually about an animal matter."

"Do you need veterinary help?" asked the woman.

"It's a bit late for that," said Angus. "The cat – this is a cat matter, you see – the cat in question is dead."

There was a brief moment of silence. Then back came the question, "Has the cat passed?"

"You could put it that way," said Angus. He had an aversion for the term *to pass*, which he considered embarrassingly euphemistic. What was wrong with *dying*? Why did people refer to *passing* when what they meant was *dying*? Passing suggested *passage* to somewhere, whereas many people who actually *passed* had no intention, nor hope perhaps, of going anywhere. Far better, he thought, to use the verb *to die*, which was unambiguous, self-explanatory, and bore with it no particular attachment to any theology or eschatology. And if it was thought a bit brutal, the verb *to die* could be replaced with *to expire*, which had the benefit of being more accurate than *to pass* and less prissy. *Passing* sounded a bit camp, in fact, as if those who *passed* actually *minced* over to the other side, wherever that was.

Then there was the good old-fashioned expression of *making a pass* at somebody. Angus had always liked that phrase, although he was never quite sure how one would make a pass. Did one walk past the object of one's desire – or, frankly, one's lust – skirting around him or her in a way which was indicative of interest? And if the pass was unwelcome, did the person passed – the *passee* – simply ignore the fact that somebody was going past her or him rather closely, or did they say *Pass*, in the way in which some people reject things, or, at bridge, decline to enter into the bidding for a contract?

"A deceased cat?" the woman asked. "Where is this cat?"

Angus did not answer for a moment. Then he said, "In my flat. In Scotland Street."

This was greeted with silence. Eventually the public health voice asked, "Is the cat your own cat, sir?"

"No," said Angus.

"So the cat came into your flat from somewhere else and became deceased whilst in your flat? Is that what happened?"

Angus sighed. "No. I brought it in already deceased, so to speak. Dead, in fact – if you'll forgive my being so blunt."

"You're in possession of this late cat?"

"Yes, and I need to find out how to dispose of it."

It became obvious that the public health department had no suggestions to make, and Angus was once again told that he was being escalated.

"But I've already been escalated," he protested. "I was escalated to you."

"That may be," said the voice. "But there are further possibilities for escalation. They are at a higher level, I assure you." There was a pause. "May I put you on hold for a few moments? It won't be long."

"More 'Für Elise'?" Angus asked.

There was a further silence, while the hidden pianist sat down at the keyboard, and then "Für Elise" began again. After a couple of minutes, Angus found himself talking to the Chief Executive of the city. Once more he explained what had happened. "I think this needs to be escalated," said the Chief Executive. "Hold the line a moment, will you."

And that was how Angus eventually reached the Lord Provost himself.

"I'm so sorry to hear about your cat," said the Lord Provost. "This is most unfortunate."

"It wasn't actually my cat," said Angus.

"Even so," said the Provost, "you can become attached to a cat who belongs to somebody else. We're very fond of a cat that lives next door to us."

Angus sensed an opportunity. "But what if that cat were to expire in your house? What would you do?"

Now, he thought, here is my opportunity for a definitive ruling, given at the highest level.

"It would be very upsetting," said the Lord Provost. "But, as I said, I'm sorry to hear about this cat of yours."

Angus sighed. This was getting nowhere. He decided to seize his opportunity. "Lord Provost, now that you're on the line, I'd like to talk to you about the trams."

There was complete silence at the other end of the line, followed, after a sudden click, by the strains of "Für Elise", so gentle, so haunting, so calming.

56
Cryptological Anthropology

When Angus had put down the telephone receiver on "Für Elise", he had taken a deep breath. Through no fault of his own, he had stumbled into a Kafkaesque situation in which he had a dead cat on his hands and no idea of how to dispose of it legally and, importantly for him, decently. Surveying the corpse on the table, he had felt as if he were a character from one of Patricia Highsmith's chilling novels – landed with a body and needing to dispose of it before Nemesis struck. Winged Nemesis, armed with her dagger, was constantly on the lookout for people with bodies on their hands, her radar being finely tuned, perhaps, to the waves of anxiety emanating from such people, and remorseless was she in her stalking of them once alerted to their presence.

It was Domenica who had suggested to him that he should telephone officialdom for advice. He had tried that, and now he went through to her study to report to her that he had failed. When he entered her room, a book-lined retreat in which Domenica conducted her anthropological research, he found her sitting at her desk, reading an article from the *Journal of the Royal Anthropological Institute*.

She looked up as Angus came in. "This is fascinating," she said, gesturing to the journal in front of her. "Cryptological anthropology. What do you think that entails?"

"Decrypting things," said Angus.

"Well, yes. But what precisely?"

Angus shrugged. "The things that people do."

Domenica shook her head. "That's the task of anthropology

as a whole. This is a specialised branch of it." She paused. "Language. It's the decrypting of language with the intention of finding out about the people who spoke it."

"I see," said Angus.

"Quite fascinating," Domenica continued. "It's a relatively new discipline."

Angus glanced over her shoulder at the journal cover. *Ideographic signs in Linear B*, he read. *A new conjecture as to social relation categorisation terms.*

"Linear B? Wasn't that very early Greek?"

Domenica nodded. "It was. Tremendously early."

"So not something one hears today in the tavernas of Kos?"

Domenica laughed. "Certainly not. You would definitely *not* be understood should you attempt to order your retsina in Linear B. They would look blank, I imagine." She paused. "Just as the Greeks at first looked blank when British officers addressed them in classical Greek in the war. Patrick Leigh Fermor and the like. They were classicists."

"Brave men," said Angus.

"Oh, they were," said Domenica. "And some of them were Scots. I met one of them. Ian Ross. A great man. He hid up in the mountains and blew up bridges with the Greek resistance. He was very courageous – if the Germans had caught him, they would have shot him out of hand."

Angus ran an eye down the journal's list of contents. One of the articles stood out. *Rongorongo Decoded at Last.* He looked quizzically at Domenica. "Rongorongo?"

Domenica raised an eyebrow. "That," she said, "is debatable."

"Not everyone agrees?"

"I hae ma doots," she said. "I could be wrong, but . . ."

"But what's Rongorongo?" asked Angus.

Domenica explained that it was the script found on artefacts removed from Easter Island. "It consists of glyphs," she said.

"Most of them are etched into wooden items."

"And nobody can work out what they say?"

She nodded. "The glyphs are written according to a system of reverse boustrophedon – that is, each line goes in the opposite direction from the one above it, and alternate lines are back to front. That's boustrophedon for you, Angus." She paused, and then added, "Rather like a contemporary novel."

"And the glyphs themselves?"

"Funny little figures – rather wriggly in appearance. Some people, some animals. Very funny to look at, but not funny when translated, according to . . ."

She picked up the copy of the journal and read out the name of the author, and the degrees he held: MA (St Andrews), PhD (Edinburgh), DLitt (Oxford).

"He sounds, how shall I put it?" said Angus. "Erudite?"

"Oh yes," said Domenica. "He can walk the walk, but . . . Well, I'm not sure that he should have published this – even if he's right, which he may well be."

Angus pressed her to explain.

"Well, he claims to have deciphered the surviving passages."

"And?"

"And he says that the inscriptions are, in fact, a recipe book. People used to suggest they were genealogical, but he says no, it's recipes – an early recipe book."

"Predating Epicius?"

"Apicius," Domenica corrected him. "There's Apicius and then there's Epicurus. Don't confuse them."

"Predating him?" asked Angus again.

"No, much later. The thirteenth century, perhaps. Round about then."

Angus glanced at the journal. There were tables of glyphs, with suggested meanings.

"The embarrassing thing, though," said Domenica, lowering her voice, as if to prevent being overheard. "The embarrassing thing is this: the collection of inscriptions in question is apparently a recipe book for cannibals."

Angus's eyes widened. "You mean those ancient Easter Islanders were cannibals?"

Domenica closed her eyes briefly. "It's not so simple, Angus. And, as you might expect, these things are sensitive. Western scholars shouldn't go around accusing others of being cannibals. Every society has had its Campbells – including Scotland."

Angus frowned. He had heard of Sawney Bean, of course, but were there others? And what was this about Campbells?

"Did you say Campbells?" he asked.

Domenica shook her head. "I said cannibals."

"I thought you said Campbells."

Domenica drew in her breath. "I did not," she said. "And remember: *tout comprendre, c'est tout pardonner*."

Angus had enjoyed the joke. "What I love about you, Domenica," he said, "is your sense of humour – and your liberality of mind. Your generosity to others, even Campbells."

Domenica acknowledged the compliment gracefully. "Thank you," she said. "One would hope to err on the liberal side, Angus, while at the same time not being naïve when it came to the failings, or shall I say, in this context, the *appetites* of others."

"Absolutely," agreed Angus. "The weaker brethren . . ."

He sighed. He had not told her about his fruitless conversation with the local authorities. He would do so now, and see if she wanted to come to the small, cat-sized grave that he was planning to dig in Drummond Place Garden. So what if the committee got to hear of this? As a key-holder, he paid his share of the gardens' maintenance expenses, and was entitled to use the gardens for reasonable purposes. Burying a cat, he decided, was one such purpose.

57

Youth Passes

Out at Nine Mile Burn, as the shadows cast by the rhododendrons lengthened, Matthew and Elspeth sat down to a dinner cooked for them – and their guest, Pat Macgregor – by the ever-obliging James, their young male au pair.

"I don't know if I ever mentioned this to you, Pat," said Matthew, as James ladled soup into their plates from a large Spode soup tureen, "but James is a first-class cook. A seriously good cook, in fact."

Pat looked across the table at James, who was standing behind Elspeth, holding the tureen in one hand as he wielded the ladle with the other. She noticed his hips, which were slender, and thought: what happens to men? When do they change shape and become . . . ? The word that came to her unbidden was *gross*. Boys and young men were lithe, and then, suddenly, they seemed to fill out and their centre of gravity shifted. Mind you, she thought, everybody's centre of gravity shifts sooner or later. It was one of the great pivotal points in life – like adolescence, or the menopause – the centre of gravity shift. And it was downhill all the way from there, which was such a depressing thought, she decided.

"You're lucky," Pat remarked.

"I know," said Matthew. "Our Danish au pairs were useless when it came to cooking. They loved salted fish and little fiddly bits of seafood."

"And pink sauce," said Elspeth. "Remember the pink sauce?"

"They put pink sauce with everything," explained Matthew.

"It was like that sauce that people used to serve in prawn cocktails. Remember that stuff? Marie Rose sauce? It had mayonnaise in it – and Worcestershire sauce, I think. And tomatoes."

"And James is lucky too," added Pat. "Lucky to be able to cook."

"He was taught by his uncle," said Elspeth. "We bought this house from him – from James's uncle. The Duke of Johannesburg."

Pat smiled. "Oh, he's been in the gallery, hasn't he, Matthew?"

"He comes down there from time to time," said Matthew. "He has a flat in Gloucester Place these days. He uses that to conduct his business."

James had finished serving the soup and now sat down. He was next to Pat, and he turned and smiled at her as he took his seat. She felt a sudden pang. Yes, a pang. It was a pang. And why should I feel a pang, she thought? Because it will pass. Youth passes. A brief moment. The rose that blows and dies.

She had noticed his teeth, which he revealed in a smile that was directed at her. It was an innocent smile. Sheer pleasure, she thought. He's made for the aesthetic pleasure of others. But then she said to herself: no. No.

"I'm not a great cook," she said. "We learned a bit at school, but it was all stodgy stuff, and I forgot most of the recipes they taught us. Except for shortbread. I can still make shortbread."

"There's a secret to making good shortbread," said James. "The temperature of the mixture must be right."

"Really?" said Pat.

Then James said to her, "Matthew said that you studied history of art at university. Where was that?"

"Edinburgh," said Pat. "Right here."

"I'd love to do that," said James. "But my uncle has been trying to persuade me to do a degree in Scottish history."

"Which would be interesting too," said Matthew.

From her side of the table, and between sips of soup, Elspeth said, "Life was so interesting in the past."

Matthew stared at her. Was this a rebuke? Was this to suggest that life at Nine Mile Burn, with three young sons, was uninteresting? "We shouldn't romanticise the past," he said evenly.

Elspeth denied that she would ever do that. "Oh, I know that. In fact, the past – when you were actually living it – was quite boring. It's only later, when we look at the past through the lens of the present, that we think it was exciting. It wasn't."

James frowned. "Are you sure about that?" he said.

"I think I agree with Elspeth," Matthew said. "In fact, I'm reading a book at the moment about what it was like to live through the British Empire. Everybody thinks that the nineteenth century, when the empire was almost at its height, was a really exciting time. But this book – and its title makes the point: *Imperial Boredom* – says that it really wasn't. People were bored stiff. Nothing very much happened. People were sent out to remote places and found that once they were there there was nothing to do. They sat and played cards and suffered from the heat, and drank in clubs at night with other bored people and said the same things night after night. That was the British Empire for you." He paused, and then continued, "It was the same for the people on whom the whole thing was imposed. They found it boring because there was nothing they could do to change their situation. They ceased to be in control of their fate, which at least is one way of not being bored."

"This is really good soup, James," said Elspeth.

James smiled. "Thank you." He turned to Pat. "Do you like Vuillard? I mean, did you study him at uni?"

"A bit," said Pat. "There were lectures on French art by Professor Thomson. The best lectures I ever went to. He occasionally mentioned Vuillard and Bonnard . . . the Nabis. I rather liked them."

"They were comfortable," said Matthew. "They painted on an intimate scale. People doing things in houses – that sort of thing." He sighed. "I wish more artists today would paint pictures of people doing ordinary things in their houses. And it wasn't just the French *intimistes* who did that – the Dutch also did it in the seventeenth century. They painted people sitting about in Amsterdam and Delft, doing things in their houses or courtyards."

"Chilling," said James. "Just chilling."

"I'm not sure if they chilled in those days," Matthew said.

Pat smiled. "Perhaps they did, but didn't know they were chilling."

The conversation continued along these lines as James brought in the main course – a pheasant casserole. "I got these pheasants from my uncle," he said. "He has this Gaelic-speaking driver, you see. He gets them from somebody out at West Linton, and then passes them on to my uncle after he's plucked them."

"You have to be careful when you talk about pheasant pluckers," observed Matthew.

Elspeth shot him a glance.

"Or sea shells," said Pat.

"I'm so worried about him," said James. "I'm worried about my uncle's project."

Pat asked him what it was, and James explained about the microlight seaplane that the Duke and Padruig were making in a byre near Single Malt House. "I could show you, if you like," he said to Pat. "We could walk over there after dinner. It's not far. Only if you like, of course . . ."

"But I'd love to," said Pat. Rather too quickly, thought Elspeth.

58

Agas etc.

After Pat and James had gone off on their walk together, Matthew busied himself with the washing up. Elspeth sat in the kitchen, drinking a cup of decaffeinated coffee. She wanted to apologise to Matthew, but was finding it difficult to choose the right words. Now, addressing his back as he piled plates into the dishwasher, she said, "Matthew, darling, I'm really sorry about how I was earlier on. I shouldn't have said what I did . . . I just felt . . ." She cast her eyes down. It sounded lame, she felt, as real apologies often sound. False apologies, in all their insistence, may be too loud, while their true equivalents, the heartfelt, the sincere, are often meek and hesitant.

He turned and walked back towards her, drying his hands on the apron he had donned for the clearing up. The apron had a picture of the Pentland Hills on it and, being his favourite, it was well used. He knew that she was sorry, as was he.

He held out his arms. "You don't need to say one word more. Not one. We've already made up. You've forgiven me and I've forgiven you. Mutual forgiveness. Over."

"But I need to ask myself something," Elspeth insisted. "Why was I so crabby?"

Matthew sat down next to her and took her hands in his. "It's because you get fed up being stuck in the house. Who wouldn't?"

"Could we get somebody in to help James? To make it easier for him? A girl? So that I could go back to work?"

Matthew considered this. "You can have whatever you want," he said. "We can afford it."

"I feel guilty," she said.

"About being able to afford things?"

She sighed. "I suppose so."

"That means you've got a heart. Anybody who doesn't feel at least a little guilty about good fortune doesn't have much of a heart, if you ask me."

Elspeth thought about this. "I'm not sure. I've met people, I suppose, who seem to take it for granted. They act as if they're naturally entitled to everything they have." She looked intently at Matthew. "Matthew, I don't come from your world. We never had any money. There was never anything left over."

He smiled. "So what?"

She gestured around the kitchen, with its expensive Aga – four ovens – and its capacious German dishwasher. "It's just that we have everything – and we've had it from the beginning. There was no waiting."

"But . . ."

She cut him short. "Other people have to struggle a bit at the beginning of their marriage. Make do with things – with hand-me-downs." She paused. "We don't have a single hand-me-down. Not one."

Matthew frowned. "But we do."

"Name one. New Aga. New dining room furniture. New beds, mattresses, carpets. Curtains. Everything."

Matthew looked up at the ceiling. He was sure there was something . . . and then he remembered. "But what about that Elizabeth Blackadder above the fireplace? And that Epstein bronze?" He looked pleased that he had remembered. Both of these had been gifts from his father shortly after their marriage. "Yes, what about those?" And then his father had given them a Land Rover Discovery. That had not been new. There had been two thousand miles on the clock – Matthew remembered seeing that when he first took it out for a drive. Two thousand miles, he thought, was a long distance – from

Edinburgh to Inverness and back about six times.

Elspeth was looking at him with a mixture of pity and affection. He doesn't get it, she thought. He just doesn't get it.

"I don't think those things really count as necessities," she said mildly. "I was talking about the things one *needs*."

He was staring at her. "I can't help being . . . being me," he said quietly. "I can't help it." And then he warmed to his theme. "You know, Elspeth, there's something really unfair going on. People judge other people for things that aren't their fault. I can't help coming from where I come from, can I?"

"Nobody is judging you for that . . ."

"Aren't they?" asked Matthew. "I think they may, you know. If you have . . . well, advantages in life – an easy start, let's say – there are plenty of people who will look down on you for it."

She began to express disagreement, but he continued, "No, I'm right about this, Elspeth. Look at universities these days. They judge people by their background. They say it out loud and in the open. They try to give the places to kids who come from deprived areas. They try to avoid taking you if you've come from the wrong sort of school."

"Well, there's a reason for that, Matthew. It's because people who come from deprived areas haven't had much of a chance, have they? Everything is stacked against them from the beginning. All that the universities are doing is trying to make up for that – trying to give them a chance."

He knew she was right. "Oh, I understand that. And it's fair enough, yes, to help people in that situation. Of course it is. But what if that involves discriminating against an individual for something that he or she just can't help – who their parents were? What about that? Should you dislike somebody for being brought up in a particular way? Surely that's one thing one can't be blamed for?"

He remembered reading something in the paper that had leapt out at him. "I saw that one of the colleges at Cambridge boasted the other day about not admitting a single student that year who had been at an independent school. Not one. And they were proud of the fact."

"Well, you know what Cambridge is like . . ."

"No, that's not the point, Elspeth. It means that they turned down lots of people who had the qualifications to get in. They turned them down because of something that was nothing to do with any choice, any single choice, made by those applicants. None of them actually *chose* their social class."

Elspeth was silent for a few moments. She thought this an insidious argument, because if you accepted it, then you merely endorsed the continued privilege of those who had the best start in life. And that, she thought, was not the result you wanted to get. She had always felt that. Individual merit was all very well, but individual merit in this context merely cemented the status quo. The children of doctors and lawyers continued to have the best chance of becoming doctors and lawyers themselves. That was the way the merit principle had always worked, and that would be its result until somebody threw a spanner in the social works. Only then would things change.

Then she said, "You can't make an omelette without breaking eggs."

Matthew looked puzzled. "What's that got to do with it?" he asked.

"Everything," she said.

Matthew sighed. "And what about the Scottish universities?" he said.

"What about them?"

"They effectively discriminate against Scottish students because Scottish students don't pay fees. So it's easier to get a place if you come from somewhere else. How's that for an injustice?"

"That can't be true," Elspeth said. "I just don't believe that."

59

Temptation

Pat felt a curious excitement as she and James set off on their walk. It was not a conventional walk, as they were doing the first part of the journey – some four miles – by bicycle. Thereafter, James explained, there would be a track that led directly to Single Malt House and its outbuildings, one of which, a former byre, contained the microlight seaplane that the Duke of Johannesburg was building with his Gaelic-speaking driver.

"We can leave the bikes at a sheep farm down there," said James, pointing to the gentle fold of hills before them. "That's where the track starts."

She loved the way that Edinburgh so quickly, and so considerately, yielded to the countryside; how, within minutes, one might move from the urban to the rural and, if looking in the right direction, imagine that one was already in the deep Borders or even, on the higher ground, in the Highlands. Edinburgh lay to the north, and behind them; to the south were the Lammermuir Hills, feminine folds of attenuated blue; to the east, the land ran down towards the sea, a hazy smudge in the evening air. Pat saw in the distance the indistinct shape of the Bass Rock, a sheer, mysterious protuberance rising from the North Sea – a pointer to what? To Norway? To Denmark? Then, like an answer from the land, there was the steeply conical shape of Berwick Law, an unlikely hill that the weather had somehow forgotten to soften and corrode.

They mounted the bikes. Pat wobbled for a few moments, and James, solicitous, asked, "Are you all right?" She had not answered before he said, "Of course you are."

"I can't remember when I last rode a bike," said Pat. "Before I went to university, I think."

She immediately regretted that mention of university, because he had yet to embark on his university career, and it underlined the difference between their ages. Five years? Something like that. Was that too much? And then she thought: but I'm being ridiculous. He's just a friend, a young friend; nothing more than that. And he seemed so much more mature than the average nineteen-year-old, or whatever he was. That sometimes happened – there were people who were years older in outlook than one might expect from their chronological age. Mozart, for one . . .

"Do you like music?" she asked.

Riding beside her, he glanced at her briefly, as if surprised by the question. "Of course. Who doesn't?"

"Some people, I imagine."

"Tone-deaf people?" he asked.

"No. They sometimes love music. It's just that they can't recognise the intervals between the notes." She had had a friend at school who was like that. She listened to music a great deal, but could never hum any of the tunes she loved so much, having no sense of pitch.

He said, "When I was younger I used to think it would be great to be a rock musician. I fantasised like mad. I imagined myself playing at the Playhouse to a whole load of screaming girls."

Pat laughed. "Is that what boys fantasise about? Screaming girls?"

"I don't know. Maybe they do. Remember, I was about fifteen at the time." He paused. "What about you? What do girls fantasise about?"

"Oh, dreamy things. Having dinner with some guy who gives you a bunch of roses and then takes you for a ride in an open-top sports car along that road that goes round Arthur's Seat. And you stop and look down at the city and the lights and he says, 'I really like your hair, you know' . . ."

James smiled. "Or he says, 'Where have you been all my life?'"

"Yes, that would do. Mind you, I don't think anybody says that any more – if they ever said it at all. Nobody's said it to me."

James looked straight ahead. "Where have you been all my life?" he muttered.

She concentrated on keeping her bicycle on a straight path. But she thought: did he say that to me, or was he just going over the expression in his mind, and happened to vocalise it? She felt her heart beginning to race, and she said to herself: no. And then *no* again. This was temptation; there was no other word for it. It was like being confronted with a box of chocolates and wanting, dying, to take one. But *no*, you did not, you *could* not.

The track on which they were riding narrowed, and James had to go ahead of her as there was insufficient room for them to ride abreast of one another. He called out to her, over his shoulder, "Am I going too fast for you?"

"No. You could go faster, if you like."

She felt the wind in her hair. And the sun – she felt that too – the evening sun that would still be there almost until ten at night, as this was high summer and the longest day would be with them within a week or so. That sun now painted everything with gold: the hills; the gorse bushes in the fields on either side of the track; the thin line of cloud in the otherwise empty sky.

"Can you smell the gorse?" she shouted. "Can you smell it?"

"Yes," he shouted back. "It makes me think of . . ."

"Of coconut."

"Yes, that's it. Of coconut."

All too soon they had reached the farm where they would leave the bikes.

"I know these people," said James. "The farmer here is a friend of my uncle's."

"Of the Duke?"

"Yes. My uncle lets out some fields to him for his cattle. He has Aberdeen Angus. My uncle needs the money, as he's not really very well off. He's got a bit of money, I suppose, but he's not rolling in it."

"That doesn't matter," said Pat. "You don't need much money to be happy."

"You know that he's not a real duke? You know that?"

Pat nodded. "I've heard that. Somebody said it was the government's fault. They broke a promise."

"I think he has more fun being a bogus duke," said James. "He has a terrific time. If he were a real duke he'd have to worry about all sorts of things."

With the bicycles propped up against the wall of a sheep fank, they set off down the narrow footpath that James said would lead to Single Malt House. Pat did not want the walk to end. She wanted to be here, with this young man, on this blissful summer evening; she wanted their conversation, so easy, so relaxed, to continue. She wanted night to come upon them and for them to watch the sky darken together, and they would see the lights come up in the towns below them, and in the old mining villages, in Musselburgh, Prestonpans, and out at sea, where the ships cut through the Forth like tiny ploughs.

60

Something Happens . . . At Last

There was no sign of life at Single Malt House.

"He's away at the moment," said James, as they breasted the small hill that looked down on the house and its cluster of outbuildings.

"Are you sure?" asked Pat. She had not given much thought to it, but now she wondered whether James was entitled to show people his uncle's peculiar project.

"Yes," James replied, and sensing her anxiety went on, "He doesn't mind my looking in the byre. He's shown me what he's doing quite a few times."

"It's just that I feel this is a bit of an intrusion," said Pat. "You know . . . going to somebody's house when they're away."

James shook his head. "No, I promise you. It's all right – it really is."

Single Malt House looked to all intents and purposes like a typical Lothian farmhouse – slightly larger perhaps, but making very much the same statement that most such houses made: I am here to shelter those who work the land. I am not here to impress anybody, or intimidate them with grandeur, but don't underestimate the good conceit I have of myself.

There was a lawn to the front of the house, and at one end of this a greenhouse and a small potting shed. Croquet hoops had been set out on the lawn, and there was an abandoned mallet next to one of the hoops.

"Does he play?" asked Pat.

James grinned. "He used to play croquet for Scotland,

believe it or not. He played against Australia once – in Australia. He said that it was easy to get selected because so few people played it in Scotland and there was not much competition. But I think he was being modest."

Pat looked at James. "You're really fond of your uncle, aren't you?"

He looked down at the ground, and she realised that there was something worrying him. But he answered quite quickly, and firmly, "Yes, I am. I really am . . ." He broke off. Then, "That's why I'm worried."

"About?"

"About this stupid project of his. This plane." He paused. "And my folks are worried too. My dad has tried to persuade him to give the whole thing up. He printed out a whole set of statistics about what happened to people who made their own microlights. He said that they were an invitation to disaster. Apparently structural failure's a real issue. And if your wing collapses, then there's not much you can do."

She saw that he was distressed, and she wondered why, if he felt that way, he should have brought her here to see the thing he was so worried about.

She asked him directly. "Why show me this if you're so concerned about it?"

He did not answer immediately, but pointed to the byre. "It's over there . . ." he began. But then he stopped, and turned to her, and faced her, and said, "Because I wanted to get you out of the house. Because I wanted to go somewhere with you – anywhere. I thought that this would be an excuse."

She held her breath. The sheer delight of finding out that somebody you want to like you likes you; that old-fashioned, simple delight. Like a jolt. Like a discovery. Like a sudden burst of warmth.

She said nothing, but smiled at him, and then reached out and touched his forearm, gently, as if to seal a conspiracy between them. And then he leaned towards her and brushed her cheek with his fingers and kissed her.

She closed her eyes, and thought: impossible. Nineteen. *Nineteen.* Impossible. And then, breathing out, she thought: why? Why should it be impossible? They were both adults, and what was five years between them? And she hadn't asked for this to happen; it had simply happened, and it was not anything to be ashamed of – how could feeling this way about somebody ever be something to be ashamed of?

He said, "Sorry."

"You shouldn't say sorry. Why say sorry?"

"Because I don't know if you like me."

She laughed, and touched him again. "Of course I like you. Of course I do."

The moment passed. He pointed to the byre again, and said, "He keeps it locked, but I know where the key is. Padruig puts it under a stone over there. I'll get it."

He bounded off, and returned with a rusty padlock key. "Come on," he said, as if nothing had just happened; as if the entire landscape had not just been bathed in a benediction of light.

They went into the byre, with James leading the way. There was some natural light inside, but not much, and it was only when he had switched on the lights that she saw the aircraft properly. There it stood, on a square of concrete flooring, advanced enough in its construction as to be intelligible as a miniature seaplane. The floats, yellow oblong things, were already attached, but the engine compartment was still only half constructed.

"It looks so lovely," Pat said. "Like a dragonfly – a large dragonfly."

James shook his head. "I wish he wouldn't. I just wish . . ."

Suddenly he turned to her. "You know what I'm going to do? You know what?"

She waited.

"I'm going to take one of the parts away. I'm going to hide it – throw it away. So that they can't finish it."

She drew in her breath. "You can't. You can't do that."

"To save his life? Why not? Wouldn't you do this if it was your uncle who was being led into doing something really stupid by that driver of his?"

"Is it his idea?"

"Of course it is. Padruig's got this thing about flying around the islands. He says he wants to see Barra from the air. He goes on about it."

She did not know what to say.

James walked up to the plane. Parts were laid out, alongside tools and diagrams, beside the body of the plane. He stopped and picked up one of the larger components, putting it into an empty box lying nearby. Then he rummaged around for another part, a smaller one this time, and indicated by a nod of his head that they should leave.

"Are you sure you should do this?" said Pat.

"One hundred per cent," said James. "I'm going to save his life. It's the only way."

"But what . . ." She realised that he was not listening.

"Come on," he said. "I'm going to throw these into the lochan down the road."

She accompanied him mutely. Her heart thumped within her. She had tried to dissuade him, but not with great passion. He was, after all, probably right. If his uncle would not see reason, then something like this was justifiable. It was done out of love, after all, and that surpassed every consideration. Things done out of love cannot be wrong. Tough love, she thought. This was an example of that – tough love. And thinking of love – what had he said to her? She could not remember the words; in the suddenness and magic of the moment, the words had gone.

61

Angels and Metaphor

When Domenica declined to accompany Angus on his mission to provide a decent burial for the cat he had found in Drummond Place Garden, she went out of her way to be apologetic. "Do you mind?" she said. "It's just that . . . well, I find these things so harrowing. That poor creature . . ."

He assured her that he understood. "I don't mind at all. I know how you feel." He remembered how, as a boy, he had helped his father bury their much-loved family dog, and how he had wept and wept until there were simply no more tears to come. And recalling this later, in adulthood, he had asked himself whether such grief stemmed from the fact that there was no comforting notion of an afterlife for animals. We invented an afterlife for ourselves, but it did not occur to us to extend the privilege to other species: the eschatology of a cat's life was a very small subject.

Now he reminded Domenica, "I think I told you about how upset I was when we buried our family dog. I was ten at the time."

"You did. Yes."

"And I wonder now whether it was because nothing was said about heaven."

Domenica looked thoughtful. "I came across a rather charming children's book the other day. I was in the bookshop and it was on display. It was all about what happens to dogs when they die."

"And what did it say?"

"That they go to a dogs' heaven – a typical heavenly

landscape, you know, parkland and so on – but then they're allocated to watch over somebody down below. When they come down, they follow us to keep an eye on us. We can't see them, of course, but they are there – ready to protect us."

Angus smiled. "Guardian angels?"

"That sort of thing. Guardian dogs."

He looked at her. "Do you believe in angels, Domenica?"

She looked at him with surprise. "Do I look like the sort to believe in such things?"

"Well, no, not really." He paused. "What do you think they look like – people who believe in angels?"

"Optimistic? Hopeful? Trusting?"

He nodded. "It's such an odd thing – a belief in angels. So peculiar."

"But a serious pursuit for some nonetheless. Angelology has its enthusiasts – and a literature to match. Have you ever seen *A Dictionary of Angels*? Gustav Davidson?"

"No." He was, as always, astonished by the breadth of Domenica's reading. Sometimes it seemed that she had read *everything*.

"It's full of obscure facts about angelology. Such as the belief of the fourteenth-century Kabbalists that there were precisely 310,655,722 angels. And many of them had names – and specific responsibilities. Behemiel was in charge of tame animals; Shakziel was responsible for water insects. And so on."

"Water insects! How considerate to remember them. Water insects rarely feature in people's view of the world – or their theology."

Domenica said, "Yes. Perhaps." And then she continued, "Of course, don't underestimate the sophistication of theologians. Sometimes what they say should be interpreted in a symbolic way. Angels may represent something rather than being, well, just angels."

He waited for her to explain.

"Origen of Adamantius, for example, took the view that all men are moved by two angels – a bad one who inclines them to evil and a good one who inclines them to good . . ."

"Like Plato's dark horse and light horse, pulling in different directions?"

"Precisely. And we think this all a bit simplistic – childish even – but who hasn't had that internal conversation, that debate with self, about making a moral choice?"

Angus said that he thought one did not need to clothe such a debate in the language of angels. Could it not just be a debate on rights and wrongs? On urges?

"Yes, of course. But don't you think we need metaphor in our lives? And what about the things of metaphor: poetry and art and music? These are things that enable us to see the moral and spiritual contours of our lives. Don't these things depend on that which can't be touched or smelled or measured? Take away our gods, our angels, our myths – take all that away and what are we left with? A materialist desert."

Angus was silent. "Yes," he said. "I think you're right." And then he added, "And love too."

"Yes, and love too, which for most people – rather a lot of people, Angus – is the only thing we've got."

They sat for a moment, looking at one another in understanding. Then Angus sighed. "I have to bury that poor cat. I can't put it off." He looked about him. "Do you have a bag I can put him in?"

Domenica pointed to the bag that she had used to carry her purchases down from Stewart Christie. As she did so, she thought: tonight's the Guy Mannering night. "Will that do?"

"Perfect," said Angus.

He went back into the kitchen, where the cat had been laid out on a copy of the previous day's *Scotsman*. Gently he lifted the body from the table – it was limp, but as he moved the cat something within it clicked, a bone somewhere that was out of place and was easing back into its socket. All of life, thought Angus, is such a marvellous creation – so intricate, so beautifully designed, by whatever had designed it. Cats filled the space they occupied with such elegance, such assurance and grace – rather like Italians, thought Angus.

He tucked the tail into the bag – it had protruded – and then he closed the zip that sealed the bag just as an undertaker closes that final zip when he collects us in his body bag. A zip to end a life – in this case a small one, and a brief one. Lived down amongst the low things of a city – kerbs, the spaces under shrubs, skirting boards, the sanctuary under a sofa, the back lanes of broader streets – the places known for cats, and known to them.

He made his way, with Cyril on his lead, down the common stair and out into Scotland Street. There was nobody about, apart from a delivery van dropping off groceries at a flat on the other side of the street. There had been a brief shower of rain, and the cobblestones – the setts – were glistening. The sky had cleared and the sun was out.

He walked up Scotland Street and crossed over Drummond Place to the entrance to the garden. And just at that moment, he heard a familiar voice behind him. Cyril growled a warning.

"Mr Lordie, we see one another again."

He turned round. Sister Maria-Fiore dei Fiori di Montagna stood behind him, having emerged from a small, sporting BMW that she had just manoeuvred into a parking place. He looked at her in astonishment. What was a nun doing driving a BMW X3?

She smiled at him, and then pointed to his bag. "That's an interesting-looking bag. Are you going for a picnic in the gardens?"

He held her gaze. "That's my affair, Sister Maria-Fiore dei Fiori di Montagna," he said evenly. He knew he sounded unfriendly, but this woman was so trying – she really was. And if he encouraged her in the slightest way, there was bound to be a flood of aphorisms, for which he was in no mood.

"But we are members each of each other," said Sister Maria-Fiore dei Fiori di Montagna reproachfully. "What I have in my bag – although I do not have one at present – is for you as much as it is for me. A bag may conceal, even if does not conceal. A bag is as open as it is closed. Always." She paused, and then finished with, "That, I would have thought, is fairly obvious, don't you think, dear Mr Lordie?"

Angus did not respond. I do not have to give an account of myself, he thought; I simply do not. But then, quite unexpectedly, Sister Maria-Fiore dei Fiori di Montagna's demeanour changed. Her intrusive curiosity – and her disapproval – seemed to lift like a morning mist, to be replaced by a look of benign forgiveness. Now she was a Madonna from a painting by Raphael – gentle and compassionate, unjudgemental of humanity about her.

"Whatever mission you are embarked upon, Mr Lordie, I understand," she said. "Purity of heart and purity of purpose go hand in hand, you know, and ever have done so." She paused. "Right from the beginning, that has been the case."

Angus stared at her. She smiled back, and her smile, he felt, was like the sun upon his face. It was a benison – unasked for, but received with gratitude; a gift, an endowment of peace, bestowed in Drummond Place.

"Oh," he said.

62

A Borrowed Morgan

"It's not far now," said the fair-haired young woman in the passenger seat of Bruce Anderson's borrowed Morgan sports car. "But this car is a bit bumpy, isn't it? Is there enough air in the tyres, do you think?"

From behind the wheel, negotiating a bend in the Edinburgh to Peebles road, Bruce laughed at her question.

"A bit bumpy? Of course it's a bit bumpy – that's the whole point of a Morgan."

She looked puzzled, and slightly uncomfortable. Bruce had folded back the hood of the car and the wind was sending her hair in every direction. If she had brought a scarf she could have secured it, but he had not told her they were going to be travelling like this. It was all very well for him, with his hair *en brosse* as it was – he was much more aerodynamic than she was.

"But why would they make the tyres like that?" she asked.

"It's not the tyres, Janny," said Bruce.

She glanced at him reproachfully. "It's Jenny."

"That's what I said."

"I wish you'd say my name correctly."

Bruce took one hand off the wheel and nudged her shoulder playfully. "Sorry, Jenny." He uttered the name with elaborate care, and she blushed. "There? Was that all right?"

"You shouldn't fool around with people's names," she said.

"I said sorry," repeated Bruce. "But look, this is a Morgan. That's what Morgans feel like. It's nothing to do with the tyres – it's the suspension. These cars are different, you know.

They're really cool."

She conceded that they were pretty. "They look great. I didn't say they didn't. But why this bumpy ride?"

"Like I said, it's a Morgan. These cars are hand-made. They make them down in England, and they have a wooden frame inside them. It's all ash."

Jenny looked about her. "Why use wood to make a car?"

"What sort of question is that?" said Bruce.

"I was just asking. I wanted to know why they were so bumpy. What's that got to do with wood?"

Bruce smiled as he explained. Women were hopeless when it came to cars, he thought. He needn't even have bothered to borrow Gav's car to impress her if all she was going to do was go on about the bumpiness. It was the suspension, of course, but how did you explain suspension to somebody like this?

"People like feeling the road beneath them," he said. "They like to feel contact with it."

She shrugged. "Not everyone."

"No," Bruce said. "Clearly not everyone."

"My brother's car isn't like this," Jenny continued. "His car has a really smooth ride. If you closed your eyes you wouldn't think you were in a car."

"Different strokes for different folks," said Bruce. "People like these cars. They don't make very many of them, you know. There's a waiting list. That tells the whole story. Anything that has a waiting list is . . . you know, rather good."

He had borrowed the car from his friend Gav, who had arranged the introduction to Jenny after his friend Sally had explained that Jenny had seen Bruce at a party and had rather fancied him. At first Bruce had not been interested – so many girls fancied him, he said – but when Gav mentioned the fact that Jenny's father owned a distillery and an estate in Inverness-shire, his interest was piqued. But it was not to the distillery nor to Inverness that they were now headed, but to the family's main house – "our Edinburgh-but-not-quite-*in*-Edinburgh house" as Jenny put it. This was outside Peebles, in a small glen tucked away in the hills to the west of that Borders town. It was a part of the country that Bruce did not know and he was relying on her to navigate.

"In a couple of miles you turn off," she said. "Off to the right. And then it's about seven miles from there. The road's twisty, though, and it'll be really bumpy in this car, I bet."

He ignored that. If somebody didn't get suspension, then they didn't get suspension, he thought. Until the turn-off, they drove in silence, Jenny struggling to keep her hair under control, and Bruce relishing the sensation of driving the expensive Morgan on this cloudless summer evening with this blonde girl beside him and, well, with what could be a future ahead of him. He was tired. I've done the bachelor bit, he thought. I'm finished with that. No, really. I know I said it to myself last time, and nothing came of it, but this will be different. Time to draw stumps, as my cricketing friends would say – if I had any. Stupid game. Typical English rubbish. Blah, blah, blah, howzat! Blah, blah.

That's what he thought. And then he thought: I'm glad I don't live in England. London! People go on about London, but you'd never get me there. Never. Where would you park a Morgan in London? And where could you drive? You'd go a couple of hundred yards and then have to stop at a traffic light. What's the use of that? No, London's not for me.

They started talking again when they were well down the smaller road. She said, "You have to watch these corners. Daddy almost crashed into somebody a few months ago. This other car was coming round right in the middle of the road. Daddy had to go into the ditch – or one of his wheels did, he said. He just missed him."

"Yup," said Bruce. "You have to be careful."

He thought he had spotted the house – or what he thought

must be the house. "Is that your place over there?"

"Yes. That's it."

For a few moments Bruce said nothing. But he was a surveyor, after all, and he had to ask. "How many bedrooms?"

She frowned. "I don't know. I never counted them."

That appealed to Bruce, and he laughed.

"What's so funny?"

He lifted a hand from the wheel to make an airy gesture. "Not many people can say that. Most people know how many bedrooms they have. It's just . . . well, it's just the way it is."

"Well, I don't see what difference it makes. What if you don't care how many bedrooms you have?"

"Sure," he said. "Sure, it makes no difference. I didn't say it did. And do I turn here?"

They were approaching a set of gates.

"Yes," she said. And then she continued, "You'll like Daddy."

"I'm sure I will. He sounds great." Why, he thought, would one *not* like somebody who owned a distillery?

"He's got a good sense of humour."

And a distillery, Bruce said to himself. "That's good. There's nothing worse than somebody without a sense of humour."

They were on the drive that led to the house. Bruce thought: right, this is the business. This is *the business*.

63

Engine Capacity

Bruce parked the Morgan directly before the front door of the large, late Georgian house.

"Here we are," he said. "Mission accomplished."

"I still think you need to look at your car's springs," said Jenny.

Bruce laughed. "I told you: contact with the road. That's what these cars are about."

"Well, I think that's stupid. If people want contact with the road, they should walk. Barefoot."

"Hah!" exclaimed Bruce. "*Très drôle!* But, look, who's going to be here? Your folks and who else?"

Jenny smoothed her hair back; it had been thoroughly disorganised by the trip in the open car. What was wrong with having a roof? Surely cars should have roofs, particularly in Scotland, where there was . . . weather. There were places that did not have weather, and you could drive in open cars there, but this is Scotland, she thought, and we *do* have weather.

"Daddy's here. Mummy isn't. She's in Egypt at the moment. And my brother, Neil, might be here, but I'm not sure. He lives in Glasgow. He's probably there. He has a flat in the West End."

"Cool," said Bruce. "But what's your mother doing in Egypt?"

Jenny shrugged. "She goes to Egypt. Some people like going to Egypt."

"I'm sure they do," said Bruce. "Have you ever been to Egypt?"

"Egypt?"

"Yes, Egypt."

Jenny finished attending to her hair. "No. Not as such."

She began to walk towards the door and Bruce followed her, looking, with his trained surveyor's eye, at the state of the house's stonework. Work had recently been done on the front, where several new mullions revealed their presence by their colour. He noted, with approval, the fine tracings that the stonemasons had incised on the new sections: a nice touch, he thought – and expensive. Once inside, he looked about the entrance hall, taking in the floor, where engineered oak had replaced what must have been there before, but done so tastefully and again expensively. He looked up towards the high ceiling, and saw the elaborate cornice with its Greek-key design. He noticed the fine chinoiserie walking-stick stand. He saw the dog's bed with its tartan blanket.

Jenny's father appeared in a door at the far end of the hall. He clapped his hands together. "Darling, spot on. Exactly when I was expecting you."

Jenny said, "Bruce, this is my father, Harry."

Harry moved forward, and Bruce found himself looking up at a slightly taller man, somewhere in his late fifties, he thought, dressed in a lightweight tweed suit and wearing a tie. Bruce fingered at his own open-neck shirt, and wondered whether he was underdressed.

Harry extended a hand, giving Bruce a look of appraisal as he did so.

"So, you're Bruce," said Harry.

There was no confusing the accent. Three words had been enough. Glenalmond, Bruce thought (or possibly Fettes, Merchiston Castle at a pinch); St Andrews (possibly Oxbridge); Gleneagles, New Club, Muirfield (handicap of ten), British Airways Gold Lounge, etc., etc. All as expected, Bruce said to himself.

"Yes," said Bruce. "How do you do?" And Bruce thought: I know not to say *Pleased to meet you*. I know not to say that.

"Pleased to meet you," said Harry.

Bruce's eyes narrowed. A trap? A deliberate solecism?

Harry said, "I see you have a Morgan. Nice car."

Bruce smiled diffidently. "Not everybody likes them, but I do." He glanced at Jenny.

"Oh, I think they're terrific," said Harry. "Have you seen the three-wheeler they're making now? They used to have that wonderful little car, and now it's in production again."

Bruce had seen one. "Yes. But they don't have a hood, do they? I'm not sure how practical they are."

"Oh, immensely impractical," said Harry. "That's their charm." He paused. "Yours is a Plus 4 110, isn't it?"

Bruce froze. Was it? "Yes," he said. "I like that model."

"Nice," said Harry.

Jenny interrupted. "Why do men always talk about cars? There's not much you can say about a car, surely?"

Harry smiled indulgently. "That's what she thinks," he said to Bruce.

"Oh well," said Bruce, eager to get off the subject. "I suppose it's better than talking about politics."

"Yes," said Harry. "I'd agree with that. And cars . . . well, I confess I like them. As you obviously do."

"I do," said Bruce. "What's not to like in a car?"

"What indeed?" Harry said. "But tell me, what do you have under the bonnet out there? What size of engine do they put in the Plus 4?"

Bruce stared at him. "Engine?" he said.

"Yes. Two litre? Something like that?"

Bruce nodded. "Yes."

"Not three? Or is that the Roadster? They make a Roadster, don't they? It looks a little bit more rounded than the Plus 4, if I remember correctly."

"Yes," said Bruce.

"So . . . two litre?"

Bruce tried to sound convincing. "Three."

Harry frowned. "But I thought . . . I thought that the Roadster was three litre. Are you sure?"

Bruce decided to brazen it out. "Yes. It's three."

Harry, he noticed, gave him a sideways glance. But then the older man said, "Well, I suppose you must know what your own engine size is."

Bruce laughed. "Oh well, these are technical details." He looked at Jenny apologetically. "I won't talk about cars. Promise."

She seemed pleased. "Good."

Harry now said, "My wife's in Egypt, I'm afraid. She'll be sorry to have missed you."

"Egypt?" said Bruce.

Harry did not answer. "Mrs Thing's cooked dinner for us," he said.

Jenny scolded him. "You shouldn't call her that. You shouldn't."

Harry was unabashed. "It's affectionate. You see, Bruce, I find her name difficult to get my tongue round. It's Polish."

"She's called Mrs Wisniewska," said Jenny. "You wouldn't find it hard if you at least tried. You should get her to teach you how to say it properly."

"Thing's easier," said Harry. "And she doesn't mind. She laughs when I call her that. She knows I can't manage Wis— whatever."

"She works here," explained Jenny. "And she's a terrific cook."

"Her son does my IT," said Harry. "He's a nice boy. A bit unkempt, but who isn't these days? Wears very odd glasses. He's been going to Telford College to do some computer course and he knows what's what. He keeps everything running – e-mail, the cloud, the works. Terrific geek."

"Daddy!"

"Geek is not a term of abuse," Harry protested. "It can be a compliment." He rubbed his hands together. "But we shouldn't stand here in the hall. Let's go through to the drawing room and then in due course we'll see what Mrs Thing has prepared for us."

He led the way through into the adjoining room. Bruce glanced at Jenny, and winked.

64

Here Comes the Sun

With Bertie at Ranald Braveheart Macpherson's house and Ulysses with Nicola in Northumberland Street, Stuart found himself alone in the flat. He had, he reckoned, several hours at his disposal, a rare luxury, as Nicola would not bring the boys back until at least seven o'clock and it was now only three.

He looked out of the window at the street below, and then up at the sky. It was one of those days that could go either way – and probably would: a thin veil of rain was descending over the rooftops of the New Town, a muslin-thin whiteness, but behind it the sky seemed to be clearing. He saw that there was sun on the tops of the trees around the old marshalling yards and, in the distance, on stone and slate. The benediction of sun: in spite of the rain and clouds and inconstancy of Scotland's weather, the sun still bestowed its blessing. A line of song came to him, *Here comes the sun*, and for a few moments he was back where he was when he had listened to that so often, every day in fact, while he was working, as a student, in a summer job on a potato farm in Angus. *Here comes the sun*, and he had not imagined that life would hold the complications it would prove to have, and he thought that he would always be happy.

He moved away from the window and looked at the muddle of papers on the kitchen table – the newspaper, dismembered and crumpled, the boys' colouring books, scribbled upon and abandoned, the book he had been trying to read, *Middlemarch*, because he had read in some newspaper one of those shaming, destabilising remarks about how, if one hadn't read *Middlemarch*, one could not claim to be well read. He disagreed with that sort of thing, because it seemed to him to be so limiting, so prescriptive – akin in a way to the statement of some Victorian missionary that if people had not been introduced to Christianity they were benighted and there would be no hope for them. That was absurd, he felt – how could anybody, from any perspective, claim that they were in possession of exclusive truth? The Hindus didn't claim that, he understood – nor Quakers, for that matter. There were any number of routes to spiritual enlightenment, and nobody had the patent on how to get there. And yet he had gone off to buy a copy of the Everyman edition of *Middlemarch*, with its fine stitching and endpapers and its eight hundred pages.

But there was another reason to read *Middlemarch*, and that was because Katie had said something about *Middlemarch* being her favourite novel. He had said at the time, "Oh yes? I'm not surprised" – a meaningless remark but one that would not reveal that he himself had not read *Middlemarch*. He remembered the exchange vividly, because they had been drinking peppermint tea at the time, and he had looked at her over the rim of his cup and the scent of peppermint had been strong in his nostrils.

Middlemarch was on a side table, and he picked it up now, and paged through it. He could not concentrate; he could think of nothing other than Katie, and about how she had said, at the end of that dinner party, "I'm sure I'll see you again." He had reflected on that all the way back to Scotland Street, and the next day he had thought about it again, trying to extract every possible scrap of meaning out of the few words. Had it meant anything at all, or was it simply one of those meaningless things we say to people, like *see you*, or *see you later*? People in Scotland said *see you later* instead of goodbye. You said it even after the most cursory contact, when you knew that you would never see the other person again, but you still said *see you later. Later* there meant *never*, but we prefer to avoid the finality of the complete goodbye.

He had been unable to decide whether she wanted to see him again. He had sensed that there was still something between them, especially when the two of them had briefly absented themselves from the company of the other guests at her dinner party, including George, and had talked in the kitchen, where she had made him peppermint tea. There had been an intimacy about that interlude, and he had sensed that she was cross with George, or, if not actually cross, then at least irritated by him. He wondered whether she was ashamed of him – after all, he was one of those types who were so confident and full of themselves when the world really was an uncertain and tragic place. How can you be so self-assured when there is so much pain and sheer regret wherever you turned – wherever? It was there, great wells of pain and unhappiness, and you couldn't be glib and pleased with yourself and make disparaging remarks about other people's shoes when all that was going on. Or tell stories about a poor Albanian who had only one leg and wanted to dance in Glasgow. How could you think of that as being anything other than tragic? Maybe she saw all that and wanted to get away from George and his world; from his smart friends and their certainties. There was a good chance that that was the way she thought because poetry *hurt*, and she wanted to devote her life to poetry. And he would love to help her in that; he would love to . . .

He took his telephone out of his pocket. He had entered her number in his contacts list, and all he had to do was press the screen twice to bring her voice into the flat and his into hers. He did that, and she answered almost immediately, saying, "Stuart?"

How did she know? Because her phone was intelligent and recognised the number and warned her. And she could have ignored the call if she had not wanted to speak to him, but instead she had said *Stuart* in a tone that told him that she did.

"I wondered if you would like to drop by?"

She did not answer immediately, and he closed his eyes, imagining her annoyance at his presumption. She was seeing somebody else. George might be right there, sitting next to her, while he phoned and asked her whether she would like to come round to Scotland Street.

"I'd love to."

He hardly heard. "What did you say?"

"I'd love to. But what number?"

He opened his eyes. "Forty-four. Come for a cup of peppermint tea."

"Of course. Why not?"

They said goodbye, although he thought: now, of all times, I could have said *see you later*, or anything, really, because any words he uttered would have done to express the joy he felt and the excitement. Here comes the sun, he whispered. *Here comes the sun.*

65

Never Gush

He stood behind the door. He looked at the panels. He stared at the brass surround of the letterbox and at the letter that lay in the wire-mesh basket underneath it, the recipient of their mail. That letter had arrived that morning, but he had not noticed it for some reason; now he fished it out and saw that it was addressed to Ms Irene Pollock, and that it came from the Edinburgh Carl Gustav Jung Drop-in Centre. He tossed it aside, sending it fluttering and failing to reach the small table to which he had intended to consign it, along with a selection of other letters due for redirection to Aberdeen. He immediately felt guilty: she was his wife, even if she had left him, and he owed her the courtesy that he would show to anybody, and to the letters of anybody. And then there was the Edinburgh Carl Gustav Jung Drop-in Centre, with which he had no quarrel, and which, when all was said and done, was only trying to help people. That it was not particularly helpful to try to analyse the dreams of people who dropped in in the belief that they would be offered a free cup of coffee was not the point: there were many ways of trying to make the world a better place, even if some of them were patently misguided.

He bent down to retrieve the letter, and as he did so he heard a sound. It was a familiar noise, one to which he would not normally pay a great deal of attention, but that now made his heart miss a beat. It was the sound of the stair's front door being opened, the door that led out onto the street, the very door by which Katie would enter the building when she came to drink peppermint tea with him.

Quickly placing the letter on the table, Stuart moved into position a few feet from the door, ready to step forward and open the door when the bell sounded. He had rehearsed what he would do. He would stand there and wait for a few seconds after the bell was rung, as he did not want to give the impression of being too eager. Then he would step forward to open the door, slowly and casually, almost as if he had forgotten that he was expecting somebody and was slightly surprised to see Katie standing before him.

Calmly, casually, he would say, "Oh, Katie, of course." That would be all. The "of course" would be welcoming and friendly, but it would not be too gushing. When starting a relationship one should never gush; Stuart had read that in a copy of *GQ* he had found in the hairdresser's salon. There had been an article entitled *How to play it cool with hot chicks*. One should not give the slightest hint of desperation, the article advised: "Desperate guys are seriously tragic," it continued. "So, if you want to avoid registering high on the tragimeter, avoid giving the impression that you're too keen. Experts are unanimous: excessive keenness is a proven turn-off . . ." Stuart had smiled when he read that article and drawn it to the attention of Kenny, his barber, who had laughed and said, "Very funny, but it could be true, you know. Never be too obvious."

Now, as he heard footsteps on the stair below, it was just too much for Stuart, and he moved towards the door. He waited. Was she outside? And, if she was, then why had she not rung the bell? He waited another agony-filled minute. There were no further steps. Had she gone? Were those steps he had heard the sound of her retracing her way back down the stair, having decided for some reason that she was not going to come after all?

Stuart crouched down, and very carefully began to lift the flap of the letterbox. Through the slit he would be able to see

out onto the landing and would see Katie, or the lower part
of Katie, if she were standing outside. But what happened was
that he found himself peering directly into Katie's face, eyeball
to eyeball, as she had, at the same time as he, entertained
exactly the same idea. She had decided, for whatever reason,
to peer into the flat just as he had decided to peer out.

Both drew back in shock. Then Stuart, standing up, fumbling
with the door handle, opened the door and exclaimed, "Got
you!"

It was exactly the right thing to say, as it converted a tense
moment of mutual embarrassment into one of good-natured
humour. And Katie, for her part, responded in similar vein,
naturally and skilfully. "*Touché*," she said.

He invited her in. She looked about. She said, "These flats
are really pretty. I've always liked Scotland Street."

He said, "I've lived here for ages." He did not say *we've*
lived here for ages. Aberdeen receded. All the humiliation and
oppression was becoming distant, like a vaguely remembered
dream. Over.

"I knew somebody who lived on the other side of the
street," said Katie. "He was a great yachtsman and free
diver. And I knew Iseabail Macleod, who used to work on
The Scottish National Dictionary. She lived on this side of the
street, I think."

"She did," said Stuart. "Dear Iseabail – everyone liked her."

"Edinburgh is like that," said Katie. "People know one
another. There are all sorts of links, all sorts of bonds between
people."

"Citizenship," said Stuart. "We feel as if we're citizens of
the same . . . the same . . ."

"Place," suggested Katie.

"Yes, place."

He looked at her. "I was so looking forward to seeing you,"
he said. It was directly contrary to the advice proffered by

GQ magazine. But what did they know? What did they know about how you felt when you had waited for years to be free of something that hung over you and made you miserable, and then, when you were free, you discovered somebody who seemed to like you, and who was beautiful, and who was doing a PhD in Scottish poetry? What did *GQ* magazine know about Scottish poetry? Precisely nothing.

And she did not answer, but suddenly reached out and touched him, and he touched her back, and then she said, "I would love that peppermint tea you mentioned." And they both laughed, and drank peppermint tea together, and were still sitting there in the kitchen two hours later when there was a sound of a small boy hammering on the door and a man's voice, that of Angus Lordie, saying, "If nobody's in, Bertie, you can wait upstairs with Domenica and me. We'll take good care of . . ." But the rest was mumbled and was lost.

66

The Lost Art of Gentlemanliness

The fact that the voice of Angus Lordie was to be heard on the stair was the result of an unusual series of events that had taken place in Drummond Place slightly earlier that afternoon while Stuart and Katie, over several cups of peppermint tea, were planning, allusively and tactfully, but with growing sense of anticipation, indeed with a knowledge of blessedness, a future life together. Suddenly a future was opened to Stuart, a future to be revealed to the accompaniment of delight and gratitude, as a gift wrapped in silver paper is laid bare, layer after layer, and enchants the recipient.

Angus had set out to bury the unfortunate cat that he had discovered in Drummond Place Garden. While on this melancholy errand, he had been intercepted by Sister Maria-Fiore dei Fiori di Montagna just at the point at which he was about to open the garden gate. She had asked if he was going for a picnic, and he had been short with her – an unusual thing with Angus, who was normally punctiliously polite, but the nun's intrusive questioning had particularly irritated him.

"That's my affair," he had said abruptly. But almost immediately he had regretted the pettiness of the exchange, and on his side, more disturbingly, its lack of gentlemanliness. That quality had been drummed into him as a boy by his father, a Perthshire farmer, a Church of Scotland elder, and, for five years, an officer in the Argyll and Sutherland Highlanders who had been captured by the Japanese in Malaya and had been subjected to the brutality in which they excelled. In spite of that, he had never spoken ill of the Japanese, enduring their lack of apology and attributing it, so tactfully, to a quirk of culture, a deficiency in language.

Angus had been told by his father what a gentleman did and what he did not do; that he never complained, that he never expected more than anybody else was given, and that he never spoke rudely or impatiently, particularly to people who were less fortunate than himself. And of course there were other things: about doors being opened for others, about walking on the outside of the pavement when escorting a woman, about removing one's hat the moment one crossed a threshold, and about not wearing suede shoes. Those minor rules – superstitions, thought Angus – had made him laugh: not to his father's face, because his father was too kind to be mocked, but secretly.

And when he had gone to art college he had tried to unlearn the things that marked him out as belonging to a lost world. He had abandoned the black brogues his father had bought him and put on, instead, a pair of tobacco-coloured suede shoes. He had taken off his tie and affected a red bandanna, tied loosely about his neck. He had given his hat to a man who asked him for the price of a cup of tea on the street. But the core value, the sense of not wanting to hurt others, or the world for that matter, survived within him, stubbornly, like a memory of home. It survived in spite of all the coarsening of our public life; it had survived the epidemic of swearing that infected our ordinary language; it survived all the mockery and casual disregard and selfishness; it survived the boasting, self-aggrandisement and shallowness of a celebrity-focused culture; it survived the loss of social decency and obligation. It survived the crude, bar-room assertion that there was no such thing as society. Oh, there was, there was, and there was still a Church of Scotland that put its arms about people in their sorrow and their suffering, and there was still a National Health Service, and there were still those who believed in society.

He had immediately relented. He imagined what his father might think of being short with a *nun*, even to one quite as irritating as Sister Maria-Fiore dei Fiori di Montagna. He would have smiled indulgently – just the hint of a smile – and said of the encounter, "Well, she is Italian, and in this life one has to make allowances. Italians are an excitable people; very talented and amusing, but distinctly excitable, Angus. And a gentleman is *never* rude to a nun, you know . . ."

And then Sister Maria-Fiore's face had broken into a smile, and her smile, he thought, was like a blessing, and he received it as such. He nodded, and made his way through the gate that led into the garden. Once inside, he set off briskly along one of the paths that led towards the London Street end. He looked over his shoulder once or twice to see if Sister Maria-Fiore was following him, but there was no sign of her. "Climb every mountain", he muttered under his breath, smiling a little, and then, "How do you solve a problem like Maria-Fiore?" Don't, he said to himself. She is Italian. She is a nun. She is only seeking the good – as she sees it. That, of course, was a general problem with humanity: people so often had misguided ideas of the good. In fact, most people's vision of the good left something to be desired, thought Angus.

But he had other things to think about: he had to find a place to bury a cat. He had an idea where that would be, and now he headed for it. He felt sad – close to tears, indeed – for the death of this cat, this small thing, but also for a whole lot of other things that we had lost, and they were much bigger, and deserved more tears than he would ever manage.

67

Bruce in Conversation

"What will you have to drink, Bruce?" asked Harry, as he led the way into the drawing room. "We've got . . . well, I suppose we have most things."

Bruce looked about him. Yes, he thought, most things – in abundance, he imagined. He noticed the picture hanging over the fireplace, an ornately framed Highland scene. "Glencoe?" he asked.

Harry gave him an amused glance. "Glencoe? Oh, that. No, not Glencoe. The Highlands certainly, but why would you say Glencoe?"

Bruce smiled. "Isn't that . . ." He pointed at the hill in the foreground, an exaggerated conical peak surrounded with swirling mists. "Ben . . . Ben . . ." He looked to Jenny in a mute appeal for assistance, but she simply shrugged.

"Ben?" asked Harry.

"Ben . . . You know, the one on the left as you go down towards . . . towards the place with the bridge, before you get to that ferry at . . ."

"Corran?" prompted Harry. "Are you thinking about the Corran Ferry?"

"Yes. The one that goes over to Mull. To that place . . . Fish . . ."

"Fishnish? That's not the Corran Ferry, no. The Corran Ferry crosses the Corran Narrows. It goes nowhere near Mull."

"Ah," said Bruce. "I was thinking of another ferry."

"I think you were."

Bruce smiled nervously. "There are all those ferries over there, aren't there? Going all over the place."

"Well, they actually follow fairly well-defined routes," said Harry.

"And they're always ploughing them into things, aren't they?" said Bruce. "Those stupid MacBrayne captains. They're always hitting bits of island."

Harry stared at him. "Not really," he said. "Not these days. My godfather was a MacBrayne skipper. He was a very good friend of my father's. They fished together."

"Ah. Well, I wasn't thinking of him."

"Clearly not," said Harry.

"No, I can see it's not Glencoe," said Bruce, moving closer to the painting and peering at it. "Funny. It looked like it." He turned to Harry. "So where is it?"

"It's invented," said Harry. "Nowhere in particular. The Victorians had a romantic idea of the Highlands – a non-specific romantic idea. They created a landscape of the mind. They increased the height of the mountains. That painting is somewhat like that. We thought it might be somewhere near Loch Katrine, but it isn't really. It's Horatio McCulloch."

"Ah," said Bruce. "I thought so too. Ben McCulloch. Of course."

Harry glanced at his daughter, who busied herself with turning on a standard lamp.

"Now then, what will you have?" Harry asked again.

"A G and T?" said Bruce.

Harry hesitated. "You're driving back to Edinburgh after dinner?"

Bruce nodded. "Yes." He had to get the Morgan back to Gav, of course – not that he was planning to reveal that. Cinderella, he thought. The coach has to get back before it becomes a pumpkin again. Ridiculous story.

"I thought you might want something soft," said Harry. "If

you're driving."

Bruce pursed his lips. "Yes, I wasn't going to ask you for a G and T. I was just wondering whether you had it."

"Oh, we definitely have gin," said Harry. "We make some, in fact."

Bruce raised an eyebrow. "Here?"

Harry laughed. "No, at a small gin distillery we have over in Falkirk."

"Hah!" said Bruce. "Falkirk."

"So, can I get you something soft?"

Bruce nodded. "A Diet Coke maybe."

"No, we don't have that, I'm afraid. Water? We have plenty of water."

I bet you do, thought Bruce. You'll have a loch or two, I imagine. And a river.

Harry changed the subject. "Jenny tells me you're interested in whisky," he said.

"Yes," Bruce answered. "You could say that."

"Any favourites?" asked Harry.

Bruce hesitated. Then, "Talisker. I like Talisker. Give me an Islay whisky any day."

There was a brief silence. Then Harry said, "Actually, Skye. You're thinking of Skye."

Bruce laughed. "Of course I was. All those distilleries on Skye – I get them mixed up."

"I think there are only two on Skye," said Harry. "Three if you count Raasay."

"Yes. Three," said Bruce quickly. "I don't like too much peat, naturally."

"And yet you like Talisker?"

"And there's nothing wrong with Glenfiddich," said Bruce.

"Not my taste exactly," said Harry. "I know it's very popular, but don't you find it a bit sweet?"

"It depends," said Bruce.

Jenny now joined in. "Show Bruce that special bottle you bought the other day, Daddy." Then, turning to Bruce, she said, "He's got a collection of really old whiskies."

Harry demurred. "I'm not sure that Bruce would be all that interested."

"Oh, I am," said Bruce. "I love old whisky."

"I'm not planning to open this one," said Harry, smiling. "It's part of a collection."

Harry moved to a glass-fronted cupboard at the side of the room and took out a curiously shaped bottle cradled on a small wooden stand. He passed it carefully to Bruce. "75-year-old Mortlach," he said. "Taken from the cask seventy-five years on. This was made in 1939, would you believe?"

"It's the oldest whisky there is," said Jenny. "1939."

"Have you tried it?" asked Bruce.

Harry smiled again. "I don't think many people will be drinking that," he said. "There were about a hundred bottles. Cask number 2475. They took it to the market a few years ago."

"Goodness," said Bruce.

"Charlie MacLean's written about it," said Harry. "He's your man when it comes to whisky. Known throughout the world. You read his stuff?"

"Of course," said Bruce. Charlie MacLean?

"He talks about Mortlach's famously rich and complex style. It's the way they made it in those days. He says that they would still have been using brewer's yeast back in 1939."

"So they would," said Bruce. What other yeast was there? He was not at all sure. In fact, why did they use yeast? Did you have to?

Jenny pointed to the bottle. "I would never pay what Daddy paid for that. I couldn't believe it. Tell him, Daddy."

Harry made a self-effacing gesture. "Oh, we don't need to go into that . . ."

"No, tell Bruce. Tell him what that's worth."

"He won't be interested."

"No, I am," said Bruce. "Let me guess. Eight hundred?"

Harry smiled, but clearly found discussion of price uncomfortable.

"Twenty-five thousand pounds," said Jenny. "Can you believe it? Twenty-five thousand for . . ."

Bruce looked down at the bottle in his hands. And then, just as he tried to make out the script incised in the glass, the bottle slipped from his hands. Curving a tiny parabola, the 75-year-old Mortlach tumbled down, to land just at the edge of the Kashan rug underfoot, but slightly on the wrong side of that, so that it hit the stone of the hearth. And shattered. The stain of the spilled whisky spread quickly. It was round at first and then, uncannily, became the same shape as Scotland itself, with outlying droplets being the smaller islands.

Harry watched, transfixed. Jenny gave a yelp and bent down, hopelessly, to pick up a shard of glass that had landed at her feet. Bruce caught his breath.

"Oh," he said. And then, once again, "Oh."

When he left after dinner that evening, Bruce was by himself, Jenny having elected to stay with her father. Bruce was not invited. She went out with him, though, to say goodbye as he drove away.

"I'm sorry about that . . ." Bruce began.

"That whisky?" Jenny shrugged. "He has other bottles."

There was something in her manner that suggested to Bruce that she wanted him to leave as soon as possible.

"I wish you were coming back to town," said Bruce. "I really do."

"I have to wash my hair," Jenny said.

Bruce climbed into the Morgan. He did not have to plead with women to come back to Edinburgh – who did she think she was? As he put the Morgan into gear, he felt himself fuming. Your loss, honey, he thought; your loss.

He chose the wrong gear by mistake: reverse. As he lifted his foot off the clutch, the highly charged sports car gave a lurch backwards, narrowly missing Jenny but hitting a large lead garden figure – Diana the Huntress, by the look of it, the head of which was toppled by the shock. This tumbled onto the back of the Morgan, gravely denting the bodywork.

"Oops!" said Jenny.

Watching from the window, her father allowed himself a smile. He was not a vindictive man, though, and so the smile was mixed with a look of sympathy. Lead statues could be repaired, even if bottles of 75-year-old Mortlach could not. He sighed, and turned away. Poor boy – the car clearly belonged to somebody else, which meant there would be some explaining to do. Oh, well.

68

On the 23 Bus

Bertie and his friend, Ranald Braveheart Macpherson, caught the 23 bus after it had crested the hill opposite the Church Hill Theatre. That theatre, tucked away in the quiet interstitial zone between Holy Corner and deep Morningside, proclaimed no performance of anything that day, or indeed that week. In little over a fortnight's time, though, the Edinburgh Grand Opera, an enthusiastic amateur group, would be presenting *Cavalleria Rusticana* by Mascagni, without its usual accompaniment of *Pagliacci*. Some of those singing in *Cav* might remember the former glories of the Church Hill, including the notable production of Gilbert and Sullivan's *The Gondoliers*, in which the late Ramsey Dunbarton, a well-known Edinburgh lawyer, had sung the part of the Duke of Plaza-Toro, to the great delight of that large cohort of the audience who were members of the Society of Writers to Her Majesty's Signet, a legal organisation of which Ramsey had been a prominent member. They had been encouraged by Ramsey to attend, indeed been given complimentary tickets, and had rewarded his performance with prolonged applause at the end, persisting in their clapping well past the point that other members of the cast thought appropriate for the Church Hill Theatre.

"Really!" muttered a disgruntled member of the chorus. "You'd think we were down in the Playhouse . . . or even somewhere in Leith, the way they're going on."

"Clapping as if they were trying to revive Tinkerbell," whispered a fellow member. "And what about us?"

"Oh, nobody applauds the chorus," sighed the other.

"You'd think we'd done nothing, just standing here doing nothing. You'd really think that."

Ramsey had taken another bow, a deep bow, as befitted, he thought, a nobleman such as the Duke of Plaza-Toro. This had led to more applause and even a cry of *Bravo* from one of the partners in the firm of Shepherd and Wedderburn, who lived nearby and had recently acted with Ramsey in a complicated Contract of Excambion.

"*Bravo* indeed!" hissed the first member of the chorus. "Why not *Bravissimo* while we're about it?"

On the impassive façade of the Church Hill Theatre that day there were no signs of such past glories. Yet the poster advertising the imminent performance of *Cavalleria Rusticana* was noticed by Bertie as he and Ranald took their seats on the top deck, along with the puppy they were intent on transferring to the promised safety of Scotland Street.

"There's going to be an opera, Ranald," said Bertie. "You see that poster? That means there's going to be an opera in that theatre over there."

Ranald gave the theatre a cursory glance before it disappeared behind them. "I don't like dancing," he said.

"Opera is mostly singing, I think," said Bertie. "Sometimes they dance, maybe, but that's just to keep people from falling asleep. Then they go back to singing."

"Are there any dogs?" asked Ranald. "Do they have operas about dogs, Bertie?"

Bertie thought that they did not.

"They should," said Ranald. "They could have operas with dogs in them, Bertie. That would be good."

Bertie remembered something. "Olive says she's going to be a famous opera singer when she grows up," he said. "She says that she's already had an audition with Scottish Opera and they're looking around for a part for her. She said that the other day. I heard her."

"She's such a liar," said Ranald. "I bet she told Scottish Opera she could sing, although she can't really. I bet she lied to them."

Bertie decided not to think about Olive – it was just too distressing. His life had improved beyond measure since Irene had gone to Aberdeen, but Olive was still a presence in the background to remind him that freedom, although glimpsed, was not unconditional, nor guaranteed to be long-lived. Girls would get you – eventually. That was the realisation to which Bertie, like so many boys, was coming. No matter what you did, girls would get you.

He looked out of the window of the bus, at the people walking along the pavement, the shoppers, the passers-by making their way down to Bruntsfield, or returning in the other direction. Everyone he saw at that moment was part of a couple – a man and his wife, or a boy and his girl. They had been caught – the boys, the men, they had all been caught. And now here they were, walking along in captivity, seemingly resigned to their fate, obediently accompanying the women or girls who had got them; going into shops without argument; carrying the grocery bags without complaint; meekly heading home to houses and flats where they would be told what to do before it was time for dinner, and would then eat what was put before them, as per instructions. Was this what lay ahead, thought Bertie?

Of course, there were nice girls. He thought there were plenty of those, but for some reason they seemed to be living somewhere else and did not seem to be in his class at school. In fact, he had reservations about everybody in his class, apart from Ranald Braveheart Macpherson and a girl called Prudence, who frequently brought Turkish Delight to school and gave Bertie pieces of the glutinous rose-scented sweet during the break.

"My mummy has a Turkish lover," explained Prudence.

"He's a tall man with a moustache. He brings her Turkish Delight all the time."

"You're jolly lucky," said Bertie, licking the powdered icing sugar off his fingers.

"Does your dad like him?" asked Ranald.

"I'm not sure," said Prudence. "I don't think he's met him yet."

"You should introduce them," advised Ranald.

The bus was now gathering speed down the hill towards Lothian Road. In no time at all, they would be in Dundas Street and it would be time for them to alight. Bertie looked down at the floor beneath their feet, where their puppy had settled in apparent contentment. He could hardly believe that this was happening – that he, Bertie Pollock, was the joint owner of a real live dog. It was good fortune on a scale that he had previously thought well beyond his reach, and yet it had come to him. And he was going home with that dog. The future lay before him like a sunny meadow – warm, bright, and full of possibility of the most delicious sort.

69

Angus Says Something

Away, or so he hoped, from the curious eyes of Sister Maria-Fiore dei Fiori di Montagna, or any other passer-by, Angus sneaked around the edge of Drummond Place Garden. He was aware of the absurdity of his situation – here he was, an established portrait painter, an academician of the Royal Scottish Academy, a former Vice-President of the Scottish Arts Club, and more besides; here he was creeping around a New Town garden with a dead cat concealed in his bag. How utterly surrealistic that was, and how unbelievable it would be were some novelist to attempt to describe it. And yet it was happening; he *was* in the garden; he *was* intent on burying a cat of whose provenance he knew nothing; and he was conscious of the fact that even if Sister Maria-Fiore dei Fiori di Montagna had disappeared, there was a distinct possibility that other interested parties might take her place.

But that was not what happened. What did take place was an unexpected encounter, in which Angus came face to face with Bertie and Ranald Braveheart Macpherson, who had entered the garden from the other side of Drummond Place and seemed to be making their way towards Scotland Street with a small dog on a lead.

"My goodness," Angus exclaimed. "This is an unexpected encounter. And you have a dog, Bertie – what a surprise!"

Bertie said nothing, but Ranald Braveheart Macpherson was quick to reply. "It's our new dog, Mr Lordie. Mr MacTavish gave him to us."

Angus raised an eyebrow. "Yours?"

Bertie looked shifty. "I don't want everybody to know, Mr Lordie," he said. "I'm going to keep him in my room."

Angus waited.

"Please don't tell Bertie's father," said Ranald.

"But Bertie," said Angus, "you can't keep a dog cooped up in your bedroom. And you certainly can't keep that from your father."

Bertie stared down at the ground. "I've always wanted a dog, Mr Lordie."

Angus looked at the small boy. Of course he had always wanted a dog, and of course the possibility of a dog had been denied him. And yes, he knew what it was like to yearn for something like that; he had felt that himself when he was a boy. He had wanted a dog more than anything else he could imagine, and in his case his wish had been granted.

Suddenly Angus knew what he must do. The decision was made without any real thought, without any consideration of counter-arguments, or even practicalities. And Angus rationalised this to himself, thinking that if everybody thought too much about whether or not to have a dog, then nobody would ever have one. There were good reasons to have a dog, but there were so many equally good reasons not to have one, and if people ever engaged in any calculation of benefit and convenience there would be no place for dogs in our lives. But that was not the way it was; people took on dogs out of love, without questioning whether it was the right time or the right place for love. Love simply took over and prompted one to act there and then. That was how dogs were taken into our lives; in that spirit of spontaneous affection, and not because we had considered and approved their case. Their case was messy and inconvenient and demanding – and yet we did it; we took on dogs, as Angus now did with this puppy on its lead and its two unrealistic young owners.

"I've got an idea, boys," he said. "Cyril could do with some company. He's getting on a bit and it would be good for him to have a younger dog to keep him on his toes."

Bertie was staring at him. "You mean . . . ?"

"Yes," said Angus. "Why don't I look after your dog? I'm already looking after Cyril, as you know, and another dog wouldn't be too much of a problem."

Bertie looked at Ranald, who nodded his agreement to the unspoken question.

"Do you think you could?" asked Bertie. "I'll give you my pocket money to buy him food."

Angus smiled. "That won't be necessary, Bertie. He can share Cyril's pay and rations. And although he'll live with us, he'll be your dog, and you – and Ranald, of course – can take him out as much as you like."

Bertie's face broke into a broad smile of pleasure. "You're very kind, Mr Lordie."

"Well, it'll suit us both," said Angus. "But now, I have to do something. I've a poor cat here who needs to be buried, and I can't put it off."

"We'll help you, Mr Lordie," said Bertie.

So it was that the small procession made its way to a spot at the end of the gardens where, under a tree and partly sheltered by a laurel bush, the body of an unknown cat was laid in a grave that Angus excavated with the trowel he had brought with him in his bag. Bertie held the cat briefly, cradling it, as if to comfort it before its committal. Then he handed the body over to Angus, while Ranald held the puppy in check.

"I suppose I should say something," said Angus. But even as he spoke, he was not sure whom he was addressing: he was talking to the boys, perhaps, although he feared they were too young to understand what he wanted to say; or to the sky, or to himself, or to that vague otherness that could be anything, even God, if that is what you chose to call it. I suppose I might say something about how the life of every creature counts for something – no matter how small it is. I suppose I should say something about how all we want, whoever we are, whatever we are, whether we are a person or an animal, like this poor cat, we all want just to get through this life without too much pain and unhappiness, and that we also want love, if at all possible, and that we should help one another to find that love, if we can, that is, which we can't always do. I suppose I should say something like that.

He closed his eyes and spoke. Did it matter where that urge to love came from – from what myth, from what fanciful cosmology? The important thing was that it was there, and we could all sense it, and all knew that it was a thing of awe. That was what mattered.

He laid the cat in the earth, and looked at the two small boys who were watching him so intently. And he said to them, "Do you understand what I've just said, Bertie? Ranald?"

They both nodded. Ranald had no idea, but Bertie had an inkling: Angus had said that we should try to make other people happy, which had always been his own philosophy anyway – the cornerstone of his theology too. And while Bertie thought this, Angus began to cover the body of the cat with soil. Fur and earth intermingled. A small foot, clawed and with dark pads, tiny circles, was for a few moments exposed, before it, too, was covered. Then, with more earth piled on it, the grave was closed and Angus, having crouched for his task, stood up, brushing the soil from his hands.

"I think we should go home now, Bertie," he said. "Cyril needs to get used to his new friend. How about that, boys?"

70

Big Lou Gets an Offer

On the following Monday, Matthew left Pat in charge of the gallery while he went across for his morning coffee at Big Lou's. He was vaguely cross with Pat that morning, for two unconnected reasons. He knew that by lunchtime he would have forgiven her, and all would be back to normal, but for now, feeling inclined to show her that he was mildly displeased, he pointedly went over to Big Lou's by himself without inviting her.

"Would you mind watching things while I go for coffee?" he said, picking up his copy of *The Scotsman*. Pat looked up from her perusal of the *Burlington Magazine*. She was reading about Gaspard Dughet, who had married Nicolas Poussin's sister, and therefore become brother-in-law of the more famous painter. After his marriage, he became known as Gaspard Poussin.

"Would you change your name for professional reasons?" she asked. "Would you change yourself from Dughet into Poussin?"

"No," said Matthew. "And anyway, I'm going for coffee."

He was displeased with Pat for what he saw as her antisocial behaviour at dinner a few nights previously. When he had invited her to Nine Mile Burn, he had done so to cheer her up, and while he had entertained the possibility that she and James might get on, he had not envisaged the chemistry working quite so quickly, to the extent that the two of them went off for a walk together even before coffee was served. That, he thought, bordered on the rude, as if his company, and that of Elspeth, was somehow tedious.

Then there was a strictly professional matter. When he and Pat had gone to the sale at Lyon & Turnbull, Matthew had successfully bid for a painting that, although described simply as *Scottish School*, was in his view probably by one of the better Scottish painters of the late eighteenth century. Pat had been doubtful and only that morning had discovered, after close examination of the lower right-hand corner of the painting, the signature of the artist. And this was not a name that anybody with a knowledge of Scottish painting would recognise. *Scottish School* was therefore anything but a misattribution; it was quite correct and meant that Matthew had overpaid for it.

Matthew might have been grateful to Pat for making the discovery, but instead he felt embarrassed, and rather resented the fact that she was right and he was wrong. This resentment, together with his feelings about her abandoning their dinner party, had resulted in a certain froideur in his attitude when she came in to work that morning. By the time he reached Big Lou's, however, he was beginning to thaw, and had decided that when he returned after coffee he would congratulate her in a rather warmer way over her discovery of the signature.

Big Lou greeted him cheerfully. "The usual, Matthew?"

Matthew nodded. He looked at Big Lou. He had not yet had the opportunity to discuss with her the news that she had accepted an offer for her coffee bar. Now, seeing Big Lou in her accustomed position behind the bar, ministering with such practised confidence to the needs of her customers, he felt a momentary pang. The world was full of unwanted change: people stopped doing the thing they were doing just when you got used to them doing whatever it was they were doing; people moved to different towns and cities, with scant regard for those they left behind; people retired – so selfishly, we sometimes think; they died, equally selfishly, in some cases.

And all the time we wanted nothing other than stability and predictability – for things to be the same as they always had been.

He watched Lou as she steamed the milk for his *latte*.

"So, what's this I hear, Lou?" he asked.

Big Lou did not turn round. "You heard something, Matthew? Aboot what? Aboot the cat's mither?"

Matthew laughed. "Oh, that's old hat, that news. No, about you, Lou. Are you selling this place?"

Big Lou finished preparing the milk, and now poured it into the waiting cup of coffee. "Aye," she said. "I've had an offer, and I'm going to accept it."

Matthew did not conceal his dismay. "But why, Lou? Why give up . . ." He made a gesture of hopelessness. "Why give up all this?"

Big Lou slid the cup of coffee across the bar. "Because this place doesn't really make much money, Matthew. Even after I started making those haggis rolls . . ."

"Which we all love so much," said Matthew.

"You dinnae buy them," said Lou, accusingly.

"I like *smelling* them," said Matthew.

"Well, that doesn't help my profits, does it, Matthew? No, I need to get my hands on some money, and that's the way to do it. Sell."

Matthew took a sip of his coffee. Big Lou had always made it exactly the way he liked it. What would he do in the future – the future without Big Lou?

"You see," Big Lou continued, "I'm going to be sending wee Finlay to ballet school. And that costs a lot, Matthew. That's why."

Matthew looked into his coffee cup.

"And if you weren't sending him to this . . . this ballet place . . . what then? Would you stay?"

"Of course. I wouldn't need the money."

Matthew looked into his coffee cup again. How many years were we on this earth? It depended on our luck. But however lucky we were, it was not all that long. And during that brief time we might have a few chances, now and then, to do something that was really worthwhile. These chances sometimes occurred when we were not expecting them, as when we were drinking coffee and thinking about how sad it was that something we liked might come to a stop.

He looked at Lou. "I'll pay," he said.

"But you haven't had your second cup," said Lou.

"No. I'll pay Finlay's fees. I can easily afford to. In fact, I want to."

Big Lou stared at him. "I couldn't let you, Matthew. It's awfie kind of you, but . . ."

"Lou," said Matthew. "I mean this as much as I've ever meant anything. And all I'd say to you is that I really want to do this. And I'll get something in return."

Big Lou frowned. "What could I possibly give in return?"

"Elspeth's bored," said Matthew. "She's a great cook. She likes making coffee. Take her on as a partner in the business, Lou."

Big Lou said nothing. She looked up at the ceiling, and then down at the floor. She loved her coffee bar. She loved this place. She did not want it to come to an end. Big Lou liked Elspeth, and she could understand how she must feel, cooped up with those triplets at Nine Mile Burn.

"Why not?" said Big Lou, with a smile.

71

The Duke of Johannesburg Aloft

Travelling in a green truck that he had borrowed for the occasion from his sheep-farmer cousin, and driven by his Gaelic-speaking driver, Padruig, the Duke of Johannesburg made his way a week later from Edinburgh towards the Morvern peninsula in Argyll. The two of them had finished constructing their microlight seaplane only two days earlier, and were now transporting it to a sea loch from which they proposed to take off on their inaugural flight. It had been a long process – building a plane, however small, is not an easy task, and its construction had not been without difficulties. In the earlier stages, everything had gone well enough, but latterly, when it came to finishing the project, there appeared to be a discrepancy between what the plans indicated and the parts that they had laid out beside the fuselage. Padruig had been concerned about this, but the Duke had insisted that the drawings must be mistaken, and they had made do with what they had.

"These things are often over-engineered," he said. "It's like the Forth Bridge – the rail one. Far too much steel. More girders than a gallon of Irn Bru."

"Hah!" said Padruig.

"Thank you," said the Duke. "But a serious point nonetheless. They design these things with too many parts – just to be on the safe side. But as long as the whole thing hangs together reasonably well, you're home and dry. We don't need absolutely everything."

"I'm a bit concerned," Padruig began, only to be silenced by the Duke.

"Haud your wheesht, man. It'll be fine. Look at it. As sturdy as anything. There's nothing wrong with this plane."

Neither of them knew, of course, that the missing parts had been deliberately taken by the Duke's godson, James, in an attempt to halt the construction of the plane. And it had not occurred to James that the Duke's response to finding certain parts missing would be to carry on regardless. So in this whole affair nobody was at fault, strictly speaking, although, speaking not quite so strictly, everybody was.

Now, as the truck carrying the plane climbed up towards Rannoch Moor, the Duke opened his window and breathed in the fresh Highland air. "Not far now, Padruig," he said. "And smell that air. Soon we'll be up there, soaring over the Sound of Mull, kept aloft by Bernoulli's principle."

Padruig said something in Gaelic that the Duke did not catch, and for the next half hour they travelled in companionable silence until they took the sharp turning down to the Corran Ferry, ready to embark on the last stage of their journey.

Their destination was Loch Teacuis, a small sea loch that fingered into the land from the larger Loch Sunart. The Duke had been told that this would be a good place to take the seaplane on its test flight, as the loch was well sheltered from the prevailing south-westerlies and would provide a good jumping-off point for a flight over to Mull and then on to Coll. If all went well, they would then turn north towards Muck and land in Gallanach Bay. There would be lunch in the tearoom, a walk down to the pontoon at Port Mhor, and then the return flight to Loch Teacuis. It would be a full and exciting day.

Padruig would be at the controls. He was, after all, the Duke's driver, but it was not just his road skills that would stand him in good stead – he had attended a series of flying lessons at East Fortune Airport, and was now licensed to fly microlights.

"It's a fine day for a flight," said Padruig, as, having disembarked from the ferry, they set off on the road towards Morvern.

"I can't wait," said the Duke, looking up at the high, empty sky. "This is the end of an auld sang, Padruig."

The road to Loch Teacuis was no more than a single track, punctuated by regular passing places. This meant that the final stage of the journey took rather longer than they expected, but even with the delays they arrived at the loch shortly before two in the afternoon. That would give them time to unload the seaplane, re-attach its wings, and wheel it into the water. The engine had already been tested, and fired well enough; all that needed to be done, then, was to tighten a few screws, check that the floats were watertight, and then climb into the seats. The Duke would navigate, allowing Padruig to concentrate on the task of becoming – and remaining – airborne.

They had chosen Loch Teacuis for the test flight not only because of its sheltered nature, but because the Duke had a friend who lived within sight of the loch. This was Loafy Weir, whom the Duke had known when he lived in Glasgow, and who was always game for an adventure. If the test flight went well, the Duke had promised that Padruig would take Loafy on a flight over Tiree, returning by way of the Sound of Iona, on which they could, if tidal conditions were right, land for a brief visit.

Loafy was on hand to help them re-assemble the plane and push it into the water. "This is a beautiful wee machine," he said. "Do you think it flies?"

The Duke laughed. "Of course it flies, Loafy. And anyway, if it doesn't we'll have a grand little boat."

"True enough," said Loafy. "Well, here's hoping."

Padruig climbed into the pilot's seat, followed by the Duke, who secured himself in the passenger seat and gave a thumbs-up sign to Loafy, who was still standing on the shore.

"Fire her up, Padruig," said the Duke.

The engine, take from a small Volkswagen, spluttered into life. As it did so, the frame of the aircraft shook violently.

"That's her responding," shouted the Duke. "She's raring to go."

Spray whipped up behind them, a white cloud that was soon dispersed by the thrust of air from the propeller. Now, as Padruig increased the supply of fuel to the engine, the seaplane began to move slowly across the water. At the other end of the loch, disturbed by the noise, a flock of Canada geese took to the air, flying low at first, honking instructions to each other, gradually climbing in controlled formation.

"There they go," said the Duke. "Look at them. Just look at them."

The flight of geese wheeled slightly, as if to inspect the would-be intruders in their airy element. Padruig smiled, and saluted them. He loved geese; he always had.

The seaplane gathered speed. Now they were travelling at ten knots, now at twenty. The air roared; the spray arose in a flurry of droplets; the water, with its tiny wavelets, was a bumpy runway. White, thought the Duke, this is a world of white: white water, white cloud, a white line of vapour where, high above them, a jet made its way towards Greenland and North America.

More white. More liquid. More air. More movement through all of these; a wild dash, witnessed, in surprise, by hidden eyes: an otter, a curious seal, tenants both of the element that now hosted a glorious headlong hurtle, one that seemed to be finding difficulty in freeing itself from the embrace of the water. It was as if the water were protesting *Stop, don't leave me yet.* And then whispering, in a voice made up of spray and of foam, *You are still mine, just as I am yours – just as I am yours.*

72

A Subtle Love Affair

And then it was time for Angus and Domenica to hold the party that they had spoken about for weeks, if not months, but only now got around to organising.

"Our party," said Angus one morning over breakfast. "I was thinking . . ."

Domenica interrupted him. "You're right," she said. "We must hold it."

"People have come to expect it," said Angus.

"They have," agreed Domenica. "And we should not disappoint them."

Preparations would be required. The guests would want something to eat, but their expectations would not go beyond cheese and olives and slices of quiche; and plates of smoked oysters and hard-boiled quail eggs with celery salt in which to dip them; and slices of Melton Mowbray pie and Italian salami from Valvona & Crolla; and cheese straws and figs soaked in syrup. And to drink they would want Brunello di Montalcino and Haut-Médoc and something from the Barossa Valley; and coffee, of course, and the things that went with coffee, such as *petits fours* and macaroons from La Barantine bakery and slices of *panforte di Siena*, again from Valvona & Crolla, and small *biscotti* to immerse in glasses of Sambuca.

That was all there for them when they arrived, and Angus ushered them in from the hall, into the kitchen, where the food was laid out, or into the living room, where there was more room to sit down.

"You're looking smart," said Big Lou, as she greeted Angus.

"New outfit?"

Angus looked confused. "Not really," he said. "Much the same as usual."

Big Lou raised an eyebrow, but said nothing. She had spotted Elspeth in the kitchen and wanted to have a word with her about their plans for the coffee bar. She joined her there, but before anything was said about coffee bar affairs she whispered in Elspeth's ear, "Your man . . ."

Elspeth waited. "Yes?"

"Your man is the kindest, best, most wonderful man there is. You know that?"

Elspeth hesitated. Then she said, "I know that, Lou. There might have been times in the past when I forgot it, but not now. I know that very well." She paused. "And thank you for telling me."

Other guests were congregating in the living room. James Holloway, nursing a plate of smoked oysters, was telling Domenica's friend Dilly Emslie about his plan to ride his motorbike through the remote New Guinea Highlands – a plan that Dilly agreed would be extremely interesting, although possibly fatal. "Domenica was telling me about head-hunters," she said. "So many anthropologists have rued the day they embarked on fieldwork in New Guinea . . ."

But James was having none of this caution. "One needs a challenge," he said. "We all do."

Dilly inclined her head towards Angus, who was now standing talking to Matthew on the other side of the room. "Angus is looking smart, isn't he?" she said.

"New clothes by the look of it," said James. "First time in years."

The conversation shifted to the Duke of Johannesburg. "He's out of hospital already," said James. "Fortunately he only broke a couple of small bones, and nobody else was hurt at all. Apparently the plane never really left the water. There was an almighty bang when they hit the shore, but the Duke and his factotum just picked themselves up and walked away. The Duke was very philosophical about the whole thing and is talking of converting what's left of the seaplane into a machine that stacks peat."

"Why do people want to fly?" asked Dilly. "We're not really designed for flight."

Pat arrived, followed by an attractive young man. "That's the Duke's nephew," said James. "He helps Elspeth with those triplets of hers. Apparently he's a great cook."

"So kind of Pat to take him under her wing," said Dilly.

"Exactly," said James.

Bertie was helping to pass round the plates of food. Now he was on hand to offer quail eggs to James and Dilly.

"I hear you have a dog now," said James. "You must be pleased, Bertie."

Bertie nodded. "He's a shared dog, Mr Holloway. I share him with my friend Ranald Braveheart Macpherson."

"Ah yes," said James. "Ranald's been a good friend to you, hasn't he, Bertie?"

Bertie nodded. "He's my best friend, I think."

Dilly and James exchanged glances. Neither had much time for Irene, and for years both had felt sympathetic towards Bertie. Now, as Bertie moved on, Dilly said, "That woman! Thanks heavens for his grandmother. Is that her over there?"

It was. Nicola had arrived, along with Stuart, and with Stuart was Katie.

"Look at that," whispered James. "At long, long last."

"I hope she makes him happy," said Dilly. "He deserves it."

"She will," said James. "Look at the body language. Just look." He paused before imparting further news to Dilly. "Katie used to have a boyfriend called George," he whispered. "No longer. History. And Stuart's much better for her, they say."

They both looked across the room and watched as Katie touched Stuart lightly on the forearm as she said something to him. He returned the gesture with a look of fondness.

"There," said James. "You see?"

A few minutes later, when a momentary silence fell on the party, James took a spoon and struck the side of his glass. "Everybody knows what I'm going to suggest," he said.

"We do," said Matthew.

"It's an old tradition," said James. "It's an old tradition that Angus says something about . . . about where we are."

"It is," said Matthew.

Everybody looked at Angus. "Oh," he said. "Do you really want me to?"

There were murmurs of assent, and then expectant silence.

Angus stepped into the middle of the room. He closed his eyes. Then he began to speak. "I've written something about the fragile beauty of Edinburgh, of our city," he said. "And it *is* fragile, you know. And it could so easily be wrecked by insensitivity and greed."

There was silence. Everyone present knew he was right.

"So," he said, "here it is." And then he added, "And afterwards, there is a short poem about love in general."

"Two poems?" said James. "Never before . . ."

"Why not?" said Angus. "Life has been a bit – how shall we put it? – trying of late. Two poems might help."

This city [he began] *woos you gently,*
As a tactful lover does,
One who says, yes, I am listening,
But do not overwhelm me
With excessive praise;
Do not expect me to respond
To ebullient adjectives;
Over-statement will get you nowhere

In a subtle love affair.

Rather, this city promises
Gentle heartbreak; you will not find
In this city's repertoire
The grand architectural gesture,
Echoing squares, statements
Of imperial ambition;
But you will find harmony here,
You will find the quiet
Resolved beauty of streets
That go somewhere with modesty,
Not in too great a rush
To get to their destination;
You will find skies that transform
Themselves hourly, if not by the minute,
As if changing, deliberately,
The circumstances of an assignation.

This city is a reserved lover,
No advocate of concupiscence,
The greys of its time-darkened stone
Are attenuated by reticence;
It has a quiet and fragile beauty:
There are other places
That can shout; this city whispers.

And its words are sometimes missed
By those not paying attention:
Edinburgh says: look, I am here,
I am yours; for your love,
And your individual cherishing,
Only that, my dear, only that;
Please do not use me otherwise.

There was silence. Then Angus began his second poem.

No words are necessary for love,
Nor are words enough;
Love that works its way unseen
Into the fabric of all we do,
Asks for no grounding
Beyond a disposition of the heart,
Which is the natural abode of love;
For the heart is capable
Of accommodating a hundred times
Its volume of those things
That are connected with love,
And that mark, as milestones do,
Our progress through life;
For love is a thing
Of many occasions,
From the infant's first embrace
Of mother, to the unselfish love
Of the philosopher for truth –
These things are called love,
These things are written within us,
As natural as breathing,
And as important – always there.

They listened carefully, and gravely. In their hearts they knew that Angus was right, and in their hearts they felt the presence of the city, and of its people, and of so many things they wished to speak about now, or later on, with those whom they loved.

The end (for the time being)